Lori's Miracle

John L. White

First printing

ISBN: 1-58851-931-7
PUBLISHED BY AMERICA HOUSE BOOK PUBLISHERS
www.publishamerica.com
Baltimore

Printed in the United States of America

Dedicated

To all the Neonatal Intensive Care nurses
Who rock and sing to the little babies while they die.
You are my heroes

Acknowledgments

A book such as this one, based on factual experiences, is replete with a host of people to whom one is eternally grateful. Everyone who played a part is honored in my memory, but some do stand out.

First and foremost, thanks to my wife, Andrea, who not only was central to Lori's Miracle by being Lori's mother, but who was an indispensable help in getting the book on paper and the one who kept the faith that one day it would be published. Next, my deep appreciation to Donna Reagan, my original editor who edited with an ax, but reasoned with her heart. Thanks for believing in me, and in us.

And of course, the grandmothers, Ursula and Ella Mae, were really "grand". They gave us courage when we were afraid, advice when we were lost, and love, when we needed it most. We love you both more than we can every say. Thank you for everything.

Heart felt thanks to all the doctors who worked with us and, who each in his own way, helped realize Lori's miracle of life; Dr. Neal Green, Chair of pediatric-orthopedic surgery, Vanderbilt Hospital; Dr. Jay Werkhaven, Otolaryngologist; Dr. Shah, pediatric internal medicine; and most of all, Dr. David E. Hill, urologist, who reminded everyone at a critical moment, "first, do no harm", and then shepherded us through the long years thereafter. Thanks to each and every one of you, you will always be saints to us.

My warmest thanks goes out to all the nurses at Vanderbilt Hospital, from the Neonatal unit nurse heroes who endure the suffering of the new born everyday, to the surg nurses on Medical East, and in that latter group a special thanks to Carol Rogers, R.N. who cared for us as much as she cared for Lori. All we can say Carol is, we love you for all you did.

To Stanley Newton, my old boss, who understood even when he did not, and without whom we could not have given Lori all the time and attention she needed. We'll never forget what you meant to us. Thanks to Lane Roberts who picked up the slack for me, and to Mona Lafferty and Henry Vernon who helped him do it; thanks a bunch, guys, you helped pull us through. Thanks to Linda Holley, who we ran crazy with the insurance, you were a jewel, and a big thanks to Dr. Doug Haney. We simply could not have made it without you, Dr. Haney, or your nurse Melissa. Thanks from the bottom of our hearts. You aw us through some terribly rough spots, and many times you helped just because you believed in us when we didn't believe in ourselves all that much.

Many thanks to our church "family", Choates Creek United Methodist, who prayed for us, and to Brother "Ray" who baptized Lori.

And Last, but not least, to "weezie" (Betty Louise Chapman) our neighbor, and best friend, who was always there during the dark nights and long days with good advice and an optimistic laugh. You got us through what both of us doubted we could survive. Way to go, Weezer!

An added note. All conversations in this book have been replicated as closely as possibly to the original, as best my poor memory serve me. If there is error to be found, let it rest with me. I did the best I could.

Introduction

I would like to share a story with you. It is a story about our life and the little girl who came into it so dramatically in 1990. In many ways it is a hard story to tell, filled with pain and regrets, tears and anxieties, fatigue and stress. But at the same time it is also a story of a profound spiritual journey and of the miraculous things that happened to each of us. It is a story of trial and personal tribulation, reported as faithfully as possible. It was an experience that I would not go through again for anything on Earth, but, having lived through it, it is an experience I would not exchange for anything on Earth.

In the end, if indeed there ever will be an end; I would like to think I came out a better person. But whether I am better or not for having lived through the drama, one thing is for certain, I am a different man than I was when I began this amazing journey. I have experienced events which I once thought were inconceivable and changed in ways that I could never have predicted. The story has proved to me the old adage is true: That which does not destroy us only makes us stronger.

Join me as I recount the story of our family and the truly marvelous adventures we encountered when Lori came into our lives. Then perhaps you too will benefit from Lori's Miracle.

Chapter I
In The Beginning

It has been my experience that the truly spectacular events of our lives grow from the most unpretentious origins. No heroic fanfare precedes our greatest triumphs, just as no dour warnings announce horrific episodes, which befall us. And so it was in my own life. There was no spectral harbinger preceding the dramatic calamity that befell my family, nor was there an angelic warning to introduce the miraculous journey that would so drastically change our lives. It all began in the most commonplace fashion, and in the most common of places.

By late fall of 1989 my life seemed settled. I had been a police officer with the City of Pulaski, Tennessee, for seventeen years. For the last twelve of those years I was a Detective Sergeant in charge of criminal investigations. I added another dimension to my life teaching criminal justice at a nearby university, and I was in the second year of a doctoral program in Public Administration at Tennessee State University. Andrea and I had been married for six years. Our five-year-old son, Little John, was the apple of his grandparents' eyes and the pride of our life. Everything seemed to be going our way. When Andrea learned that she was pregnant with our second child, we believed this was only one more blessing designed to enrich our already full lives. As things turned out it was a blessing all right, but the definition of a "full life" was about to undergo a drastic revision.

One Fall day a coworker and his wife joined Andrea and me for lunch. I had chauffeured them in an unmarked investigative unit to the radio station where Andrea was working. Parked on the opposite side of the street, we waited for Andrea to appear. We were all in good spirits, talking and laughing easily.

I looked up from the conversation with my friends just in time to see Andrea emerge from the entrance of the radio station and cross the sidewalk. She smiled and waved as she stepped from the curb. She was wearing a pair of low heel shoes that had a small tap on the heels. As she passed from the sidewalk onto the pavement, she instinctively looked to her left. Seeing a car approaching on her side of the street she stepped backwards and as she did the metal tap on her heel skidded on the pavement and caused her to slip. She lost her balance and sat down with a jolt on the pavement. The fall did not appear to be serious but it did elicit a chorus of gasps from my passengers. Andrea quickly got back to her feet. Highly embarrassed, she looked around to see who might have witnessed her spill. Seeing that no one else had noticed she brushed off the seat of her pants and hurried across the street to join us. She assured us that she had not suffered any damage to anything other than her pride and we relieved our anxieties by making light of the incident as we drove to the restaurant.

After being seated, our guests excused themselves to cruise the buffet. While they were gone, Andrea confided to me that despite her apparent dismissal of the event she was concerned about the fall. She said she had decided to go to the hospital to have an ultrasound to reassure herself there was nothing wrong. The pregnancy plan with the doctor's office, Andrea pointed out, provided for one free ultrasound to determine the sex of the baby. Always taking the frugal approach, Andrea said she thought the imaging would be an inexpensive way to see if the fall had caused any problems. For her peace of mind, I knew the checkup would be a worthwhile investment of the time and trouble because she was still haunted by the near fatal experience of our son's birth.

Five years earlier she had been in labor all day when, suddenly, the monitor recording our son's heartbeat began to fade. What had happened was known as an abruption. An abruption is a condition where the placenta pulls apart from the wall of the womb prior to delivery, instead of following the birth of the child, as is its normal sequence of occurrence. The near loss of our son was a trauma, which had overshadowed her present pregnancy. I knew how much she worried about the new baby. I also knew that nothing would really set her mind at ease, but anything that could offer the least amount of solace was preferable to her constant anxiety.

The next day Andrea went to the hospital and had the ultrasound performed. When the procedure was completed she was given a copy of the video that had been made during the session. When I got home from work that afternoon she excitedly demanded that I sit down to watch it. She proudly put the tape into the VCR and set about explaining the gray and black images moving about the TV screen as they had been explained to her. She proudly announced the baby was a girl, but she cautioned that the staff had told her they could not be 100% certain. I really did not care whether the baby was a boy or a girl I told her, I only wanted it to be healthy. She agreed.

As I sat there watching those ghostly images float about the TV screen, there emerged from the swirling mass a group of three dark spots swimming amid the grayish sea, two blobs smaller than the third. They moved about for some time until the two smaller splotches hovered above the third one, forming the classic design of a skull's eyes and nose. A cold feeling of dread swept over me. I remember thinking that I had made a terrible interpretation of the images. I tried to push the thought from my mind, but the idea persisted. An uneasy feeling crept over me. I thought, "Is this some sort of omen?" It was the preamble to a reality that was far worse and more frightening than any thing I could have imagined.

What I was seeing, but did not understand at the time, was the genesis of trouble. The dark spots were two kidneys and a bladder.

In my experiences with law enforcement I had tracked armed, desperate men, gone into darkened buildings after criminals, and plunged into fights without thought for my personal safety. Over the years I had entertained myself with the idea that I knew what fear was all about, but nothing I had ever experienced could prepare me for the fears I would soon face. In the months and years to come I was going to discover that there were horrors I had not dreamed of and suffering beyond anything I could conceive. A malaise seeped into the pit of my stomach as I watched the video of our future daughter, a disquiet washed about my entrails like hearing something crawl behind your chair on a dark night and being too afraid to put your hand behind you to see what it is.

Several days after undergoing the ultrasound Andrea had stopped by Dr. Fitts' office, her OBGYN at the time, to drop off a Christmas gift for him. When the receptionist saw her enter the office she alerted Dr. Fitts who broke off an examination to come to the front desk and asked Andrea to stay. He said he had something he wanted to discuss with her. When he was finished with the patient he had been examining, Dr. Fitts took Andrea into his personal office and told her that the ultrasound tech had alerted him to some anomalies she had detected during the test. He said she had brought the tape to his office and that he had viewed the ultrasound. Based upon his examination of the tape he told Andrea he believed there was a problem with the baby. His initial opinion was that it was some sort of abdominal obstruction, certainly cause for concern, but in his opinion not extremely serious. He suggested we go to Vanderbilt University Hospital in Nashville and have another, more extensive, ultrasound examination. He pointed out that Vanderbilt's ultrasound technology was far superior to that of our local hospital. He told her that Vanderbilt was one of the leading research hospitals in the nation and possessed some of the best equipment and specialists to be found in the Southeast.

Going to Vanderbilt was simply a precaution and nothing more. What could possibly be wrong? This was our baby, not someone else's. Other people have serious problems, not us. I confidently reassured Andrea before we went that everything would be all right. I even speculated that the tests would probably show that there was no problem at all, only that the equipment at the local hospital was faulty. I treated the trip as if the only problem we would have would be a wasted day away from work, a nuisance more than anything else.

Andrea prides herself on being pessimistic. She believes that if she anticipates the worst, then she cannot be disappointed. She said she prepared herself for the worst, but nothing in my life, or hers, could have possibly prepared us for what "the worst" would turn out to be.

Christmas was approaching as we drove the seventy-five miles to Nashville that gray day in December 1989, but the joy and anticipation of the season was far removed from our thoughts as we made our way toward the Vanderbilt complex that afternoon. Once in Nashville, we searched through unfamiliar streets to find equally unfamiliar parking lots. Leaving our car in a parking space we crossed the street in front of the hospital and entered a huge, brown brick building that ingested and discharged people in a dispassionate process, which concealed the eminent proportions of human drama taking place inside the structure. We proceeded from information desk to reception area, answered questions, filled out forms, and waited as if it were just any other day in our lives. We made small talk to disguise our anxiety. Soon a nurse came and led us down a corridor to a room filled with strange equipment. A young technician came in and massaged Andrea's stomach with some sort of gelatinous goo. She then took a hand-held ultrasound monitor and placed it on the prepared region of Andrea's lower abdomen. Although Andrea was only about four months pregnant she had developed a noticeably swelled stomach. The young technician started the examination by adjusting the hand held monitor to the side of the lower abdominal slope. On the TV screen gray images grew, shifted, and changed. I could discern nothing intelligible from the shadows and shapes appearing on screen. The monitor produced images that changed with the slightest movement of the technician's hand. Shapes developed, melted into other shapes, and disappeared only to be replaced by other images that floated silently across the screen.

I stood in the darkened room looking from Andrea to the screen. When the examination was complete the technician got up and excused herself. We were left alone in the room; the monitor had been left turned on like a blind eye glaring into the semi-darkened room. I told myself the technician would come back soon, smiling to relieve our tension. Everything would be all right. It was then that I realized that I had not seen the technician smile, not even when she left, but I thought I must have been mistaken. Surely she must have smiled. People automatically smile. It is a social practice, if nothing else, but a part of me kept reminding myself that I had not seen the tech smile, especially when she left.

Soon a man entered and crisply introduced himself as Dr. Chantee. He sat down at the ultrasound board and picked up the hand scanner and promptly began his own examination. Probably just a minor thing I told myself, something the tech did not recognize immediately. I thought she was probably new at the job and not yet as experienced as Dr. Chantee was. That was all, I told myself like whistling in a cemetery, there was no reason to be concerned. We waited, watching him retrace the scanner over the mound of Andrea's stomach. Andrea looked at me inquiringly, but all I could do was shrug. I wanted to reassure her, but really didn't know how. All I kept telling myself was that everything would be all right once they got the kinks worked out.

The gray and black images appeared and changed, just as they had before, but I noticed that the doctor lingered at certain points, leaning forward to examine the screen intently. I found myself wishing that I knew what he was seeing. To me the whole thing was a meaningless morass of grays and blacks but I knew his experienced eyes were seeing things that I had no knowledge about. I desperately wished I could see like the doctor, to know what it was I was looking at, to understand what it all meant.

Dr. Chantce took some individual pictures of certain areas, studied the screen closely again and moved on. I have no idea how long the examination lasted, whether it was ten minutes or two hours. Time was an absent thing, I did not even know if it was evening or night. Since our entry into the little room, the small dark place had become our world and the monitor screen the center of our universe. After a time he stopped, put down the hand scanner and stood up. Turning on the room lights he gave Andrea some towels to wipe off the gelatin and told her she could pull down her blouse.

Dr. Chantee was from Northern Europe and his heavy accent made his speech somewhat difficult to understand. When he began trying to explain what he had discovered, I strained to catch his words, failing at most, but grabbing hold of enough to understand that the problem was not the bowel obstruction that we had been sent to have confirmed. I understood enough to learn that in actuality the problem was a bladder seal. I had never heard of a bladder seal before, but then I had never heard of an abdominal obstruction either. We asked what a bladder seal was. He explained that it was a condition where the bladder is blocked by the collapse of a weakened sidewall obstructing the neck of the bladder so that urine cannot escape. Without the urine, which makes up the amniotic fluid in the uterus, the fetus is endangered. The amniotic fluid creates the atmosphere in which the fetus exists. The baby cannot survive without it.

I was startled. Had I heard correctly? "...Cannot survive." Survive? My mind raced to catch up. We had come to have a minor problem confirmed and taken care of; we did not come here to talk about not surviving.

He told us about the structure of the kidneys and how they produce urine, which is emptied into the bladder. The bladder, when full, empties out of the baby's body into the womb. The unborn baby exists in an atmosphere of this fluid. Without it, the baby perishes. Human beings come into life breathing liquid because baby's lungs are not completely formed until the latter stages of development. Without an adequate supply of the life-giving fluid the fetus dies. In our baby's case the bladder was blocked by a portion of the bladder wall, which had developed a hole in it. The hole allowed the fluid to get between the lining of the bladder and the bladder's outer wall. As the fluid seeped inside the hole it caused the lining to expand, and as the lining expanded it blocked the mouth of the bladder.

The urine was trapped in the slowly expanding bladder without an avenue of escape. But even though the trapped fluid had nowhere to go, the kidneys were continuing to produce more urine. This caused the bladder to swell ever larger and the baby's stomach was bulging. To complicate matters even further, the backed up urine was in the process of destroying the kidneys. If the kidneys were destroyed, then no new fluid would be produced. The crisis was enhanced by the fact that the baby was only four months along in its development and needed the life-giving fluids for five more months. The early stage of development prevented any intervention in the form of surgery to remove the baby.

When he had finished his explanation I did not know what to say, my mind could not take it all in and process the information as it should. Andrea repeated that Dr. Fitts had said it was an abdominal obstruction as if the idea might suggest an alternative to the diagnosis we had just heard.

Dr. Chantee shook his head, saying that an abdominal obstruction had nothing to do with the problem he had discovered. I asked how common this sort of thing was, hoping, I suppose, that if I could establish some sort of commonality to the condition that it would some how ease the troubling news we had been given. Dr. Chantee said that it was not uncommon and happened in a given number of pregnancies.

"What happened to the other babies who had this condition," I asked, banking on the idea that the customary scenario would be our best bet for progress.

"The fetus is a girl baby," he informed us, and my first thought was who cares! That is not what I asked. I wanted to know what happened to other babies with this condition not what sex the baby is, but Chantee immediately clarified his reason for telling us a seemingly unimportant fact.

"No girl babies have ever survived," he said with a flat, emotionless voice.

My first thought was that my hearing had gone bad. Did he say no girl babies have ever survived? No, he couldn't have said that, surely not that. Some giddy part of my mind wanted to ask the inferentially implied alternative to the answer, if no girls have survived then does that mean boys have survived? And if they did, why? But it was an absurd question. I should not ask absurd questions I told myself. I looked at Andrea and saw terror in her eyes, and something else, something deep and dark, sadness so profound it frightened me. It was sadness as ageless as motherhood, a melancholy of doom shared by all mothers. My young wife had suddenly connected with the horror of mothers throughout the ages, and from that seminal connection she had instantly grown older, but old in the sense of dread, not of years. I would come to know that sad countenance much better as time went on. I was to see that look in the faces of countless "old" young women as they anguished over their dying babies, flanked by their equally "old" husbands of tender years. At that moment all I knew was that it shocked me. Looking into Andrea's terror-filled eyes I wondered if her face was a mirror of my own fear.

As I was grappling with the implications of what he had said, Dr. Chantee excused himself, mumbling something about checking with another doctor on the matter. He showed us out into the hallway and directed us to a waiting area.

The waiting area was nothing more than a wide space in the hallway equipped with chairs. Black and white photographs of landscapes adorned the walls. Neither of us could speak at first, we just sat there and held hands. I remember looking at the photos on the wall. I love art and beauty but at that moment I could not find any there. My gaze drifted about the room, *"... no girl babies have survived ..."*, to the walls and the floor. Some other people were there, waiting, I suppose, on other doctors, but I paid little attention to them, *"... no girl babies have survived ..."*.

I wished the others were gone one minute and the next I wanted to go over to them and say ... *They tell us it is a little girl, did you know we're expecting a little girl, but no girl babies have survived, do you understand?* But I knew they would not understand, just as I could not have understood ten minutes earlier if someone had said it to me. During my career people have brought me their fears and terrors and I thought I had understood, but at that moment I knew that I had never understood, not in the least, because now I was truly beginning to understand - really understand what it meant to be afraid because, "No girl babies have survived."

I said something to Andrea, something stupid I suppose, because I could not recall what it was I said, I just wanted to say something to help her, help me, but what could I say? I just wanted them to fix it. Then I remembered a strange encounter I had had when I was in the sixth or seventh grade.

There had been a carnival at the elementary school I attended with games and toys and booths. It was one of those early attempts to raise money for the school, and classes were dismissed for the last half of the day so that all the children could enjoy the carnival before going home. The free time was used to get the kids to have fun so that they would go home and nag their parents into bringing them back that night to spend more money. I was in the gym when the incident happened. There was a kid in a lower grade that had several physical defects. Back then he was called mentally retarded, now I suppose he would be referred to as mentally challenged, or perhaps slow. The other children considered him to be some sort of monster. His face was large and mis-shapened, with thick dark eyebrows. He was short and fat, and was usually accompanied by an additional distinct body odor which the order served as a deterrent to socialization. Perhaps the single most repulsive thing about the boy, as far as the other children were concerned, was his hands. The fingers on both hands were fused together, and the nails were wide, flat, and badly formed.

The affliction was bad enough, but what really made the children fearful of him was a rumor that went around school that claimed if you touched him your fingers would grow together like his. For this reason other children would not go near him. If he tried to play with them they would usually run away. He had a sister or two in the same school and he sometimes played with them, when they would let him, but he usually played alone, an outcast on the playground, in the lunchroom, or wherever he might be found.

As I walked across the gym floor that particular day I was suddenly stopped dead in my tracks by the malformed youngster running up to me with a balloon in his hands, those horrible, deformed hands. The balloon had been attached to a thin stick but it had come off. He cut off my path with his shuffling, awkward gate, breathing hard and sweating with excitement.

"Fix it," he lisped, thrusting out the balloon in one hand and the stick in the other. "Fix it."

It was a simple, pitiful appeal rising up from the deep well of his physical helplessness. He neither knew of, nor cared for, my fear of him. He had only one thing on his mind; his balloon had broken and he wanted it fixed. I did not know if I was the only one he had asked to help him or if others had chased him away or turned their backs on him. All I knew was that he was holding out that balloon in a hand full of welded together fingers with the long slender stick grasped firmly in the other repeating his heart breaking plea over and over, in his lisping, broken speech, "Fix it, fix it."

I remember being so afraid. Ashamed too, I suppose, in some way that I did not immediately understand. Very mindful of my unreasonable fear I reached out and took the balloon and stick from him, certain my hands would grow into similarly grotesque shapes.

It was a simple matter to tie the balloon back to the stick and I handed it back to him. His eyes were bright with excitement as he quickly retrieved his repaired toy. He thanked me in his lisping, high-pitched voice, as he raced off at breakneck speed to immerse himself in the newly restored wonder of his bright, pretty treasure.

I had fixed the balloon because I knew he was too poor to have bought it himself and that some teacher had probably felt sorry for him and given it to him. It was the only toy I ever saw him with and the only time I ever saw him so happy. I remember taking a quick look around to see if anyone had seen me help him, fearful that some of the others would think that I now was tainted and that they would shun me out of fear that I might transmit to them the horror of the melted hands. No one had seen me and I went quickly on my way, his plaintive words forever echoing in my mind.

Sitting there in that waiting area I kept hearing the lisping, pathetic voice again, pleading, "Fix it", only this time it was not the sweating little boy with a broken balloon pleading for me to aid him, this time I knew that the powerless, pleading voice was coming from within me. I was that helpless child swallowed up in the murky depths of inadequacies. This time it was I begging the plaintive appeal for someone to, "Fix it, fix it."

I sat there wishing for the white-coated savior with the magic of science to sweep down the hall, smile benevolently, and explain in a knowing, condescending tone how this problem was nothing more than a minor glitch, a trifling thing, really, something they corrected everyday here in the wonderland called, Vanderbilt.

Andrea sat quietly, as lost within herself, as I was lost within my own misery. The only thing that we could do was to hold hands and be there for one another. We carefully scrutinized each person who came down the hall. Was this the one, we wondered, the doctor with the possible answers? As each one passed we fell back into our miserable silence.

At long last Dr. Chantee came striding down the hall with another man matching his pace. The newcomer was slender beneath his white coat. He was dark skinned with immaculately trimmed black hair. As they approached, we stood to greet them. Dr. Chantee introduced the man as Dr. Shah, a neonatal specialist. Dr. Shah briefly reviewed what

Chantee had explained to us earlier. Shah was even more difficult to understand than Chantee was at times. Both practiced the art of mingling their descriptions with medical terminology as if we were proficient in "medicalese". But we understood enough to know there were no simple answers. He told us that the survival rate of such a condition was rare and that the odds were that the baby would not survive to term, because the supply of amniotic fluids would gradually decrease until the fetus died. Chantee commented at that point in Shah's explanation that there was a lot of fluid present, a condition for which he had no ready justification. Shah agreed that this was highly unusual but did not hold out any hope that this would continue. He only said that they would do more tests and try to determine why the fluid was being produced despite the bladder seal while searching for some way to intercede in the problem.

At the end of the discussion we were simply told to go home and wait. They wanted us to come back in two weeks so that they could perform another ultrasound. Dr. Shah promised they would see what they could do to save our baby.

We walked out of the hospital to discover the day had fled away from us, leaving the night as our companion. The ordeal had taken all afternoon. We located our car and threaded our way out of the parking lot. As we drove onto the street Andrea held her stomach in both arms, as if by cradling the baby inside her she could comfort her. Holding her stomach in her arms as though she held a fully born child, she began talking to the baby as tears rolled down her cheeks.

"You're not going to die," she said softly. "I won't let you."

I kept driving, resolutely watching the road ahead of us. I could not, would not, give in to the throbbing desire to start crying right along with her. I refused to succumb to the emotions that threatened to engulf me.

"She's not going to die, is she?" Andrea asked, as if by our mutual agreement we could stave off the inevitable if only we banded together in a refusal not to believe in it.

"I don't know." It was all I could say. I was determined to concentrate on driving, doing something, anything that would keep my mind busy.

"We're not going to let her die, are we?" she asked. Her voice was a challenge now, not a question. Her tone had taken on a fierce determination and I knew she meant it. I knew her too well, she was preparing herself to face death and she was resolved to fight it. Death would not have her child.

"Not if we can help it," I said, offering what support I could logically afford.

Andrea had never faced death in a personal, intimate battle. She did not know its awesome ferocity, but she was preparing herself as best she could to fight it and I knew, without thinking about the alternatives, that I would join that battle with her. I was afraid, but I too was prepared to fight. I just was not prepared to deny it.

It was a silent drive home, heavy and oppressive, each of us prisoners of our thoughts. That first terrible drive home was a forerunner of many similar trips that were to develop into a way of life for us. We would discover that people could adjust to living a life of constant fear, dread and anxiety just as readily as they adjust to lives filled with everyday trivialities.

Chapter II
The Ordeal Begins

Breaking the news to the grandparents was difficult. My mother cried when she heard that her granddaughter was not supposed to live to be born. She held Andrea as they both wept and reassured her that everything would be all right. Andrea's father exhibited a stoic resignation. He was the kind of man who manifests little external indication of his private thoughts and feelings. Upon learning of her granddaughter's serious condition and probable fate, Andrea's mother, Ursula, became a tide of optimistic grit. She exhibited the same tenacity Andrea demonstrated.

As a child, Ursula grew up surviving daily Allied air raids and the privations of Hitler's Germany. She had lost her father, before she was old enough to know him, to a firing squad in a concentration camp. She had watched as rescuers pulled the remains of her mother from a collapsed cellar where she had been boiled alive by hot water tanks that had ruptured when an American bomb had hit the building where they had taken cover during an air raid. Her earliest memories were of emergency techniques designed to enhance the odds of surviving the constant aerial bombings and of later fleeing across a ravaged country to escape the horrors of the advancing Allies. She had learned how to fight to survive in hostile environments at a tender age, a skill that served her well both during and after the war.

When friends and coworkers asked about Andrea and the baby I spoke optimistically. When pressed for details I would explain and then watch as pain and discomfort settled upon their faces. The news simply made everyone who heard it uncomfortable.

What I eventually learned to do was to carry the conversation on my own. Whether it was out of fear or just the need to fill the voids I don't really know, all I did know was that when asked about the situation I just kept talking, always pointing out that the predicament was not normal and that things were not happening as they usually did in such a condition. I admitted that I was not sure what could be done about the problems, and that there were other tests and appointments to be completed which might hold information that could change the prognosis. Talking became a form of verbal confidence for me, a sort of verbal equivalent of whistling in the dark.

The days following our initial examination at Vanderbilt seemed like a small eternity as they dragged slowly along. Eventually Dr. Shah's office contacted us. On the appointed day we made the trek back to Vanderbilt Hospital, arriving a little ahead of schedule. The medical clinic attached to Vanderbilt Hospital is a small, self-contained red brick extension of the main hospital building, four stories high, filled with a bewildering array of specialists.

Walking the efficiently designed clinic hallways we encountered a depressing parade of patients, far too many of which were babies and small children. I had never really looked closely before at afflicted children, but I began to look at these children of misfortune. Some were in wheelchairs with deformed limbs, twisted bodies, or distorted faces. Many had no hair or were bloated, symptoms I would later come to know as the appalling signs of chemotherapy. With each child I encountered I wondered if I was looking into our future. Later I found that I had developed a superstitious habit of not stepping on wheelchair ramps as I crossed sidewalks or entered buildings. I had developed a sort of ritual avoidance the ramps, as if not touching them physically could prevent my ever having to use them.

I began to wonder if death might be preferable for our baby. I was ashamed to think such a terrible thing about my own unborn child, but deep inside I knew I must confront such a horrid question. Was life so precious that we would prefer it to death at all costs, or were there some costs, which we were not prepared to pay? Somewhere the dim thought roamed about the periphery of my mind, what if I have to make that choice? What do I choose? How do I choose? Would I have to make a decision whether or not my child would live or die, and by letting it live was I sentencing it to a life of pain and suffering? Intellectually, I knew that such choices are made by people all the time, but by me? Not me. Surely, God, not me. This is something other people must do, but please, not me!

We tramped the halls, counting down the numbers on the walls and reading the titles attached to doors and waiting areas. We finally located Dr. Shah's office, signed in at the reception desk and selected a seat. We waited, just like ordinary people doing ordinary things, as we tried to make ourselves comfortable in the uncomfortable chairs.

Other patients sat, scattered about the room, waiting their turn as they flipped through magazines or stared out the windows as if everything were normal. All the while I sat there, a part of me wanted to jump up and yell at everyone sitting so contentedly about the room, "Everything's not normal, O.K.? So let's stop pretending that it is! Stop acting like everything's O.K.! Can't you see that it isn't, that we're plugged into some awful nightmare here and no one can wake us up? Stop pretending that everything's all right because it isn't! It isn't and we know it, but we just can't stop pretending!"

But I said nothing, did nothing. Like all the rest, we sat there quietly and waited. In the months to come, as our experience in waiting rooms grew, we got very good at acting like everything was normal, even when sheer terrifying insanity peeked around the corner and grinned its maniacal smile, we acted as if nothing was wrong. One of the great lessons we learned was that people could become articulate liars when life necessitates.

After an interminable length of time Dr. Shah was free to see us. We went into his inner office and were seated in front of his desk. Proudly displayed on the wall behind his chair were his graduate degrees and licenses to practice. He began the session by reciting the familiar circumstances of our present predicament, which served as an educational tool as well as a refresher of the facts.

Shah covered the same ground that Chantee had days before, the baby was female, no female babies with a bladder seal had ever survived. In the unlikely event she lived long enough to be born she would die very soon thereafter. Shah's conclusion was that something must be done, but the problem was, practically speaking there was very little that could be done about such a condition. He told us that he knew of only one other case where a female baby with a bladder seal was surviving like ours. The case was in California, in the San Francisco Bay area. He said that he believed there was a chance of success for a procedure to pierce the bladder seal externally and relieve the obstruction. The procedure was rare. He said he knew of a doctor in California who had done the operation before. Shah mentioned that he had done a similar procedure only once himself. He offered to contact the California doctor and see if he could lend any assistance.

In short, what Dr. Shah proposed was that we agree to an experimental outpatient surgery, to be performed at Vanderbilt. The fetus' stomach would be pierced with a long needle. Once inside the fetus the needle would be used to puncture the bladder and break the seal. If the needle could slash holes in the seal the trapped fluid would be able to escape. Later, after birth, the seal could be surgically removed with ease. It was clear that without some such surgical intervention there was no hope for the baby's survival.

Andrea looked at me. I could tell that she had made up her mind to try the surgery, and consulting me with her eyes was nothing more than polite formality. I nodded and she turned back to Dr. Shah.

"When do we do it?" It was her way of agreeing to the procedure.

"As soon as possible," Shah replied, his immediate response reflecting the urgency of the matter. "I will have my staff set up the necessary arrangements. They will call you."

Smiling confidently, he ushered us out of the room. I wanted to believe that all this conjecture was true. Just a simple procedure, that's all it was going to be. All they had to do was pierce the bladder and break the seal! It sounded so easy, so simple. Admittedly the approach was uncommon but it was easy, something I could comprehend. This I could understand! My hopes soared.

As Andrea and I drove home that day I cheered her lagging spirits with the bright prospects of what Shah had described. Things were not as grave as they had seemed. There was hope and between Shah and the unnamed doctor in California this problem could be solved. With Christmas only days away, this was the best present we could have been given. We drove home in the best frame of mind we had enjoyed since the ordeal began.

* * * * * * *

It was dreadfully cold as we set off toward Vanderbilt the morning of the operation. The windows on the inside of our car were frozen over. It was so frigid that the car's heater refused to work. Believing that it was broken we borrowed a car to make the drive but the borrowed vehicle was no warmer than our own. We drove bundled in layers of coats, shivering in the bitter cold. I chipped at the ice coating the inside of the windshield as we went. We drove cautiously, wary of icy spots on the road, but in truth the ice-covered highway did not concern us as much as the fear of the unknown awaiting us at the hospital.

The warmth inside the reception area of Vanderbilt hospital was a relief. When we arrived on the surgical floor and presented ourselves at the nursing station a pleasant, sympathetic young nurse who showed us to our room and assisted us in making preparations attended us. Her cheerful and upbeat attitude put us at ease.

Not long after Andrea donned her surgical gown Dr. Shah strode into the room dressed in an expensive heavy topcoat and confident smile. He related that he had made contact with the doctor in San Francisco who had done this type operation before but since that the doctor had only performed the operation once. Shah discarded the idea of referring us to him, "Even I have this much experience," he proudly proclaimed. "So, I decided I will do it myself."

Chantee stuck his head in the door as Shah was informing us of his plans. The two doctors exchanged pleasantries and wandered out of the room immersed in a private discussion obscured by medical terminology concerning the upcoming surgery. I stood by the bed, trying to reassure Andrea. In a few minutes our nurse pushed open the door, smiled at Andrea and told her it was time to go. Andrea looked at me with a mixture of false bravery and evident fear. I assured her that everything would be all right, and when I reminded her that she was doing this for the baby she switched on her determined maternal mood.

"Let's go," she said, immediately ready for surgery.

After Andrea had been wheeled out of the room I felt terribly alone. I could not stay in the room by myself so I walked out into the hall. Once in the hallway I knew nowhere to go. I stopped and looked aimlessly about. Coming toward me down the hall were Shah and Chantee. They had changed into green surgical scrubs and looked like an odd set of twins. When Shah saw me standing in the corridor he stopped and came toward me.

"What are you doing here?" he demanded in his clipped speech.

I mumbled something about waiting for them to return and he snapped a curt order at a nearby nurse, "Get him some scrubs." He then turned back to me abruptly.

"No, no, you suit up and go on in. Here, here," he waved at a nurse coming down the hall with a bundle of green scrubs under her arm. "You put these on and come along, quickly."

I hurried back into our room and pulled on the unfamiliar clothing. My hands shook as I fumbled to tie the pants in place. I pulled on the top easily and tried to put on the sterile mask as I rushed out of the room, hurrying down the hallway. Tying on a mask while rushing down a hall always looked good in the movies but in real life it is not so easy to accomplish. When I pulled up short at the operating room door I still had not tied the mask in place. A nurse appeared and helped me secure the mask before opening the doors.

The room in which the surgery was to take place was a small rectangle dominated by an examination table on which Andrea had been placed, covered by a sheet. Dr. Chantee was busy setting up the monitor and ultrasound equipment on the far side of the examination table. The nurse who had helped me with the mask moved about unobtrusively assisting each doctor in silent efficiency. Dr. Shah was sitting on a stool to Andrea's left, by her knees. Beside Shah sat a much younger man dressed in scrubs. Dr. Shah was quietly instructing the younger man about the implements scattered over a tray placed nearby. For a moment I could not understand the younger man's reason for being present until I recalled that Vanderbilt was a teaching hospital and this was undoubtedly a very fortunate young doctor who was about to experience an operation which had been attempted only a couple of times in modern medicine.

I walked to the head of the table and looked down at Andrea. She was trying to be brave amid all these strangers. I knew she must have been terrified but she was courageously holding up on her own. I stood over her for some time before she looked up at me. At first she gave me a brief glance, but her eyes quickly returned to my face. She stared at me for a long time, then tried to turn her head sideways for a better look.

"John," she finally asked, as if she could not believe what her eyes told her.

I wiggled my fingers at her in a mock, childish wave and her mood brightened instantly.

"John, it is you?" she exclaimed with tears welling up in her eyes.

I slipped the mask down to the bottom of my nose so she could see who it was and then quickly pushed it back in place.

"What are you doing here?" she asked.

"They told me to come in," I shrugged.

She reached above her head with both hands and caught hold of mine, she squeezed my fingers in a grip that made me grimace beneath the mask.

"I'm so glad," she giggled like a small child. It was an endearing trait I loved in her.

I just nodded, afraid to say too much in this alien environment. Activity inside the small room was growing by the second. Comments were passed to the young doctor in training as the door continued to open and close, each time admitting one, two or more young medical students who were quietly beginning to line the walls. Within minutes the room was crammed with students standing shoulder to shoulder as they leaned against the walls and murmured among themselves.

"Who are all these people?" Andrea asked me, after motioning me to lean forward so she could whisper her question.

"Doctors," I whispered back.

"No," she shook her head, her eyes growing serious as she scanned the room, "they're too young."

"They're doctors," I reaffirmed.

"They can't be," she persisted, "they're younger than me!"

"And you'll be 31 next year," I reminder her.

Her eyes flashed with the fire of her temper. Andrea does not like to be reminded of her age.

"They're still younger than me." She stressed the 'younger' part, and I knew what she meant.

"Yes, late twenties," I calculated out loud for her benefit, "is about right to be finishing their medical training. They're all doctors, don't worry."

"I'm not worried," she started to turn her head and then spun it back around at me, squinting up at an angle, "and I'm not old!"

"No," I agreed, "you're not old."

Although Andrea is touchy about her age I knew that was not her reason for engaging me in a discussion. Just before she had turned her attention to me she had seen, as had I, Dr. Shah extract a very long needle from the implement tray. It looked to be well over a foot long. He was discussing something with the assisting trainee as he held the needle casually in his hand. Andrea and I both wanted our attention diverted away from that gruesome puncturing device.

Hearing us talking in hushed tones the attending nurse leaned over the table between Andrea's face and mine, and said,

"I just took a head count and there are 25 people in this room beside the three of us."

Andrea told her we were just discussing that fact.

"And he," glancing up at me, "says they're all doctors. I was just telling him that they're too young to be doctors."

The nurse smiled behind her mask, making her eyes crinkle. "They're doctors."

Dr. Shah spoke up to let everyone know that they were ready. He informed everyone present that they had administered a local anesthetic to Andrea's lower abdomen to dampen the pain. He said that she might feel a slight pressure, but that would be all. He exchanged a few directions with Dr. Chantee concerning the placement of the ultrasound devise and the procedure commenced.

Dr. Shah handed the needle to the young doctor beside him and gave instructions about the initial entry as he indicated the area on Andrea's stomach with his finger. He directed the young man's attention to the monitor screen hanging above Andrea's head and to her right. He cautioned him about the depth of entry and then told him to begin.

The young man placed the needle out of sight against the bottom of Andrea's distended abdomen. She looked up at me in fear. I tried to reassure her quietly but did not know what to say other than to keep repeating, "It's all right, it's all right."

On the TV screen I could see the grayish ghostly outline that I instantly recognized as my daughter, small and composed of light gray lines and oddly shaped dark splotches. From the many ultrasounds we had in the past weeks I knew what she looked like, I'd even seen her face. I had watched her suck her thumb and kick her feet. I knew the ominous outlines of the enlarged bladder, that oblong black spot in her stomach that meant that the bladder seal was still in place.

I watched and waited, holding my breath. Then I saw it, the edge of the needle slowly poked into view. On the screen it seemed larger. Slowly it moved closer to the baby reclining in the streaks of gray lines, the enlarged stomach forcing the body to extend rather than curl in the familiar fetal position. The needle moved closer to the rounded hump of the troublesome stomach accentuated by the large black area filled with trapped amniotic fluid.

I was struck by the surreal absurdity of it all: men in white coats sticking long needles into Andrea's rounded abdomen, piercing it in an attempt to stick it into a smaller rounded abdomen. Stomach within stomach, a needle connecting them together like a straight line on a painting, a bizarre Mondrain design, so unreal yet appallingly too real. I remembered Edward Munch's painting, "The Scream", but it was not a scream I was joined to now, it was madness and I was the insane, floating, distorted screamer. How could we have come to this? This was pure insanity, sticking pregnant women with needles so that you could pierce their unborn babies! Madness, but there was no escaping it, so I watched with a prisoner's fascination as the needle came closer and closer to the sacrificial stomach within a stomach.

I heard Dr. Shah say that he would take over now. The needle wavered, steadied, and then drove relentlessly forward into the gray outline of the baby's stomach. The image blurred for an instant. The baby, my baby, grabbed at the needle and her body jerked with pain and surprise (could the unborn be surprised, I wondered). I thought of how sorry I was to let these men, these strangers I did not know, hurt my baby for a reason that it could not understand. Part of my whole reason for being was to keep people from hurting my child and here I was holding Andrea's hand and letting these men pierce my baby's tiny tummy with a huge needle. What kind of father was I? What kind of madness was this? I thought of the painting of the scream again. For the first time I understood how a person could scream until the world wavered and undulated, and yet not make a sound. As the needle penetrated the tiny tummy, its contents exploded, causing the stomach to diminish in size and collapse into a normal configuration.

"We have relieved the bladder pressure," Dr. Shah announced, adding something about having missed the bladder seal.

Dr. Chantee leaned over the table, working the monitor screen slightly to his right; "Can you see all right?" he asked Andrea.

"I don't want to see," Andrea gritted her teeth, her bravado completely gone now.

"Are you all right?" Dr. Shah asked, hearing her comment.

"It just feels...I feel funny," Andrea struggled for words. "It hurts," she added, "It's starting to hurt."

Her grip on my fingers was like bands of steel cutting into my flesh. Shah said something about almost being through, the needle dipped again, back into the baby stomach's inner regions. The baby jumped and pushed at the needle. Back down the needle plunged, digging at the seal, the baby pushed outward, striking out at the invading pain. Back down the needle drove, insistently digging, digging at the elusive seal.

Andrea cried out, the pain growing as the baby moved. Were they experiencing the same pain I wondered? Transferring pain from one to the other somehow? Shah tried again but grumbled something about not getting it, that the reduction of the pressure had made the seal pliable and unyielding to the needle. Andrea was stiff, and she appeared to be at the end of her endurance.

Sensing that Andrea could bear no more Dr. Shah called an end to the operation and began withdrawing the needle. When the steel sliver was extracted from her stomach Andrea did not ease immediately. Shah and Chantee put away their equipment and gave instructions that the operation was at an end. The nurse started unhooking Andrea from the various devices to which she had been attached and we were soon outside the operating theater and headed back to the outpatient room where we had started.

Once inside the room Andrea's pain eased, her color returned and she asked questions about how the surgery had gone. I had no answers and the nurses that came and went put her off, deferring to the surgeon who would see her shortly and explain it all.

After a time, Dr. Shah entered the outpatient room. He slowly explained, in his clipped English, that he was not certain that the operation had been a success. The bladder had collapsed and taken with it the rigidity that he needed to penetrate the seal. He feared that the seal was still in place. He said that he was leaving directions for our next ultrasound visit for an appraisal of the condition. He mentioned that he had taken a sample from Andrea's womb that he had sent for testing. This sample would alert us to conditions the baby might have, such as Downs Syndrome. We would not know the test results for three days. We would have to endure Christmas with that uncertainty.

I gathered up our belongings. Andrea sat up slowly on the bedside and touched her head.

"Are you all right?" I asked, knowing there was no way she could possibly be all right.

"I feel dizzy," she rocked slightly from side to side.

"Just take it easy," I warned her and pulled our things to her bedside.

Our nurse came back in with something wrapped in a blanket.

"Here," she said, handing me the bulky item with a smile, "it's a bottle of sterile water. We heated it up in the microwave at the nurses' station. Keep it wrapped in this towel and when you get in the car put it around her feet. It'll help keep her warm on the way home."

Of all the duties she had performed that day the nurse had remembered how cold we said we had been coming to the hospital that morning. Her simple human kindness was touching. We found many more nurses at Vanderbilt like her. It was the nurses, in the end, who made it all bearable for us.

The trip home was difficult. Andrea had not eaten all day, so we stopped at a burger place to get something to go. As we were leaving Nashville Andrea became sick to her stomach and threw up. She apologized like a child whose illness has ruined everyone else's outing. But the warm water bottle around her feet gave a sense of comfort as we drove home through the cold night.

Andrea's sickness faded as we left Davidson County but she had vomited so hard that her face was splotched with broken blood vessels. She celebrated Christmas with bluish patches over her face and under her eyes. She looked like she had been in a fistfight and lost. To this day her terrible appearance is the thing she remembers the most about those lamentable Christmas days of 1989. Like a lot of the other unpleasant things that we experienced during our ordeal I do not recall the splotches on her face. What I recall is her courageous endurance of the operation and my admiration of her tenacity in the face of fear so great that it would have paralyzed many other people.

The holiday season was a very difficult time for all of us. Christmas came and was celebrated with as much cheer as we could muster. For Little John's sake we set aside our concerns and made Christmas a happy time. We unwrapped presents, ate the traditional dinner, and watched "It's a Wonderful Life" on TV, but all we could think about was what the tests might reveal

Finally, Monday came and I made the call from my office to find out the test results. The technician who answered the phone did not have the results and told me that she would have to call back. I gave her my number and tried to get some work done while I waited. In a few minutes the technician called back.

"It's a girl!" The woman on the other end of the phone cheerfully announced.

"What?" I was not prepared for the announcement, and certainly not in so excited a voice.

"It's a little girl," she repeated.

"I know that," I told her in a reply that I believe might have been a bit too curt, "What else?"

"Uh.. nothing, nothing else." The tech stumbled over her words. She seemed not to know what to say.

"Nothing else?" I struggled to keep my voice calm. "What do you mean, nothing else?"

"Well, uh..that's all the report has, the sex of the baby." She sounded as if she were rereading the report on the other end of the line.

"Oh," I felt I should apologize for snapping at her, and I tried to explain, "we already know what sex she is, we are waiting for the test results to see if she had any other problems, like Downs Syndrome."

"Oh no," her voice regained its original excitement, "the test results were negative. She's fine."

"Great!" I exhaled an audible sign of relief.

"I'm sorry," the young woman on the other end of the line picked up on the obvious relief in my voice, "usually people want to know the sex of their child from these tests, I didn't know you were wanting anything else. I'm sorry."

"No, please don't be sorry," I told her, "We've waited all through Christmas to hear this news. This is the best Christmas present you could have given us even better than finding out what sex she is. Thanks, really."

"Oh, you're welcome," she said.

I hung up and quickly relayed the news to our families. Everyone was happy to find that we had no other problems. The happiness would last just three months.

Chapter III

Awaiting Lori's Arrival

The results of the next ultrasound test proved that the experimental surgery had been a failure. Doctors' Shah and Chantee immediately launched into an exploration of potentially promising new approaches that might be tried. While they were engaged in seeking out other options Andrea had to appear every other week for ultrasound examinations to "monitor the progress" of the baby. The intent of the phraseology was not lost on us. Monitoring the progress of the baby was nothing more than a polite euphemism for periodic spot checks to see if the baby was dead yet. It was not a question of if she would die, only when.

On one of these biweekly visits Dr. Chantee described an approach he and Shah wanted to try. They had decided on another experimental operation. In the proposed procedure they would insert a device into the womb and pierce the baby's stomach again. This time the instrument to be used would have small teeth that could be manipulated externally by the surgeon. In theory the teeth of this device would chew into the bladder seal, tear it open and release the trapped fluid. Chantee was excited about the possibilities, but we were not so keen about the prospect of undergoing another experimental surgery.

Chantee also offered an alternative possibility of another type of operation in which the womb could be opened and the baby extracted so that the surgeons could work directly on the fetus. Chantee said that this procedure was now being tried on the West Coast, but that it was more prone to induce abortion than the other procedures they were considering. Some years later we saw a news broadcast in which the open womb procedure was reported to have been used successfully in a landmark operation. Although we were happy for the parents of the fetus that had been repaired and rescued by that method, we were very glad that we had not been the first parents to undergo this type of experimental surgery.

The next time we went to Vanderbilt for our "check-up Chantee told us that there had been a meeting of hospital personnel to discuss our case. According to him, seventeen doctors representing various specialties, two hospital attorneys, and a medical ethicist debated the facts of our case at length. One doctor had significantly argued down all proposed experimental surgeries. Dr. David E. Hill, a urologist on staff at Vanderbilt, based his opposition upon simple logic; there was too much amniotic fluid present in the womb for this case to be a traditional bladder seal. Therefore, he reasoned, there was something at work which none of the people at Vanderbilt as yet understood. His proposal was to simply leave the situation alone and keeping monitoring the baby's condition. The ultimate defense of his "do nothing" position was a recitation of the Hippocratic oath, which warns doctors, "First, do no harm..." He contended that no one in that room could conclusively prove that they were not doing harm, and they certainly could not claim that they were accomplishing anything. The meeting, according to Chantee, ended with a stalemate. Dr. Hill had succeeded.

We kept going back every other week to "check the condition" of the baby for three more months. The trips became routine, but the pressure was anything but routine. Each ultrasound was a junket into a womb fraught with fear. Was the baby's condition worse than the last time? Had she died yet? The stress was unrelenting. But an unexpected benefit of the ultrasounds was that we got to know our baby much sooner than most parents.

It was during this time that we named our daughter. Our son, Little John, gave her the name Lori. One of his playmates at the baby-sitter's was named Lori. He liked the name and wanted his sister to have it. But it was her middle name we labored over. Believing that she should be given a name of significance, we looked for one that befitted her strong sense of survival and defiance of difficult physiology. Finally we settled on Ariella as a middle name. Going through some books on names, we discovered an old Hebrew name for a woman, Ariellia, which means "a strong spirit". It seemed to fit, Lori certainly had a strong spirit, but Andrea felt that Ariellia would put too many vowels in her names so we adopted Ariella.

Having named her helped us to think of her as a person. Andrea always spoke to her by name. When we went to the ultrasound appointments she began to refer to the grayish figure on the screen as "Lori". By giving her a name we had given her an identity. She became a real child, in an emotional sense.

On the ultrasounds we watched Lori suck her thumb, kick her feet, and move her little fingers. At times she was playful, at others she seemed restive or asleep. On one occasion the ultrasound staff made snap shots of Lori's face from the monitor screen. They were her first baby pictures, and a treasure we cherish.

One downside to getting to know Lori so well during this time was that the doctors and staff at the hospital referred to her as "the fetus", or "baby White". The references were objective and I am sure helped keep their objectivity in tact when making decisions about her. The problem with the reference was that it irritated Andrea. Out of their earshot Andrea would complain about their referring to Lori in vague, impersonal terms. She felt they were denying Lori her right to be human. Some of this came from the continual stress of not knowing what was going to happen, of never knowing when one of the tests was going to reveal a dead child, so I said very little about Andrea's strong reaction to the doctor's impersonal approach. But, on one occasion, the stress of the detached objectivity of their neutral comments overwhelmed Andrea to the point she exploded.

We were having a routine ultrasound, just as we had done so many times before. Two doctors were standing in the room discussing the results of the test, as they usually did. We had become used to them discussing us, and especially Lori, in the third person as if none of us were present. I knew it was a device they used to maintain their professional neutrality. From these candid discussions I learned a great deal about their suspicions and beliefs. Lori's condition was one that gave them a good deal of trouble because none of them had an explanation for her continued survival. She should not be alive, yet here she was not only alive but apparently developing normally. Normally, that is, except for her grossly distended stomach. Because of this ability to step inside their private discussion I did not resent their professional detachment, but Andrea felt entirely different about the matter.

On this particular occasion two doctors were standing apart from us, discussing Lori's perplexing condition. They were referring to her in the usual objective terms, when suddenly Andrea exploded.

"Her name is Lori!" She propped herself up on one arm from the supine position she had been lying in on the examination table. "She has a name, and I would appreciate it if you'd starting treating her like it!"

The doctors said nothing, they just looked at Andrea as if she were a very rude child that had interrupted an adult's conversation. They looked at each other, obvious signs of agitation on their faces at having been so impolitely interrupted. One cocked his head toward the hallway and they both departed to hold their discussion outside the presence of such an obviously upset woman.

I tried to calm Andrea, reasoning with her that it was their way of being objective. I tried to explain that they needed to do this so that they could do their job better, but she would not hear of it. Fetuses are babies, babies are people, and people have names she reasoned, therefore doctors should call people by their names. Not calling unborn babies by their given names lets doctors treat the baby as if it is less than, or other than, human.

* * * * * * *

A few weeks after Dr. Hill had stopped the exploration for new methods of intervention; Dr. Shah interrupted our regular schedule of ultrasounds with the announcement that he wanted us to come to his office for an appointment. He would not tell us why he had set the appointment or what we were to discuss. When we arrived we were ushered into a conference room.

Andrea and I took a seat on the North side of the room facing Dr. Shah and another man we had never seen before. The newcomer was bearded and dressed in a business suit. An obvious intellectual type, he seemed to lack the medical air that surrounded most of the M.D.s we had associated with in the past. Shah introduced him, adding that our guest was a medical ethicist.

At first we were confused as to why he was in attendance at the meeting. Shah began the session by reviewing Lori's condition, a recitation we knew all too well, then launched into a recital of their impending expectations. Emphatically, Shah stated that she could not survive to term but, if under some remarkable set of circumstances she did somehow manage to live to be born, she could not live for more than a day or two. He continued to say that if, by some miracle, she lived longer than a few days there was no way that she could live to be older than three years of age without a kidney transplant. He painted a very bleak picture of her future. I had heard such discussions before, usually in hushed tone and by people who did not think that I overheard, but never anything so out rightly awful as this recitation. Andrea looked shocked.

I was confused. Why was Shah doing this? What was his point? We knew all this, had gone over it many times with him as well as other doctors. What was he leading up to? And why was this other man here for this? As if in answer to my silent questions the man introduced to us as the ethicist leaned forward and told us in even, calm tones that Vanderbilt would do all that it could to keep our situation out of the media. He promised all the support the hospital could muster and counseling for us afterwards. Suddenly it hit me. I knew why we were having this meeting and why the ethicist had been invited to attend. They were talking about aborting the baby.

No one had used the word "abortion". Lori was too far along for a legal, traditional abortion, but what they had cited were the exceptional circumstances that would justify abortion in this particular case. The ethicist was offering not solace but cover. Aborting a baby at this stage would be news, and might set off a heated controversy. Without uttering the dreaded word the issue lay naked on the table before us.

"I'm not going to abort Lori," Andrea suddenly declared.

She sat straighter in her chair as she spoke, defying them as well as their logic.

Dr. Shah started to recite the difficulties again that awaited us if the pregnancy continued but Andrea cut him off.

"I don't care what you say," her German ire was up, and at times like these I have a clear appreciation of how people from such a small country could take on the world twice in the space of only twenty years and almost win each time. "I'm not going to kill Lori!"

In response Dr. Shah adopted the old 'you don't understand' tact, citing the dangers and certain death that lay ahead. Andrea remained unmoved. Shah pressed his tact but only succeeded in angering me, treating Andrea as if she were some stupid child who could not appreciate her dire predicament.

"Lori can't live to term," I said. "She will die soon. If she does live to be born she can't live more than one or two days, and if she were to be able to live any longer than that she could not possibility live longer than three years." I looked from Shah to the ethicist. "Isn't that about it?"

"I believe he has a good grasp of the situation," the ethicist said, as much to me as to Shah.

"I believe we do," I nodded sharply.

"Well," Shah's clipped English cut into the silence, "if that's your decision."

"That's our decision," Andrea said flatly, ending the discussion.

As quickly as the session had begun it was over and we all four walked out of the conference room together. Shah abruptly seemed in good spirits once again. It was obvious that he had done what he thought was necessary to explore all possible alternatives with us. He had done his job thoroughly and completely. He had no personal stake in the outcome and had only done what he believed to be the right thing. He made an odd comment as we walked out of the office.

"I am actually a pro-choice advocate," he said to the ethicist as we were walking down the hallway. "Most people don't believe that."

I wondered about the statement and thought how odd it was coming from a man dedicated to fetal medicine. Later I would learn that many neonatal doctors were pro-choice, and for good reason. In their careers they come in contact with so many infants who are either victims of their parents or nature that the emotional drain appeared to force them toward the pro-choice point of view. Dr. Shah had admitted to a belief diametrically opposed to his profession's basic mission, but one, which came from years of experiencing daily tragedy.

Andrea adamantly maintained her pro-life position. As we walked down the hall the discussion between the four of us was light and friendly, an amazing feat after the intense session we had just experienced.

Listening to these people calmly discuss their position on abortion I realized that on this very day there were hundreds of people manning both sides of the barricades on this issue across the country. I thought that there were many who stood ready to die for their convictions on this issue, and some were just as ready to kill to defend their position, but here we were four people who had actually discussed the event in practical terms and we were calmly discussing it as if we were a debate team on break. The friendly atmosphere aside, I knew there were deep issues at work here that made the fight over the political question of abortion appear simplistic and pallid.

What I did not tell them as we walked down the corridor was that I had always been a pro-choice advocate. It was not just the mother's body argument that I supported but the belief that people have a right to make all the mistakes they want. I firmly believe that true freedom carries with it the right to be wrong just as much as it carries the privilege to be right. True freedom means that we have an equal opportunity to destroy ourselves with our decisions just as we potentially possess the ability to enhance our conditions.

Related to my belief in a person's right to choose I also believed that people have the inherent responsibility to live with the consequences of their choices. The right of Adam and Eve to be free to make choices carried with it the inference that they must then live with the consequences of their act, as must their successors for all time. We have a right to choose, and a right to be wrong, but we also must be able to live with those choices once they are made.

These were my beliefs, but in that room just moments ago there had not really been a choice. We would not, could not kill Lori, no matter what the consequences might be. She was a part of us, a member of our family, and if she had problems, they were our problems by right of heritage. We had no "right" to refuse our own, to reject our child simply because she was less than perfect. But I wondered had we subjected ourselves, and this child, to a life of misery? Would we live to regret this decision? I was troubled by these questions, but never once did I really entertain taking the "choice" offered. As far as I was concerned there was no "choice". This pro-choice man had no choice when it came down to him and his child.

Andrea and I are fighters. In that respect we are the perfect compliments to one another. Some might say that we have a tendency to tilt at windmills, but we like to think that we both fight for principles, and moral issues. God had given us this child. I did not know why. Why was not important, only that we had this responsibility and I could not forego the responsibility. In the "for better or worse" part of the marriage vows this was the "worse" part and I had to live up to that promise.

As we left the office Shah confirmed that we were to keep up the ultrasound appointments. He told us he would have a team assembled and ready when Lori was due, which he believed would be late May. The team would assist him in taking her by Cesarean section.

* * * * * * *

After deciding that aborting Lori was not an option we also had to deal with the other end of that equation. What were we to do if, and when, she died? This problem faced us constantly. Andrea was the first to speak of it out loud.

One day Andrea asked me what I thought about donating Lori's organs to other babies who needed them, in the event she died. I had not given the idea much thought. Actually, I had tried not to think about the baby dying at all, but Andrea had and her solution forced me to deal with the prospect.

During the trips to Vanderbilt for the ultrasounds we had been exposed to other parents in similar situations. The doctors told us of other patients and their problems. Those conversations made Andrea think about the other people's suffering. There was a comfort that came to me when I thought that out of her suffering Lori would be able to improve the life of other babies and console their parents by helping save the lives of their children.

Our comfort from making the decision was short lived. On our next visit to Vanderbilt Andrea told Dr. Chantee about our decision. He frowned, and shook his head. He said that the gesture was very nice but that Tennessee law would not allow organ donation from a baby born with birth defects.

"But her only problem is her kidneys," Andrea protested. "Everything else is perfectly fine, her heart, her lungs..."

"Yes," Chantee agreed, "you are correct. There is nothing wrong with any of her other organs, but we have had this problem before. Technically, she would have died from a birth defect and the law will not allow a transplant."

We were first crushed, and then angry. We had finally found something that gave us a tiny bit of relief from our misery. The thought that we would be helping other babies and their parents with the death of our own child had given us a modicum of comfort in our time of such great distress and now we were told we are not allowed to help!

Some years later there was a story carried in the national media about a baby born without a brain that was kept alive by the parents for organ donation. There were outcries from various groups denouncing the parents for the cruelty to their baby, to keep it alive just so that its organs could be transplanted into other babies.

If Lori were to die we would have been denied the ability to use her organs to save other babies, and her death would have been twice as cruel because we would have had to grieve not only for her, but all those others we could not help to save.

I became angry with the philosophical elite who would have denied life to all those babies who could have been helped by one dying infant. Later I decided to use my anger and disappointment positively. The first thing I did after Lori was born was to go out and obtain an organ donor card. I still carry it and live in the hope that when I die something of me will be salvaged. If just one person is helped it would be worthwhile. I told Andrea they could cremate what was left; I will have no use for it.

* * * * * * *

People exhibit courage in many different ways. Some people stand and fight while others refuse to fight and both are called brave. But Andrea's daily management of Lori's impending death was a kind of deep, personal courage I have seen few people display.

At the time of Lori's conception Andrea was an afternoon jock (radio personality) on a local radio station. She worked a regular four-hour shift on the board five days a week. In addition, she made commercials and dubbed other materials for the station. One of the requisites for on air work is that the announcer must project an upbeat attitude. A good announcer never lets the public hear that they are depressed, upset, or worried. Andrea's job was to entertain people, and she believed that she should deliver 100% of the expectations of her job. She prides herself on her professional skills, for her there was never another option.

For hours each day Andrea would be on the air, cracking jokes and playing songs. She created entertaining commercials with upbeat themes, delivering her lines with energy. But after work I saw the real Andrea, drawn, pale and fatigued. The hours of acting left her so drained that she often came home to collapse in bed and cry. At other times she would go into our computer room and play a simple game called "Hack" over and over again. She played so long and so often she wore the letters off several keys. I tried to get her to quit her job, but she was adamant; she was a professional jock, she would do her job, and do it to the best of her abilities.

* * * * * * *

We kept up our biweekly schedule of trekking to Vanderbilt to "check" on Lori's condition. Even though it might seem strange to anyone who has never lived through such stressful events, you actually do get used to the routine of dreadful circumstances. But about the time we had settled into our uneasy routine, we were suddenly jolted by a startling crisis from a completely unexpected direction.

In January 1990, Andrea's father, Fred, suffered a heart attack. From the outset his condition was serious. Fred had been plagued by high blood pressure for years. A retired Air Force NCO he had become a deputy sheriff with the Giles County Sheriff's Department. He had not exhibited any outward signs of heart distress, or any other ailment for that matter, prior to the attack. His failing health was an added burden, which seemed to drag Andrea to new depths of depression. Andrea and her father were extremely close. Even though Fred was not her natural father Andrea loved him as if he were.

In February 1990, Fred went to an appointment with his cardiologist. The appointment was supposed to be nothing more than a check on his heart's condition, but when he entered the room and approached the examination table he collapsed with a massive heart attack. The doctor desperately struggled to save his life. All the cardiologist was able to do was stabilize him enough to get an ambulance to the office and rush him to Vanderbilt. He was admitted to Vandy's CIC unit. A team of cardiac specialists undertook his case and began tests. Their findings revealed a heart too damaged to continue functioning for much longer. There was an immediate attempt to place him on the heart transplant waiting list, but Fred did not have that long left to live. On the afternoon of March 1, 1990, he and Ursula were watching TV in his room. Fred drifted off to sleep for a short time. When he awoke he told Ursula not to worry about Lori, that she would be all right. In a few minutes he drifted off back to sleep, and then was gone. The staff tried to revive him when he flat-lined, but were unsuccessful. Fred died while we were on our way to visit him.

We met Ursula at the hospital and she immediately ushered us into a tiny waiting room where she told us of Fred's death. As soon as she could, Andrea requested time to be alone with her father. Death is such a profound event. We have no power over it whatever. All we can do is observe its awesome silent power and experience its intense influence.

After making arrangements for the transfer of Fred's body back to Pulaski, we gathered up Ursula's things and stuffed them into our tiny car. The three of us set off for home. Almost as if to punctuate the macabre directions our lives had taken of late, our car began to lose power as we left Nashville. Pulling into a service station just off the interstate I checked the trouble and found that the transmission had broken down. The little car would never make the 70-odd miles back home. As I walked to a nearby pay phone to call someone to come get us, it started raining. It figured.

Dealing with Death

One of the decisions Andrea and I made early on in the tangle of emotional dilemmas over Lori's condition was that we would not hide the truth from our son. Initially Andrea was apprehensive about telling him that his unborn sister might die. We had discussed it at great length, and Andrea had mulled over its downsides for sometime before agreeing that we should tell Little John.

We told him in language he could understand, about the problems his sister was encountering, and the fact that she might not survive. It took time, and patience, but quicker than we expected John began to understand, in his own way, what was happening, and, to some extent, why his father and mother acted strangely at times and were often too emotional. We believe his understanding of what had happened helped him cope with problems that many young children would have found insurmountable.

* * * * * * *

Working our way through the days after Fred's death was difficult. Andrea busied herself with activities associated with the funeral. Losing Fred was a staggering blow, but months of waiting for her baby to die had numbed her senses to some extent and she was not as devastated as she would have been had the death happened during happier times.

Andrea was very brave during the funeral, and she even found humor during the procession to the cemetery. Because Fred was a deputy sheriff we had the customary law enforcement with its long line of police vehicles making up the funeral procession. Blue lights flashed as we proceeded slowly along the highway toward the cemetery. At one point along the way we noticed a large herd of cows in a field next to the highway. The procession of flashing lights had drawn the curious bovines toward the fence. They were all standing in a line with their heads poked out over the barbed wire watching intently as the police vehicles passed.

When Andrea saw the cows she turned to her mother and said, "Look, mom, we're attracting a crowd."

Chapter IV

Lori's Arrival

The day after Fred's funeral was a Sunday. Andrea seemed to be doing well but by midmorning she began complaining of abdominal pains. We first thought they were the byproducts of the stressful week we had just completed, but she made the comment that she felt like she was in labor. This did not seem likely because the baby was not due for almost two months. Andrea lay around on the couch for most of day desperately trying to rest, but her condition did not improve. After church I told her that we should go to the hospital and let them check her, just to be safe. I called our neighbor and asked her to keep Little John. Andrea and I set off for the local hospital. She was checked in through the emergency room and placed in the maternity ward. She was assigned a bed and a nurse checked her vital signs. She questioned Andrea about her contractions, whether they were better or worse when she walked, and whether she had other signs of labor. Her OBGYN, Dr. Fitts, was called and the information relayed to him. The nurse came back and said that they would observe her for a while. After about an hour the nurse returned and told us what Andrea had was a condition known as Braxton-Hicks; false labor. We were told to go home and the condition would soon pass.

When we got back to the house I asked our neighbor, Louise, to bring John home. A nursing student at the time, she talked with Andrea for a few minutes, then asked her, "Did they have you walk?"

"No," Andrea looked puzzled.

"They should have had you walk," Louise motioned her up off the couch, "it's the one way to tell if its Braxton-Hicks."

Louise had her walk around the living room, then looked at me and shook her head.

"She's in labor," Louise said solemnly.

"No, I'm not," Andrea protested. "It'll be O.K."

Louise insisted, but Andrea became stubborn about it. Finally Louise relented, but before she left she whispered a warning to me at the door.

"If she keeps hurting you get her back to the hospital. She's in labor."

As the night wore on Andrea's pains became much more severe and frequent. I became concerned and asked her to get ready to go back to the hospital. She insisted that she would be all right. For hours we argued about it, but by 10 p.m. she was in such pain she relented. I called Louise to keep John again and we were off to the hospital once more.

This time Dr. Fitts was called and he came to the hospital. Dr. Fitts is a tall, good-natured man who cares a great deal about his patients. He questioned Andrea about her symptoms and performed a quick physical examination. Sitting on the side of the bed he snapped off his rubber gloves and announced,

"She's dilated to eight centimeters."

From past experience I knew that 10 centimeters was birthing time, so I quickly said that we needed to get enroute to Vanderbilt. I knew that a team was ready to take Lori in a month or more so I felt that the groundwork was probably already in place there.

"You don't have time," Fitts cut me off. "We've got to take the baby now, here."

I was stunned. Lori was a problem baby, there were difficulties expected and I felt uneasy about having her delivered in Pulaski, so far from the specialists I felt we needed.

"We're supposed to have her taken by a team at Vanderbilt," I reminded him.

"I know," he nodded, "but we don't have time. Don't worry I'll call Vanderbilt and have them enroute to get her while I'm operating. This is a minor detour."

Fitts looked up at me. As I have said, he cares about his patients and I was as much his patient as Andrea and he wanted my opinion as well. Fitts is one of the kindest and most empathic physicians I have ever met. Earlier, when Andrea and I were awash with speculation about what was going to happen with Lori, Fitts had told Andrea to bring me to her next appointment. I went with her and found out what it is like to be the only man in an OBGYN's office. You get a lot of very strange looks from the other patients. What Fitts wanted was to talk to us both. He took us into his office and sat us down.

"What I see is," he began, without preamble, "in about five years a little girl with a lot of scars on her stomach out playing with the other kids and being as normal as any five year old little girl."

We were confused. Andrea and I looked at one another and tried to grasp what he was saying.

"Now," he went on, "you have my opinion. I'm a doctor and that's my opinion, and what you have from the other doctors are their opinions. My opinion is as valid as theirs. The fact is that no one knows what's going to happen to Lori and I have just as good a chance of being right as the other doctors do. It all depends on what you want to believe."

Suddenly it became clear, in his own way he was trying to relieve some of the anxiety and fears that we were going through. He was offering an alternative to the gloom and doom we had been getting in Nashville. Many doctors heal the body, and they are good at what they do, but very few concern themselves with the souls of their patients, but Fitts was different. He cared about what Andrea and I were going through, and he was taking the time of address our emotional well being just as he looked after Andrea's physical health.

You can buy good medical advice, but what Fitts gave us is not for sale.

"Now," he smiled at Andrea, "I'm going to take her by C section. We're not going to wait for natural birth, there's too many potential complications involved."

Andrea frowned, and he caught her reaction quickly.

"What's the matter?"

"I'll have another scar," she pouted, "and my stomach already looks terrible."

"No," Fitts consoled her; "you won't have another scar. We'll go in the old one."

"But I thought you couldn't cut a scar," Andrea brightened some what at the news, "I was told that it wouldn't heal back."

"No," he smiled, "that's an old wives tale. You can open a scar several times. There's no problem. I've done it many times."

Andrea brightened considerably at the news. Fitts made his final preparations and she was wheeled out of the room.

"You can wait over here." Fitts pointed me toward the waiting room in the hallway. "I'll be out in a few minutes." He reassured me as he left.

I used the time to make two phone calls; both grandmothers needed to know that plans were abruptly being altered in the middle of the night. I woke both women, while each sounded less than pleased at the news, both were encouraged by the prospects of a quick birth and transport to Vanderbilt. I assured them that everything would be all right.

After I disconnected from the last call I heard a "Code Blue" alert over the hospital P.A. system. I knew that a "Code Blue" meant there was an emergency in which someone, somewhere is not breathing. Feet scurried down hallways, doors opened and banged closed, and people were rushing somewhere beyond my vision. I remember thinking that with my luck the code blue was for Andrea.

Shortly Fitts came down the hall in long, urgent strides, his face glum and tinged with anger. He drew up short at the waiting room door.

"The baby's not breathing," he said curtly. "I don't know why. We've inserted a tube. That's under control, but Andrea's awake. She woke up when we took the baby and I can't get her back to sleep." Then he added quickly, "And Vanderbilt says they won't come for the baby." This last comment extracted a flash of anger from him.

"What?" I was shocked. "We've been going up there for months, everything's all set."

"I know, but now they say they're not coming for her. I don't know what's going on, but I'm going to find out, you can bet on that." He looked furtively down the hall from which he had come. "I'm going to call them back, but if they keep on insisting that she's not theirs I'm going to call Huntsville General, they've got a helicopter and they can be here in 30 minutes."

I nodded, Huntsville was something new, but if Fitts thought it was what we should do I was ready to go along with him. At the moment I had no other choices.

"I'm going to give Andrea one more shot." He looked anxious. "If that doesn't work I'm not sure what we can do. If I give her any more it could kill her."

"But you can't just let her lie there in pain," I protested.

"I'll try one more," he nodded as if agreeing with some decision he had made mentally, "but that's all." He started off down the hall. "I'll be back," he called as he dove back toward the operating room.

I did not know what to think or do. Andrea was wide awake with her abdomen split open. Lori was out but was not breathing. Vanderbilt was acting as if they had never heard of us and for months we had banked on their expertise to pull us through this terrible birth process. If Huntsville came for Lori they had no experience with her and we had no one we knew in Huntsville General that we could talk to. My mind rocked back and forth from worrying about Andrea to worrying about what we were going to do with Lori. If Lori's chances of survival were doubtful at a medical facility where the experts had worked with her for months, what were her chances in a hospital where no one knew anything about her case? If Andrea could not be put back to sleep what was going to happen to her? Could she survive such an experience?

It was then that the thought hit me, what if I lost both of them? The thought made my knees go weak and I sat down. The waiting room was empty except for God and me, We sat there in silence. In the beginning I had made a decision, about Lori and us. I remembered my old sixth grade teacher's story about her son and the night he almost died. This was back when you could talk about God in the classroom just as if He was a real part of everyday life, and court decisions and civil actions did not restrain teachers. She had told us about how she had prayed the Lord's Prayer and had gotten to the part that said, *"Thy will be done."* At that point she had realized that this was truly what must happen and that she must abide with His decision on the matter.

In the early days of waiting to see if Lori was going to live or die the pressure had gotten unbearable. I was pushed to the limit, and then I realized something very fundamental. All my life I had said that I believed in God. It was not an intellectualization. It was a fact. All my life I had prayed to God, as people are want to do, during good times and bad. Like most people, I was given to asking for things I wanted to make my life easier, better, safer, wealthier, or smoother. But I had never been in a predicament like this. As we went to

Vanderbilt to have the check ups week after week, I wanted God to make things all right, make the bad things go away.

But one day I realized a fundamental truth - God would do what God would do. My problem was not persuading God to do what I wanted him to do. My problem was, if I believed in God like I professed, then I must accept His decision; "Thy will be done." Moreover, I knew that whatever the decision, not only must I accept it, but also I must believe that it was the right decision! In other words, if my baby died, it was O.K. with me because it was what God wanted to do, or needed to do, for His own purposes!

It all comes down to a basic understanding between God and me, I would believe in Him and He would do the right thing. But even with all my faith, I was dreadfully afraid. I felt like a young student learning how to drive for the first time, fearful of the twists and turns that waited up ahead, while a benevolent instructor guided me in the right paths.

After awhile Dr. Fitts came down the hall once again. Stopping at the waiting room door he leaned on the doorframe. He appeared exhausted.

"We got her knocked out for the time being," he smiled, referring to Andrea. "Vandy still maintains that Lori is not theirs. I got tired of arguing with them. Huntsville General's helicopter is on the way. They should be here in a few minutes. They have an adequate neonatal unit," he added in a consoling way.

Fitts pushed off the doorframe.

"I'll check in with her later." He started down the hallway. "She'll be in her room in a minute. They'll come and get you when she's ready." And he was gone.

More time passed. I could hear activities far removed in other rooms but no one came by. After what seemed like an eternity a nurse came and told me that Andrea was in her room and I could go in.

I entered the maternity ward and pushed open the door to Andrea's room. She looked pale and drawn, but at least she was sleeping now. I stood by her bed and waited until she opened her eyes. She forced a smile.

"We had some problems," her voice was weak.

"I heard."

"What's wrong with Lori?" she reached for my hand and I took it.

"I don't know," I shook my head.

"They said Vanderbilt wouldn't come and get her," she shifted to look at me. "What's going on?"

"I don't know," I sat down on the side of the bed. "Fitts said he talked to them and they said they knew nothing about her. Huntsville's coming to get her with a helicopter."

"A helicopter?" she raised an eyebrow.

"Yeah," I said as a nurse entered the room.

I had been unaware of the activity around us, but became aware that nurses and aids were rushing in and out. There seemed to be an air of urgency all over the ward.

"They're here," a nurse told us.

"They're hereeee." Andrea imitated the voice of the little girl on the movie Poltergeist.

The nurse smiled at the attempted humor.

"The helicopter," she informed us, "landed in the parking lot. They're in the nursery getting Lori ready to go."

I stood by Andrea's bed as we waited. We could hear strange noises but the doors to the nursery were closed. We looked from the hallway to one another.

In a few minutes the doors to the nursery swung open and a bizarre apparatus with air tanks, tubes, and valves, capped off by a Plexiglas dome was wheeled into the hallway. Inside the plastic dome lay a very small baby. I could see very little of her face, tubes and wires ran from her mouth and head out of the dome to a variety of gauges and indicators. A nurse was pulling the device behind her as she came into our room.

"We're ready to go," she smiled at Andrea.

"Flying out," Andrea spoke, her voice had gained more strength.

"Yeah," the flight nurse smiled. "She's doing fine. We have her stabilized and she's ready to go."

Andrea tried to sit up to see Lori.

"I can't see her," she said, straining.

"Don't hurt yourself," the nurse cautioned her. "Would you like to touch her?"

"Can we?" Andrea brightened instantly.

"Surc." The nurse opened a round porthole in the side of the plastic dome.

Andrea reached up and snaked a finger into the bubble. She could not see what she was doing but she reached forward until her finger encountered a tiny leg, which she caressed. When she withdrew her hand I reached inside to touch the daughter I had seen so many times in ultrasounds. I was astonished at how small she was and yet how large her belly was. The blocked bladder had ballooned her stomach to grotesque proportions. The arms and legs that I could see were doll-like, much too small for a human being. I had never seen a premature baby and I was astonished at the minuscule body inside the plastic dome. I rubbed the leg nearest me, saying a silent hello, and wishing her luck.

"We've got to go," the nurse said when I had withdrawn my hand.

She pushed the apparatus toward the door.

"Don't worry," she said as she maneuvered the transport through the doorframe. "She'll be fine. We'll take good care of her."

I found myself on the verge of tears. Andrea lay back in exhaustion, but smiled.

"We'll never keep that girl at home, you know," she said.

"Why," I was confused by the comment.

"Well, she's only been born for an hour and she's already leaving town on a helicopter." She smiled at her humorous observation and lay back against her pillow.

The nurses came in and told me that Andrea needed to sleep. I told her to get some rest and left for home. I noted that it was after 2:00 a.m. on Monday. It had been a long day, a long weekend. Fred had died on the First, we buried him on the Third, Andrea went into labor on the Fourth, and Lori was born on the Fifth. As I left the hospital I looked into the darkened sky, wondering how my daughter was doing. Reaching the car it dawned on me that it was Monday. That night I had a mid-term test in a doctoral class on organizational theory. We had been given 500 terms to know for the test. With everything else that had happened this weekend it only seemed appropriate that I would conclude the day with a huge life or death exam. It figured.

* * * * * * *

Huntsville

After a few hours sleep, a very few, I was awakened by a telephone call from the hospital. They needed me to take specimen samples to Huntsville. Because Lori was an emergency admission Huntsville General had no specimens from Andrea, and they needed them. I told them that I would be there soon. Pushing myself out of bed and into a shower I was dressed and at the hospital within the hour. The nurses gave me a collection of vials and boxes for transport and after a brief stop by Andrea's bedside I was off to find Huntsville General hospital.

The Neonatal unit at Huntsville General was a large area filled with small "beds". Each "bed" was a Plexiglas "crib". The tops were open and heat lights shined on the tiny patients. Rising over most of the cribs was a bewildering array of monitors and measuring devices. A nurse guided me through the maze of beds to a crib against the South wall. In the bed was a small body hooked up to a multitude of tubes, wires, and devices. It was difficult to see her face but I did note that her head was covered with hair. I touched her right foot and she it jerked away from me. Ticklish, I thought, just like her mother.

A nurse came up to the opposite side of the crib. She was a pleasant woman, a big lady, and as it turned out with a big heart as well. I had noticed that she was very compassionate toward the babies in her care as we made our way among their numbers.

"What's her problem," she asked. "We don't know very much about her?"

I started to explain to her about the bladder seal, the biweekly tests and trips to Vanderbilt, but as I spoke I realized I was having trouble talking. It was a strange sensation to have your body leave your control and wander off on its own, but it was happening and I could not stop it. For a moment I could not get a handle on what was wrong. I was speaking but nothing was coming out. I knew I was making my mouth move, I was forming the words and thinking the thoughts, but bubbling sounds were all I could hear coming out of my mouth, not the words and descriptions I had intended. Then it hit me, I was crying, not talking, and I could not stop. I became embarrassed. A grown man was standing there over his newborn baby bubbling and crying and trying to talk.

"It's all right," the nurse patted my hand. "You just go right ahead." She handed me a tissue and left me alone with my daughter.

* * * * * * *

When I regained my composure I returned home, changed vehicles, drove to Nashville and took the mid-term exam. After the test I told my professor, Dr. Arie Halachmi, the events of the past few days. He said, "I believe that would have been sufficient for a postponement of the test." It was about as humorous as he ever got.

The next day I returned to the hospital and told Andrea I was taking Little John and my mother down to Huntsville to see Lori. Before I left, Andrea asked if I had noticed anything wrong with Lori's eyes. I told her I had not, but she insisted.

"Somebody said there was something wrong with her eyes," she pushed up on one elbow. "Now, don't hold anything back from me. Is Lori blind?"

"No," I was astounded at the thought. I had not really looked at her eyes, they were closed the whole time I was with her, but I began thinking, was there? Could there have been and I had not noticed?

"No," I soothed Andrea, "there's nothing wrong with her eyes."

When we arrived at Huntsville I discovered that Little John was not allowed in the neonatal unit, only parents or grandparents. While I went inside to visit Lori Little John stayed with his grandmother in the hallway, looking in through a window in the wall of the neonatal room. John must have been frightened because he began crying as he peered in at the neonatal window.

While visiting Lori, my mind returned to the question Andrea had asked; was there something wrong with her eyes? She lay sleeping on her warming bed, tubes running from her mouth were taped in place, monitors clipped or stuck to various parts of her body, but I could see nothing unusual about her eyes. I leaned over the warming bed to take a closer look. Was there something, anything wrong?

As I was scrutinizing Lori's sleeping face, she opened her eyes and I almost fainted. They were solid white!! No pupils, no irises, nothing, just continuous white orbs! She was blind! Then, down out of her upper eyelids came bright, blue, beautiful eyes! They looked at me and moved around! She did have eyes. I found out later that it is not unusual for newborns to roll their eyes up in their heads because they have no control over them at such an early age. Nevertheless, the experience took at least a couple of years off my overall life expectancy.

When I returned to the hallway I tried to comfort Little John. He was frightened but could not tell me why he was so upset. When my mother came out crying I never had to ask her why, she had a reason and a right.

The next day Andrea had talked Dr. Fitts into letting her leave the hospital to visit her daughter. Dr. Fitts told me that he opposed her leaving, but that she had insisted and he felt that the strain of not being able to see Lori would only delay her recovery. Under any other circumstances he would not let a patient in her condition leave the ward. Visiting Lori might be beneficial in the long run, but he warned me to keep an eye on her. He feared she would overexert herself.

I had never seen Andrea struggle as hard as she did that day. She was in terrible pain and none of the drugs Fitts had given her seemed to help, but she would not entertain the idea we should give up and visit Lori later. She was grimly determined to see her daughter. Remembering all we had been told about her condition I could only think that Andrea was desperate to see her daughter at least one time while she was still alive. I could not deny her that wish, and so I let her press on when I knew that she was pushing herself far beyond all reasonable limits.

When we entered the neonatal unit the physician in charge took us into his office. He wanted to tell us what he had discovered since Lori had been with them. First, he explained that they had found the reason she could not breath when she was first born. He said that she had a condition called coanal atresia.

He explained that with coanal atresia a baby is born without nasal passages. Her external nose was perfect, I had seen that myself, but coanal atresia is not readily visible. The bones inside her skull had not developed openings for the nasal passages. Just inside Lori's nose the skull was solid. The problem is, babies are nasal breathers, they do not breath by mouth. If a baby's nose does not function it will suffocate. Since babies must breath while they eat, a way must be found that would allow Lori to breath through her mouth, as she was doing now with a tube down her throat. She could not nurse nor be fed other than by a tube. The neonatal chief was stymied. He said that he did not know of anything that could be done about such a condition. He assured us that he would keep searching for an answer. He even went so far as to speculate that perhaps Lori could be taught to nurse and breath alternately, but he conceded there was little hope of success.

Then he told us that he had found that she had a blocked bladder and that her kidneys were being systematically destroyed. We filled him in on the months of struggle already dedicated to the problem and told him because of the kidney problems we were supposed to have been in Vanderbilt when Lori was born. He told us that we could still try to get Lori back to Nashville if we wanted. We told him that we would look into that possibility.

Andrea said she wanted to see Lori now. He could tell that she was fading quickly as she slumped in her chair. He quickly agreed that we should spend some time with Lori and got up to let us out of the little office. When we opened the door he delayed our departure.

"Uh," he paused, as if thinking before he spoke, "there's something else, not anything serious, but something we found."

"What's that?" Andrea was suddenly alert as we froze in the door.

"It's not anything really," he started to smile, then dropped it, "she's got six fingers on her left hand."

"It's nothing," he reassured us, "I just wanted to tell you before you found it yourself. It's something that can be taken care of later, simple procedure." He waved off any concerns we might have.

"Six fingers," Andrea repeated, and he nodded.

"Eleven fingers," Andrea said, almost to herself, "and how many toes?"

"Ten," he smiled, "just ten."

"Just ten," Andrea said solemnly. "She just has ten toes." She looked at me and made a theatrics widening of her eyes, "She can only count to twenty one."

"Sad," I nodded, and we both broke into wide smiles, suppressing laughter we moved into the neonatal unit to visit our new daughter with just ten toes.

Visiting with Lori, there was very little we could do other than stand and stare at her. Tubes and wires obscured her face, monitors were clipped to her toes and taped to her chest, legs, and arms. There were so many tubes and wires that she appeared even smaller than her 6-lbs. 9 oz. The only reaction we could get from her was by touching her feet. If either of her feet were touched she drew up sharply, in an attempt to get the foot away from the irritation.

Andrea grew weaker and was not able to stay as long with Lori as she wanted. I noticed her face begin to pale and she leaned harder against me. Her strength was going fast and I had to physically support her as we left. We barely made the car before she collapsed. She should not have made the trip. It was against all reason but I could understand her driving desire to see her daughter at least one time before she died, even if only for a few minutes and even if she could not see her face. The closeness of a mother to her living child was enough, for the time being, and it had been worth the effort for Andrea and for me as well.

After getting Andrea back home, I began efforts to get Lori moved to Vanderbilt. Calls to Dr. Shah started the process and he arranged for the neonatal unit to retrieve Lori. An exploration of the initial refusal to transport her the night of her birth was still an unresolved mystery, but now we encountered another problem, fog. There was a drastic change in the weather, causing a dense ground fog that would last for twenty-four hours and caused further delay. Angel, the transportation unit for children and newborns at Vanderbilt, was anxious about making the trip from Nashville to Huntsville in such weather. They wanted to wait until it cleared. In the meantime we made the trip the next day to Huntsville to visit Lori and check her condition.

We met with the doctor heading up the neonatal unit. He again asked us into his office to brief us on the progress he had made. He reported that he had spoken with all of the surgeons at the hospital. None of them knew of an answer for Lori's coanal atresia. He said that he would check with Birmingham's University of Alabama Hospital if we wished, but he held out little hope.

"It looks like they could just drill holes," Andrea offered an idea, "like with a drimmel tool or something?"

The doctor's smile was grim. We had hit a brick wall. Our little girl had another condition that seemingly had no relief. Leaving the office we visited with Lori for a few minutes, checked her progress with her nurse, and went home. She had beaten tremendous odds just to be born. As yet she had not succumbed to the kidney failure that we had been told would kill her, but now she had developed another condition that was equally as hopeless as the one we had faced initially. Even if we could escape one condition, how could we possibly get past two such insurmountable ailments? No matter how we looked at it, our future appeared very bleak.

Chapter V
Vanderbilt Neonatal

After three days the Angel crew felt secure enough about the weather to make the trip to Huntsville General Hospital for Lori. We went to Nashville to meet them when they arrived. The fog between Nashville and Huntsville was still bad, occasional rain and mist shrouded the Interstate.

At Vanderbilt's neonatal center Andrea and I were ushered into the office of the pediatrician in charge of the unit. He was a young man, with dark curly hair and an expressive, friendly personality. He seated us opposite him in the small cubical that served as an office situated at the far end of the Neonatal Intensive Care Unit complex. He immediately offered an apology, explaining they had discovered the cause of our original rejection when Dr. Fitts had called for admittance the night Lori was born.

"The letter detailing your baby's condition and the preparations for her admission was never given to me when I took charge of the unit at the beginning of March," he shrugged, helplessly. "I didn't know. Since then we've found the letter. It just didn't get passed along."

"For the want of a nail...," I thought. The simple fact that a letter was not passed from one man to another had created three days of hardship and pain, not to mention the anguish Monday morning during the birth when we could get no assistance from the people we had depended upon. A bureaucratic slip-up had wreaked havoc on our lives for days, but I realized he was right. There was nothing neither he, nor we, could do now to correct the past error. What was done was done and we had to accept our current situation and move on. After clearing up the mystery the pediatrician switched the conversation to a discussion of Lori's condition. We found that the staff at Vandy's NICU had discovered a complication.

Someone in Huntsville Neonatal had given Lori a barium enema. The Vandy staff suspected it was done to conduct an examination of some sort. Usually this was not a problem, except in our case it did. The barium was still in Lori therefore the Vanderbilt doctors were prevented from doing their work at relieving the bladder seal until the barium could be eliminated.

Passing on to another topic the doctor explained that waste materials in urine are called creatinine, the levels of creatinine in the body can affect the health of the individual. Lori's creatinine levels were very high, because the bladder seal made it impossible for urine to pass so it backed up into her kidneys. The high levels of creatinine were a life-threat. If the levels did not fall, and soon, she could not survive. In addition, it seemed that Lori's kidneys, or more correctly the parts of her kidneys that were still functioning, were working too fast.

Andrea offered the explanation that perhaps her kidneys had adapted to their adverse condition in the womb by speeding up their functions to compensate for the blocked bladder. The doctor conceded that it might be possible, but he had little conviction in his voice when he agreed. He also told us that Lori's blood was thick, caused by a high saline content. This too was cause for worry.

He explained that as Lori stabilized they would run more tests on her to better assess her condition. At that point Andrea asked about the coanal atresia. He nodded and said that they would look into that. Andrea offered her thought about drilling holes for her to breath and the doctor smiled, but was not very committal about the proposed procedure. We asked if there was anything else they had found. He looked thoughtful, then said there was not.

"She's got six fingers on her left hand." Andrea smirked, pleased to know more than the pediatrician about Lori's condition on at least one count.

"That's not too serious," he shrugged. "It's an easy procedure to remove it.

"Can I see my baby now," Andrea concluded the meeting.

The doctor apologized once more for the foul-up in not admitting Lori as soon as she was born and showed us into the neonatal unit.

Vanderbilt's Neonatal Intensive Care Unit is essentially one large room filled with rows of warming beds, each surrounded by a perplexing array of monitoring and life support equipment. At first view there does not seem to be any system or logic behind the arrangement of beds and equipment, but as you become accustomed to the needs of each patient you begin to understand that it is the patient's needs that dictate the basis of placement of equipment, not any logical arrangement. Each child in the unit has a nurse. Each nurse cares for only two children. Except for one man, almost all the nurses were women and almost all of them were what are called "master" nurses, or nurses with master degrees.

Neonatal nursing is a specialty of more than medical expertise, I was to discover. One major personal quality that each nurse possessed was the ability to continually deal emotionally with the most serious medical aliments imaginable to newborn infants. Frequently this involved the deaths of the babies they cared for. Often, when a nurse's patient had died the nurse was given time off, but many times the nurses pressed ahead, putting aside their personal feelings as they continued to care for the babies in their charge.

I cannot say enough about the work of NICU nurses. During our time there I discovered that when one of the babies in their charge is about to die, and no one from the baby's family is present to attend it, the charge nurse unhooks the baby from its monitors, drags a rocking chair to the bedside, picks the baby up in her arms and sits down in the chair. She gently rocks the baby, sometimes talking to it or singing to it, as it dies so that it will not die alone.

I used to think we cops were brave for all the dangerous things we do, and firemen for the dangers of their job. In the past I have done both, but I can tell you that there are no braver people, or more courageous workers than neonatal nurses and doctors. How they can do their jobs, day after day, without going insane I will never know. I have heard many people talk about overpaid doctors and medical personnel, and in some cases I have agreed, but you can never overpay a neonatal nurse for what she or he does on a daily basis. Over the weeks we were in the neonatal unit I watched those nurses calmly, and efficiently deal with some of the worse cases of birth defects imaginable. They never complained or asked for assistance. They always had time for the parents' questions, no matter how simple or silly those questions or requests might be. All the while they treated everyone with dignity and respect.

On one of those visits after Lori had been in the neonatal unit for a couple of days Andrea made the comment that she had never had a chance to hold Lori. Every time we had seen her she was on the warming bed hooked up to her monitors and tubes. Lori's nurse overheard the comment.

"Would you like to hold her," she asked, stopping what she was doing and turning to Andrea.

"Oh, yes!" Andrea's eyes grew large with anticipation, "Could I?"

"Why, sure you can," the nurse said, calling to another nurse across the room to come help her.

I thought she would pick Lori up and give her to Andrea, but it was not that simple. Dragging over a rocking chair and placing it beside Lori's bed, the attending nurse told the other nurse that Andrea had not had an opportunity to hold Lori since she was born. The other nurse dove right in, picking up cables and tubes, moving wires and equipment. It took a minute or two for the two women to get all the wires and devices positioned for the transfer of Lori from her bed to Andrea's waiting arms where she sat in the rocking chair.

Placing Lori in Andrea's arms the nurse stepped back and helped the other woman with the tangle of wires and tubes. Andrea sat and rocked our baby for the very first time, almost two weeks after she was born. It was a touching scene and I will never forget those nurses standing there patiently holding up those wires.

Lori was to spend the next thirty days of her life in the Neonatal Intensive Care Unit (NICU) at Vanderbilt Hospital. Andrea learned early on that she could decipher most of the notations made on the charts hanging on the foot of Lori's bed. It turned out to be a handy skill. When she could not be with Lori for a few hours, or she had to go home overnight to care for Little John, upon her return to NICU she could conduct her own briefing by reading the chart notations.

The creatinine levels were the first priority in Lori's recovery. Radical surgery might be required to address the situation, but Dr. Hill had noted one significant factor that led him to believe there could be hope. Lori's creatinine level had consistently fallen since her admission to Vanderbilt. He was not sure why this had occurred, but whatever had caused the drop, slight, as it might be, he hoped the process would continue. If the levels did continue to fall he felt that her body was better suited to deal with the crisis than external intervention methods. He explained the situation to us and we joined him in a "wait and see" posture. Meanwhile, Dr. Hill used the time to discover as much additional information about her condition as possible.

On the second day in NICU Dr. Hill had Lori examined by a pediatric radiologist, Dr. Sharon Stein. Her discoveries, and his examinations, revealed startling information. The lower half of Lori's left kidney was completely destroyed by the trapped urine (a condition known as hydronuphrosis), but the upper half, as had been detected before birth during the many examinations we underwent, was perfectly healthy and functioning. That upper pole had not been affected at all by the bladder seal. We had no idea why the upper pole remained unaffected. The right kidney was found by Dr. Stein to be larger than initially projected. The upper pole of the right kidney extended up into Lori's chest and had grown so large it caused the collapse of the lower half of her right lung. Bad news on top of bad news, but Hill was not concerned about the lung because he felt that it would develop normally once the kidney shrank or was removed.

The one piece of good news that came out of Dr. Stein's examination was that she had found something everyone else had missed, Lori's lower right kidney had a very small piece of unaffected, functioning tissue at its base. The reason no one had found this small piece of kidney before was that they had not looked in the right place. The right kidney was so large, because of the expanding urine backup, that it had not only grown upward, colliding with the lung, it had also expanded downward, into the pelvic cradle. There, nestled in the pelvic cradle, was a tiny piece of undamaged kidney. That minuscule piece of kidney had lain in her pelvis for all this time silently doing its job, helping keep her alive. The piece of kidney was so small that Hill did not believe it would be able to support her system alone, but any piece of kidney tissue that he could save was valuable. The one thing he didn't know was how long these two pieces of kidney tissue could keep Lori alive.

Newborns are too small for transplants, even if they are not premature and, as Hill explained, dialysis is not possible on infants whether they are premature or not. If Lori's kidney tissue could not keep her alive on its own, then her chances for survival were nil. The indicator of where Lori stood in this daily battle for life was her creatinine level. If her creatinine remained high Hill would be forced to do something about it, such as emergency surgery, but he admitted this was not an attractive option.

Thus began our constant monitoring of Lori's creatinine level. Several times a day we would ask her nurses about it, and if we had been gone from NICU for any length of time it was the first thing we inquired about. For the first few days the creatinine dropped slowly, but steadily. Point by point the creatinine plummeted, until it reached normal ranges, and then dropped toward the bottom of those. Within a week Lori's pieces of kidney had worked so well together they had brought her completely out of danger from kidney failure. We heaved a sign of relief. We were over one hurdle, but we still had a long way to go.

When her condition permitted, Dr. Hill scheduled her for surgery and cut the bladder seal, allowing her body to begin to drain off the accumulated fluids. Seeing her after the surgery was a shock. Over the first few days of her life we had become accustomed to seeing our balloon-bellied little girl lying on her warming bed, her distended stomach protruding beyond her chest and sides. But after the surgery we walked into the NICU to be confronted by a shriveled, wrinkled little baby. Lori had lost two pounds of fluid and now weighed a little less than five pounds.

Over the next few days she would lose even more body fluids as her system depleted itself of the stored liquids. We were assured that this condition would resolve itself as she adjusted and her body replaced the lost fluids, but for the time being she looked like a miniature ancient woman, dressed in loose fitting, elephantine like skin.

Late in the afternoon on the day Dr. Hill completed the bladder surgery he stopped by NICU to see us. We stepped into the hallway to discuss Lori's situation.

"I think we know how she survived the seal," he said. "When I went in I noticed what looked like a passage on the interior walls of her urethra. After cutting the seal I looked at it again before coming out. I think what has happened is that Lori has one ureter on the left side that went around the bladder and connected in the urethra." He was using his hands to demonstrate how the tube from the kidney circumvented the bladder and connected to the urethra leading out of the bladder. "If I'm right about this it explains why she was able to keep producing amniotic fluid all the time she had the bladder seal in place."

"Why does that happen?" I asked.

"I don't know," he shrugged. "It's not really too rare, but it does happen that some children are born with more than two ureters." He explained that in most cases the ureters join together before they attach to the bladder. That condition is called, bilateral duplication. In Lori's case one ureter completely bypassed the bladder. The other kidney may have done the same thing that would explain why the lower half of the right kidney also survived. It is possible she developed four ureters that are independent of each other, that's known as true bilateral duplication, and that is much more unusual than simple bilateral duplication. He continued, " I could see two ureters connected to the bladder after I cut the seal. I haven't found the lower right ureter yet but if it developed its own ureter, like the left kidney did, it probably connected below the bladder too."

"It's not unknown, but it's highly unusual," he smiled brightly, "But it worked for us this time. Without it the bladder seal would have shut down the amniotic fluid and she would not have been able to survive to term. True bilateral duplication doesn't hurt anyone. You can live a normal life with it. All it really means is that at some time in the future we will need to resite the ureters to a location higher up on the bladder. I'll probably do that when we excise the destroyed portions of each kidney. It's a simple procedure." He dismissed our concerns about the ureter problems by refocusing us on the much more important problems "Our first concern is whether the remaining pieces of kidney can support her on their own."

A medical rarity had occurred which produced the true bilateral condition, but the miracle had occurred when one of those ureters by-passed the bladder entirely. What we were to learn later was that there had been yet another miracle occur with the ureter connected to the small piece of lower right kidney that had been found in her pelvis. That small piece of kidney had survived despite the fact that its ureter connected to the bladder above the bladder seal! When I asked Dr. Hill why this small piece of kidney had been able to survive when the other two lobes, whose ureters were connected above the seal, had been destroyed, he only smiled and simply said that he did not know.

It is said that God makes fools of wise men. I have come to believe that He does not do this with large, grandiose things, like we would ordinarily expect. But I think he does his confounding with small things, like little pieces of kidneys that should be dead but are not, small, sometimes unnoticed contradictions in nature that cannot be logically explained. I think that sometimes, if you listen very carefully, you can hear God laugh, and in those times I think that when He laughs it sounds just like the laughter of a small child, like a child with dead kidneys that work, like a child who should not be here at all.

* * * * * * *

After we had been at Vanderbilt several days we became conscious of the fact that no one had said anything about Lori's coanal athresia. I thought they had forgot about it until one day Andrea was sitting in the waiting room and a giant of a man ducked under the door jam and introduced himself as Dr. Jay Werkhaven. He said that he was an Otolaranologist, then went on to explain that he specialized in just the area where Lori had trouble, nose and throat. Andrea quickly gave him a thumbnail sketch of what the doctors had told us in Huntsville NICU and how they had despaired of ever being able to solve Lori's affliction.

"I do it all the time," Dr. Werkhaven waved away her concern as casually as you might brush lint from your sleeve.

Werkhaven went on to explain the procedure involved opening the roof of her mouth, drilling out the solid bone that obstructed her nasal passages and installing plastic tubes to hold the passages open while they healed.

"I told them," Andrea exclaimed excitedly upon hearing this. "All they had to do was take a drill and make holes so she could breath!"

"It's not that easy," Werkhaven cautioned her, "but essentially that's what we do."

"Well, maybe not exactly like using a hand drill, but it's still the same thing," she was overjoyed. Not only was there a solution to Lori's problem, but her idea had been the right one. (Andrea likes to be right).

The operation was scheduled and Werkhaven left. That evening when I came to Vandy after work I found a bubbling Andrea who patted my arm as she recounted her visit from Dr. Werkhaven. Explaining the procedure as she had been given it she ended her recital by jumping up and down slightly as she excitedly pointed out that her solution to the problem had been the correct one all along.

"When are they going to do it?" I asked.

"In a day or two," Andrea skipped over the dreary details, "but did I tell you how I was right all the time?"

"Several times," I pointed out.

"I should have been a doctor," her eyes danced with enthusiasm.

A couple of days passed without surgery being performed. I became concerned, perhaps there was some problem which had developed that we had not been informed about. I asked Andrea if she had heard anything, but she had not. After several days I came to the hospital one evening to find that Werkhaven had dropped by to see Andrea. From what he had told her his team was not available. To press ahead he would be forced to work with a team that he had no experience with. Andrea said that she did not see the problem.

"He held his thumb out," she demonstrated with her own thumb as she offered it to me for examination, pad up, "and said that working on Lori's nasal passages was like operating on an area smaller than the pad of your thumb. Then he said, would you want me to do that with assistants I haven't worked with before?"

"I told him no," she said, then dropped her head to examine her thumb more closely. "That's not a very big place to work is it?"

I found myself looking intently at Andrea's thumb and imagining how confining a place our daughter's mouth must be to work inside. I shook my head in wonder.

"No," I agreed, "not very big at all."

"He said," Andrea continued, still scrutinizing her thumb, "he might get around to it by the end of the week if he could get the team back together."

We stood for a moment looking at Andrea's thumb and wondering. Anyone passing by would have thought she had a splinter. No one would have guessed that we were exploring the potentiality of our daughter's future surgery.

Several days passed with no word from Werkhaven, or anyone else on Lori's nasal surgery. We continued to monitor creatinine levels, bladder size, and kidney functions. Obsessed with these life threats I almost forgot about her nasal surgery until one day I came up after work to find an excited Andrea waiting for me in the hallway.

"They did it!" she squealed.

"Did what?" I asked.

"Werkhaven did her nose!" She jumped up and down like a child on Christmas morning. "Hurry, come see!"

I rushed through scrub up and gowning procedures as Andrea excitedly described how they had come to get Lori that morning for the surgery without warning. They had been out for several hours before bringing her back to NICU.

"You've got to see her tubes," she pulled me through the door into the unit, "they're so cute!"

Cute? Cute tubes? I thought Andrea had lost her grip as she pulled me around the beds and through the isles to Lori's bed.

"See!" She pointed to the tiny bundle on the warmer bed.

The first thing I noticed was the absence of the oxygen tube that had been taped to Lori's mouth. For the first time I could see her mouth. The next thing I immediately saw were two very small, white plastic tubes protruding from Lori's nose. The tubes were like tiny PVC pipe. There was small blue printing on the sides of the tubes that I could not read. The two tubes were braced apart just beyond her nose with a third piece of tubing that had been sutured into place. The tubes made her little nose turn up in piggish fashion. For a moment I was concerned that this would become permanent but we later learned that the nose would "drop" back into place.

Studying her face for the first time I could finally see my daughter. For the previous weeks an air tube that had been taped to her face, making recognition impossible. But now I could see her without hindrance. She had a sweet, kind face, but one which looked much older than her age. Andrea caught me studying Lori's face.

"Well," she began, "she doesn't look like me."

"No," I agreed, still considering the little face.

"And she doesn't look like you."

"No," I also agreed.

"But, she does look like her brother."

"Yeah," I said, turning my head so that I could get a view of Lori's face at the same angle at which she lay, "she does."

"Well, that proves it," Andrea said.

"Proves what?"

"We've had the same milkman for five years," Andrea said with a straight face.

"Yeah," I agreed seriously, "I guess we have."

We left Lori when her nurse came to do her periodic examinations. Walking down to the waiting room we sat down to discuss the latest events. As we were talking a tall man ducked under the door and extended his hand. He was dressed in surgery greens. He raked off a scrub cap as he sat down to talk with us.

"I'm Jay Werkhaven," he said as his hand engulfed my own. He wore an amiable casual attitude as he settled himself into one of the chairs. His long legs forced his knees up toward his chin as he sat perched on the edge of the cushion.

"Everything went fine," he said with a warm boyish smile, "we didn't have any problems. The stints will stay in for six weeks. Then you'll have to bring her back so we can remove them. After that you'll have to bring her by the office every couple of weeks for me to check her."

"Will this work?" I asked, somewhat leery after the experiences in Huntsville.

"I do it all the time," he smiled easily as if such a thing was a daily event. "Right now I have, " he paused as he mentally counted, "five babies with coanal atresia."

"Five?" I was surprised at the high number. "Why so many? I thought this was unusual?"

"It happens once in every five thousand births," he replied as if instructing a college class. "Most cases affect only one side. It is much more exceptional to find a case where both sides are blocked, but its not that rare."

He went on to explain that skin growing over the nasal passages rather than bony obstruction causes most atresia cases. As he talked I was impressed with his youth and informality. He struck me as the type of kid who experimented with acids and bases in his bedroom to make his own firecrackers for the Fourth of July. Later I was to learn that Werkhaven was not only an extraordinary medical doctor but had peculiar personal traits as well. His hobbies were skydiving and deep sea diving on World War II shipwrecks in the South Pacific.

Adding to the youthful impression were Werkhaven's shoes. As he talked I noticed that his surgery scrubs included shoe covers that were stretched to the breaking point over a pair of large tennis shoes. The effect of the tennis shoes poking out from the inadequate covers gave the impression of a young man who had interrupted a basketball game to run down to surgery.

But his casual appearance and relaxed manner gave us comfort. His whole visage seemed to say, 'why worry, I have everything under control.'

"I've got to go," he said as he stood up to leave.

Towering over me he again engulfed my hand in his and then Andrea's as he made his way to the door.

"Remember, come by my office two weeks after you get out of the hospital so I can check the stints," he flashed a warm smile and disappeared down the hall in long strides.

"Well, what do you think?" Andrea asked, when he had gone.

"He seems all right to me," I agreed.

"He's great," she said, looking after him.

Time would prove, Andrea's assessment of Jay Werkhaven absolutely correct. He simply was great.

Chapter VI
Families of Special Children

While we were in Vandy's NICU we were interviewed by an endless series of doctors, specialists, and researchers. We had become accustomed to odd questions and impromptu conferences. We were into our third week at the hospital and were quite weary when one day we were asked to go into a small conference room near the NICU ward.

A motherly, middle-aged woman came into the room and sat down opposite us. She had a large notebook cradled in her arms which she laid in her lap as she began to speak.

She was a soft-spoken, pleasant person who explained that she had a few questions to ask us. We assumed her questions about our families and our past were an effort to determine whether or not there were genetic links to Lori's condition. We had answered similar questions before in endless fashion, so we answered her questions by route.

Andrea explained she did not know who her father was, except that he was German and that she had been born in Kassel, West Germany. She knew of no relatives because most all of her mother's family had been killed in World War II. Her grandfather had been shot by the Nazis in a prison camp when he resisted the military draft in 1939 and her grandmother had died in a bombing raid sometime in 1943-44. Other, more distant members of her family were either dead or unavailable for comment. One great aunt was last known to live in South America after fleeing there with her SS colonel husband at the end of the war.

Then the questioning turned to me and my family. I explained that my father had died in 1980 of cancer and that my mother was still living. We were an unremarkable family of modest means, and even less celebrity.

Then she began to ask about our childhoods. Andrea had grown up all over the world, moving from one Air Force base to another, from one group of people to another. She had no childhood friendships that carried past the last base assignment. I was asked about my upbringing and I described what there is to say about growing up in a small town in the South and going through my teen years in the San Francisco Bay area.

She changed directions and asked Andrea about our relationship, how well did we get along, how close were we? During all the meetings and conferences we had endured during the long months at Vanderbilt, no one had asked us questions like these. Then she asked Andrea about our sex life. I had put up with a lot of questions in recent months which I saw no sense in, or point to, but I could see no connection between our sex life, dismal as it might be at that point in time, and our daughter's life and death struggle.

Andrea was trying to answer the question when I sat forward. "Ma'am," I interrupted, "We've answered a lot of questions that we believe were intended to help Lori, but I don't see how our sex life has anything to do with her condition."

She calmly turned to me.

"This has nothing to do with Lori," her voice was even and professional. "This is about you two. I'm with Vanderbilt Social Services and this counseling session is designed to help you, not Lori."

"Counseling session indeed," I thought. I was tired. I started to get up from the rocking chair.

"We don't need any counseling," I began, but she stopped me, motioning me back into the chair.

"Yes, you do," she insisted in a voice that was more kind than condescending. I sat back down and she continued.

"Let me explain." She looked from Andrea to me as she spoke. "Parents of children with serious birth defects have a very high rate of separation and divorce. The stress of having a seriously ill child destroys relationships. What we try to do here at Vanderbilt is give counseling to parents while they are still here in an attempt to help them get through the rough times with their marriages still intact."

I was not connecting with this line of reasoning. It had been my belief that families were drawn closer together by tragedy. The very idea that a family would fall apart because it encountered difficulty was alien to my concept of the meaning of love. You do not abandon the ones you love in times of need. I explained this to her and affirmed that I would never leave Andrea or Lori, and especially not at such a terrible time in all our lives.

"That's commendable," she smiled benevolently, "but it's not the usual experience in such situations as this. All too often one parent begins blaming the other for the child's condition. The stress on their lifestyle is so great that they soon come to believe that the best thing is to simply leave it all behind them."

"I couldn't leave Andrea," I said, incredulously, "or Lori! It's not Andrea's fault that this happened, just as it's not Lori's fault, or mine. No one is to blame for all this. I don't know why it happened, and to tell you the truth I don't really care anymore why it happened! The point is that it did and now we have to deal with it. Blaming one another will not accomplish anything, and it certainly won't help Lori." Andrea nodded in agreement.

"It's encouraging that you both seem so dedicated to Lori, and I don't believe you would blame each other, but there are stresses that will mount over time and there is a chance it could ruin your marriage," she persisted, gently.

I pointed out that Lori needed us and that I could not leave a baby who needed me.

"Let me tell you," she looked at me and I could see a sadness in her eyes that fell on her like old age, "one of my jobs is to find the parents of babies left at the NICU. Almost every week a baby will be ready to be released. They look at its status sheets and discover that no one has ever been to visit the child. Then they get me or one of the people in Social Services to go out and try to locate the parents." She seemed to brace herself as she spoke. "And do you know that often, when I finally learn where the parents live, I'll go up to the door and knock. They'll answer the door and I'll ask them if they have a baby in Vanderbilt. They'll say 'yes'. Then I tell them that their baby is ready to come home, and they say, 'You keep it' and slam the door in my face."

"I didn't know," I said.

"Most people don't," she shook her head, "just as most people don't know that most of the babies we have in NICU are crack babies, or cocaine babies, born addicted to drugs, or alcohol. We lose most of them from withdrawal, but the ones that survive...no one wants them and we have to send them to Human Services to find foster families for them until they can be adopted. But babies like that are seldom adopted because a crack baby or a baby with mental handicaps due to the mother's alcoholism has too many medical and mental problems for people to take on. Usually these babies stay in foster care until they're grown."

I looked to Andrea and saw tears welling up in her eyes. I knew what she was thinking, "Just give them to me, I'll take them all."

As time went by we began to understand that once you have a handicapped child your life would never be the same again. Time, money and other resources must be spent to assure that the child will be able to attain the best quality of life they are capable of having. That means you may have to give up one lifestyle for another. And you know that as a child gets older the parents' responsibilities will usually increase.

All parents ask themselves what will happen to their children "if" something happens, and they make provisions. Family or friends will step in and take care of the child's rearing, but who will step in if the child is handicapped? Few, if any, want the responsibility of constantly caring for a child whose needs outstrip most people's resources.

Then there are other problems that must be contended with. How do we train the child? What should we concentrate on teaching him or her? What kind of sleeping arrangements must be made, and kept, for years? What about insurance? What about nursing or special care? All of this requires selflessness.

In time, we found the social worker was absolutely correct, most parents of handicapped children suffer a great deal of stress, but it is how people handle that stress which makes the difference. You do not have to be a saint to succeed. You do not have to be more intelligent, more prosperous, or more educated. You only have to care for one another, and for each other's well being. If you care for the child, then no sacrifice is too great, no task too enormous.

The people that I have come to know who have split up over their defective, handicapped, or retarded children are most often expressing their own selfish concerns before anything else. They are incapable of living a life of total service to another person. Such people cannot give what is required of parents of handicapped children. For this reason their marriages fail, and they usually end up blaming the other parent for the failure.

* * * * * * *

One way we dealt with worry and feelings of despair was to treasure what humor we could find. And there was usually some around if you looked hard enough.

While Lori was in NICU I continued to attend night classes in the doctoral program at Tennessee State University studying Public Administration. When I had to attend class Andrea stayed home with our son trying to make his life as normal as possible during those difficult times. One particular night I had gone to class only to find it had been canceled. I took advantage of the opportunity to spend a little extra time with Lori.

When I got home Andrea looked up at me from where she was sitting on the floor and erupted into uncontrolled laughter. My first thought was that the stress had finally gotten to her. When she finally recovered enough to speak she explained.

As was her custom, when Andrea could not be with Lori personally she called every hour or so to check on her. The nurses in NICU were very accommodating and would give her an update, citing Lori's creatinine levels, oxygen stats, and other vital signs. That night had been no different. She had called the NICU to check on Lori. Her nurse had been brought to the phone to answer her questions.

"How is Lori?" Andrea asked, as soon as the nurse came on the line.

" Oh, Lori's doing fine," the young woman cheerfully replied, "why, her grandfather's with her now."

"Her grandfather?" Andrea asked, astonished, because both of Lori's grandfathers were dead before she was born.

"Well...," the suddenly troubled nurse quickly corrected herself, "could be her father, tall man, gray hair and glasses?"

With that Andrea collapsed into gales of laughter again. The difference in our ages has been a standing joke in our house for a long time. There is a twelve years difference in our ages and she constantly teases me about how old I am, never failing to point out how young she is. It was the first time Andrea had laughed out loud since this whole ordeal had begun. It was a good sign that our hearts were strong enough to resist the deterioration that so often destroys other peoples' relationships. It was a good thing to see.

* * * * * * *

But for every lighthearted moment there were many heartbreaks. Even though we had more than enough of our own to deal with, we continually recognized the sorrows of others whom we encountered on a daily basis. One night, as Andrea and I were suiting up in the scrub room adjacent to the NICU, we met a woman coming out of the unit. She pulled off her gown and dropped it in the disposal bin. We had seen her there before and knew she had a baby in the unit, but we had never spoken.

Andrea said hello and the woman responded. She opened the door to leave, stopped, hesitated and turned back to us. Without preamble she began speaking.

"They say my baby's got a hole in his heart, he's blind, and has brain damage. They say my baby's only going to live for a year and a half," she repeated the facts in a dulled voice, as if she had accepted the inevitable and had come to terms with the pain, "but I'm going to take him home with me and love him for what time he's got left."

She stood there for a moment, her eyes far away in a future I knew she must dread and fear, then she turned and left. After having opened her heart to us and let us peek at the pain and suffering which was her world, she never spoke with us again. It was the way things were in NICU.

* * * * * * *

On another night we were scrubbing up to go in the unit to visit Lori when a young couple from Kentucky joined us. The scrub room was equipped with a long sink with several faucets where all visitors were required to wash their hands before putting on one of the sterilized gowns stacked near the door. The young couple had the awkward manner of people who are not yet familiar with the scrub-up process. The woman appeared to be in her late teens and her husband was not much older. They both wore the frightened look of troubled new parents we had often seen in the NICU waiting room. They glanced nervously at us as they fumbled with the faucets. Andrea tried to make them feel more comfortable by explaining how the process worked. They warmed to us immediately and Andrea asked if they had a baby in the unit, they did. We listened in silence as they told of the debilitating heart ailment that was so severe their baby's chances of survival were virtually non existent.

I felt so sorry for them, these youngsters flung into a terror that even much older and more experienced adults were ill equipped to handle. I was struck by the way the young husband stood protectively behind his wife as she told of their child's situation.

When the young woman finished the grim recitation of their baby's condition she inquired about our baby. The litany of our recital was longer than theirs and they stood listening silently. By the time we finished we were standing at the door, scrubbed, dressed and ready to enter the unit. They looked at us for a moment in disbelief, then the woman said, in the most endearing voice I had ever heard, " We'll be praying for you."

Amid the horror of their own dilemma those two young people still thought of others, and their troubles. I was never as touched by the sincerity of others than I was by that young couple that night. I will never forget them, and I have hoped many times that their situation came to a good end. I never found out.

* * * * * * *

Little John's Acceptance

During the pregnancy we had always been truthful with Little John about his sister's condition. Usually he handled it pretty well. He would get down on the floor in front of Andrea and want her to pull up her blouse so he could "see" his sister. He would bend over her stomach, squint into her navel with one eye closed and talk to his sibling. Sometimes he would bring toys and lay in Andrea's lap for his sister to play with. They were usually Teenage Mutant Ninja Turtles, his favorite toys at the time. But as Andrea drew nearer to term John seemed to get more concerned. When the unexpected birth happened so suddenly and Lori was shipped out to Huntsville Little John's attitude changed completely.

He started saying to us, "It's Mama and Daddy and Little John's house." At first we paid little heed, but one day Andrea noticed the intent of the phrase and brought it to my attention. Little John seemed to be rejecting his sister. We discussed it and felt that probably he was rejecting the uncertainty we were all experiencing. As young as he was he had no way to really understand what was going on. His solution was to simply reject it.

We talked about it and tried to deal with it, but we made no headway with Little John. In fact, after seeing his sister in the neonatal unit at Huntsville he became worse. His oft repeated sentence took on a desperate tone. With provocation he would come up to one of us and say, "It's Mama and Daddy and Little John's house!" He was trying to push away the terror he could not comprehend, but felt so intently.

After Lori was transferred to Vanderbilt we kept Little John out of the neonatal unit, believing that the prohibition against children in NICU was universal. One of us had to always be outside in the waiting room with him while the other one visited Lori. One night we were making arrangements to keep him in the waiting room when a neonatal nurse overheard us and asked if he was Lori's big brother. We told her that he was and she said that he could come in and see his sister.

We could not believe what we had heard, so we told her that he was only five. She smiled and said that did not matter, siblings were allowed to visit in neonatal as long as they behaved themselves. Andrea promised her he would be good and the nurse told her to go ahead and bring him in. We took him into the scrub room, washed his little hands and found the smallest gown in the stack. Andrea admonished him against any outbursts. Little John promised he would be good and off he went with us into the neonatal unit to see his sister.

A first Little John was reluctant, to say the least. He seemed to be fearful of what he might find there. We encouraged him and told him that his sister wanted to see him. He went with us, but stood back from the bed when we stopped by Lori's side. Andrea engaged the nurse in an update on Lori's status as I stood to one side with Little John. I told him he could step up closer and see her, that it was all right. He took a step forward, but did not get too close to the side of the strange looking place that held his sister. Lori was still covered with monitors and wires and a sock cap was pulled over the top of her head to keep in body heat.

Lori moved on the warming bed and John watched her intently. He leaned forward a bit.

"See John," I told him, "she wants to see you."

He ventured a little closer, but stopped short of the bed. He stood there for a moment watching her squirm on her warming bed. Then he turned his head slightly, looking back toward me.

"Can I touch her?" he asked timidly.

"He wants to touch her," I told Andrea across the bed.

"Sure, Honey," Andrea smiled warmly at him. "You can touch her, just be careful."

He gingerly extended one small finger forward until it touched her leg. She jumped at the contact and so did he. Withdrawing his finger quickly, he held it against his chest as if she had burned him.

Each time we went to visit he grew bolder about touching her, then on the day that his mother was able to hold Lori for the very first time, Little John was present. At first he stood patiently while Andrea held her, then he stepped up fearlessly and leaned over Lori's tiny form.

"I want to see her eyes," he said.

We could not imagine why he made such a request, but Andrea turned her so that he could look into her face. He leaned over her, and brother and sister stared face to face with one another. After a moment he stood erect and held out his arms.

"I want to hold her," he announced.

Andrea cautioned him to be very careful and helped him hold Lori, retaining control of her under his arms. John leaned down until their noses touched, looking intently into her eyes that were as clear and blue as his own. They remained that way for a long time, then he straightened up and handed his sister back to his mother.

His interest satisfied, he was ready to go play. I told Andrea that I would take him to the waiting room and that she could stay with Lori for a while. Little John and I walked down the hall and found his toys waiting for us where he had carefully placed them before going in to scrub up. I sat down in one of the rocking chairs looking out the windows into the night beyond.

"Dad," He said, getting my attention.

"Yes, John?" I asked.

"It's Mama and Daddy and Little John and Lori's house," he said matter of factly.

"Yes, it is," I choked.

I will never understand what transpired between those two that night as they stared into one another's eyes, but whatever it was, it was enough to convert a fearful little boy into a loving and accepting brother.

Chapter VII
Tube Feeding

Toward the end of March Lori was moved from NICU to an intermediate care facility referred to as "step-down". Step-down was located, immediately next to NICU. Although the health care is not as critical as in NICU, step-down is still considered a form of intensive care. Our residence in step down lasted for several days without any apparent reason for the stay. One day when I arrived on the unit after driving to Nashville from work Andrea took me aside and told me that she had found out the reason for our lingering stay.

"The hospital in Pulaski won't take her," Andrea abruptly whispered as she visibly grappled with suppressed anger.

"What's the problem?" I asked.

"They say that because she has to be gav-fed they don't want to take her!" She threw her hands up in exasperation.

"So?" I did not get the point.

"So, here's what we're going to do," her eyes took on that "all-be-damned" look she gets when she sets her mind to something. "You pay real close attention and they're going to teach you how to gav-feed Lori, then they'll let us go home," she stated.

"What?" I was startled.

"It's easy," she patted my chest in a matronly benevolent way like a mother soothing a whimpering child, "you'll see. I've already talked to the doctors."

"But .., I mean .. I don't know anything about gav-feeding a baby!" I could feel a hot flush wash over me as I had the distinctly ominous feeling of being sucked into something very serious and very demanding. But at the same time I also knew there was no fighting the inevitable once Andrea is committed to an idea.

"Don't worry," she smiled, all cherubic innocence and light. "I've taken care of it."

"What's going on?" I tried to get some perspective on the moment by stalling and making her explain.

"I asked the nurse this morning why we were still in step-down. I mean they aren't doing anything that couldn't be done on the floor and if she is well enough to go out on the floor I didn't see any reason why she couldn't be shipped to Pulaski. It's a long drive, you're so tired all the time, and then there's Little John to think about. If we were down in Pulaski I could be home with him more. It would be better for everyone."

I nodded, agreeing with her rationale, so far.

"Anyway," she shifted gears, "the nurse said that the only reason they were keeping Lori in step down was because she had to be gav-fed."

Gav-feeding was a term the hospital staff used to refer to tube feeding. Tube feeding is a procedure where a narrow gage plastic tube is inserted down the baby's throat and into the stomach. Formula is then forced down the tube by use of a syringe attached to the end of the tube. In Lori's case this procedure had been necessitated because she had lost the sucking reflex during the time she had an airway in place waiting for surgery to relieve the coanal athresia.

"I asked one of the doctors who makes the rounds every morning if we couldn't have Lori transferred to Pulaski since the only thing keeping her in step-down was the gav-feeding. He said that he'd check on it and get back to me."

She was getting into the flow of the story and was becoming agitated again as she recited the events.

"Then a little while later he came back and said that he'd called Hillside, Pulaski's one and only hospital, and they'd refused to take her! They said that they didn't want the responsibility of a gav-fed baby! Can you believe that?" The question was rhetorical, and she did not wait for an answer. Her momentum mounting as she recounted the story.

"I can believe it," I shrugged, trying to prod her along to the heart of this tale.

"Wouldn't take her, well," she shifted to a higher gear. "I asked him if there was something we could do. I told him about the long trip up here, how our son needed me home as much as possible, and how you had to work all day and drive up here at night. He said if we had a doctor who would take responsibility for her primary care that he could teach us how to gav-feed Lori and let her go home with us!"

"I told him that I was sure Dr. Haney would agree, I mean he's so nice and he's done everything he could to help us in the past," her eyes flared with excitement. "He called and guess what!"

"What?" I asked, knowing full well what the answer must be.

"He said, sure, he'd take responsibility!" She began to bounce up and down with excitement. "So, all we have to do is go in there and let them train us in how to feed her with the tube and we're out of here!"

"Whoa," I held up a hand. Things were moving just a little too fast for me. "Now, what do you mean ... what do we have to do?"

"There's nothing to it," Andrea waved off my hesitancy as if it were not worth pursuing. "They teach you how to feed her with the tube. They'll give us all the things you need to do it with and then we're off home! Nothing to it."

"Wait just a minute," I had caught the subtle shift in pronouns. "What do you mean, all you'll need to know? What happened to them teaching us?"

"Oh, you're going to do it. I can't do that!" She acted as if I had asked a stupid question. "Now, all you have to do is listen real close to what they tell you, do what they show you, and by tomorrow we can go home. Isn't that great!"

"How'd I get saddled with this?" I asked, knowing it was a hopeless battle, but my growing fear demanded I put up some sort of struggle at least.

She patted me on the chest, "They're going to teach you. Do everything they say and we'll get out of here by tomorrow. I've already told them we would do it and they're going to start teaching us at her next feeding."

When the next feeding time approached the nurse attending Lori called us over and began our instruction. She was a kind, pleasant woman who was originally from Pulaski. She had the kind of maternal presence that permitted no nonsense when it came to her job. She was astute at her work and approached it with the same serious, down-to-earth manner that she expected out of her students. Her patience wore thin when the topic of conversation strayed from our main purpose, but her prodding's were gentle as she eased us into the skills we would need to know to keep Lori fed, and alive.

The first thing she demonstrated was how to measure the tubing to be used. She cautioned us, showing us how to locate Lori's stomach, then measure plastic tubing from her stomach to the bottom of her ear.

"Now, that's how much you will need to reach the stomach from her mouth." As she drew the tubing away from Lori's body she warned us not to let the tubing slip, or lose our placement on the tubing with our finger and thumb.

"If you lose your place, measure again," she cautioned us with a serious wag of her free finger, "don't go guessing where your place was."

Pleased with our progress, the nurse then told us that we were going to learn how to insert the tubing. She explained that we had to insert the tube quickly because it would interfere with Lori's breathing. Inserting the tube too slowly also presented the danger of misdirecting the tube into her lungs. Assuming that the tube was in place, we were to stop inserting the tube when the point marked by our fingers reached Lori's lips. The next thing we had to do was test for the proper location of the tube. She told us there were two ways to discern whether we had the tube in her stomach or in her lungs. The first method was to use a stethoscope and a syringe full of air. She took an empty syringe and pulled the plunger to the top of the barrel, leaving the barrel of the syringe filled with air. Then she pushed the tip of the syringe into the end of the plastic tube, which during feeding would be inserted down our daughter's throat, and pushed the plunger of the syringe down with her thumb.

"Now, when you do that it causes air to go down the tube and into your daughter's stomach." Seeing the look on my wife's face she quickly added. "It don't hurt her to have a little air in her stomach. When the air rushes out of the tube you'll be able to hear it with the stethoscope placed against her stomach. It makes a little 'whoosh' sound. Before we feed her I'll let you both listen when I do it."

She then went on to explain the second method of testing whether or not we had the tube in the stomach.

"You take a little bottle of water," she demonstrated with an empty baby food jar, "and you put the end of the plastic tube in the water, holding your thumb over the end of the tube. After you get it in the water, take your thumb off the end of the tube and one bubble will come out if you're in the stomach. If you're in the lung a lot of bubbles will come out."

She grew very serious at this point.

"Now, if you don't hear the air, and you try again and you don't hear it, or you use the bubble test and a lot of bubbles come out, get that tube out of her and insert it again because you're in her lungs. If you put milk in the tube when you're in her lungs you'll drown her before you can get the tube out."

Andrea looked at me, her eyes wide at the prospect that this method of feeding Lori could kill her if we made one single mistake. We had not contemplated such a possibility when we agreed to undertake the instruction. Our training now took on a fresh, somber intensity.

"Now, it ain't that bad," she caught our change in attitude. "We do it all the time and we don't get tubes in any babys' lungs, but you got to take care, that's all. Just make sure that the tube is in her stomach before you give her the milk."

With that admonition she picked up the syringe she had used to demonstrate the air injection and pulled out the plunger.

"Give her one of these full of milk, that's all," she smiled benevolently as she spoke. "People have a tendency to want to feed children more than they need and with tube feeding you can sure do it 'cause you're the one putting the food in. She doesn't have any choice about it. Just one syringe full per feeding, that's all she needs. Now," she eyed us judiciously, "I'm going to feed her and you watch closely."

She set about gathering the materials she would need for the tube feeding. When she began the process she let us measure out the tubing, first Andrea and then me. She appraised our work and deemed it competent. As she inserted the tube down Lori's throat she pointed out the method and manner as she worked, noting that she stopped inserting the tube when she had reached the point marked by her fingers. With the tube in place she was ready to test the position of the tube. Putting a stethoscope on each of us in turn she let us listen to the air rush into our daughter's stomach when she depressed the syringe plunger. I barely detected a whisper of what could have been air coming out of the end of the tube in Lori's tiny stomach. The sound of the exiting air was so faint that it might have been a "brain burp" on my part, but I nodded to indicate I had heard the sound. She then filled the syringe with milk, placed it into the plastic tubing and injected it into

Lori's protesting body. The milk rushed down the tube and was gone in an instant. As soon as the milk disappeared down the tube she immediately extracted the tubing from Lori's throat with a slight plop. As soon as the tube was taken from her mouth Lori settled down and stopped her silent crying. Before leaving us, the nurse reviewed all she had told us. She asked a few questions and, satisfied with our answers, promptly informed us that at the next feeding we would do the procedure without assistance.

Andrea and I went outside while Lori slept. After we were well out of earshot Andrea excitedly asked, "Did you hear the air?" Her eyes bore into mine with enthusiasm and animation.

I told her that I did, but admitted it had been hard to detect the trifling sound.

"Did you," I asked, more out of politeness than curiosity because she had told the nurse she had heard it.

"No, never heard it," she shook her head.

"But you told her you did," I reminded her of her statement during the training.

"Sure," she said flippantly, "if I tell them the truth, that I didn't hear the sound, they'll never let Lori come home. Besides, I told you that you're the one that's going to do this, so you better learn well. Let's go get some coffee. I need a cigarette bad."

She needed a cigarette! I had not smoked since January of 1984 and the thought that in a couple of hours I was going to have to shove a tube down my daughter's throat and pump milk into her without drowning her made me want a cigarette!

The time passed more quickly than I would have wanted and before I was ready it was time to report to Lori's bedside. When the nurse came into the cubical she had her hands full of the materials needed for tube feeding.

"Well," she set the items down on Lori's bed and turned to us, "you all ready?"

I did not speak. I knew Andrea would, and she did.

"Sure?" she chirped.

The woman nodded as she stepped back and motioned toward the materials she had brought with her.

"There it is," her hand swept over the plastic tube, syringe, and milk.

I looked at Andrea. She was confident and cheerful, because she knew, as did I, that I would be doing the actual feeding. She would go through the training, but that was it. The feeding was my responsibility. I began rehearsing each step in my mind as I examined the materials laid out on the bed next to Lori.

"Which one of you is going to be first?" The nurse held out a length of plastic tubing.

I looked at Andrea.

"I will," I agreed, and Andrea smiled like a proud parent who had just got her reluctant child to do a difficult task.

After washing my hands, I took the tube and placed one end at the point I had been told was her stomach, near the top of the navel. Letting my fingers slide up the tubing I traced the length to Lori's throat and then angled off to the bottom of her left ear. At that point I stopped.

"Good," the nurse said. "You've got the right length, now what?"

"Now, I insert it," I offered.

"Right," she nodded, "go ahead."

Lori was groggy from sleep and offered little resistance when I first put the tube in her mouth, but once she realized what I was going to do she began to squirm about and try to cry. I lost my measure, and the nurse nodded her head sympathetically.

"Measure it out again," she said.

Starting over it took only a moment for me to have the correct length located and locked between forefinger and thumb. With the nurse's praise for such quick measurement still hanging in the air I started to insert the tube down Lori's throat. Lori's attempt to cry actually made the work of forcing the tube down her throat easier than it would have been should she have kept her mouth closed. The tube slid quickly down her throat and I was left with my fingers marking the spot at the edge of her quivering lips.

"Good, good," the nurse congratulated me, but quickly added. "Now test it. You can let go of the tube, it's in."

I let go of the tube and reached for the syringe. As I inserted it into the end of the plastic tube the nurse handed me the stethoscope.

"You'll learn to put this on before you start measuring the tube." She hooked the ends of the listening device around my neck.

I had to take the syringe off the tube because I had not pulled back the plunger. After putting the syringe back into the tube I realized that I would have to have the stethoscope in my ears before I could hear the air I was about to press into the tube. Fumbling with the tube and scope I had to lay the tube down and use both hands to put the tips of the stethoscope into my ears.

The nurse smiled knowingly and said, "Don't worry it won't be long before you'll learn how to put on the stethoscope with one hand."

After adjusting the tips of the scope in my ears I was ready to press down on the plunger. Andrea held Lori still as I placed the receiver of the stethoscope against her stomach. Pushing with my thumb on the syringe plunger I listened intently. There was a slight, low whoosh sound, just barely audible in the earpieces. The sound was so faint I asked myself, did I hear it, or not?

"Did you hear it," she asked, and I hesitated. "If you didn't do it again."

I nodded, unable to speak.

"Good, now do you want to try the other test?"

I nodded. She handed me a baby food jar filled with water. I put my thumb over the end of the tube as I took off the syringe. The bottle was held at bed level and I inserted the tube into the water. One tiny bubble rose to the surface when I released my thumb from the end of the tube. That was certainly a small bubble, I thought.

"You're in," the nurse announced. "Get the milk ready."

Andrea had taken the syringe and was pouring milk into it. When she had it full she handed it to me, careful not to let it leak out the bottom of the syringe. I took the plastic syringe and introduced the open end into the end of the tube. We were ready to feed Lori.

"Go ahead," the nurse said, clearly pleased with our accomplishment up to this point.

I was surprised how easy it was for the milk to rush down the tube once I had applied the slightest pressure on the plunger. I suppose I thought I would have to press harder to get the milk on its way, but all it took was a little pressure from my thumb and the milk rushed down the tube in one swoop and disappeared.

"All right," the nurse said, breaking my concentration on what I had just accomplished, "you can take the tube out now."

I had been so thrilled at having accomplished the task that I had forgotten it was necessary to take the tube out. Grasping the plastic tube just beyond Lori's quivering lips I began pulling at the long clear tube. It slid out of my daughter much easier than it had gone into her.

"You can pull it faster than that," the nurse informed me in a motherly tone, "but not too fast."

I increased the draw on the tube and it immediately popped out of Lori's soundless, crying mouth. I stood looking at the wet tubing for a moment, trying to fully appreciate what I had just achieved.

"Good job," she said, with a quick nod of her head.

"Thanks." I felt sort of stunned that things had gone so well.

"See you in two hours." She gathered up her articles and swept out of the room to attend other duties.

The pride of accomplishment immediately vanished with her parting words, two hours and I would have to do this again! Andrea smiled and patted me on the arm.

"Let's go get something to eat," she ushered me out of the room and down the hall.

Chapter VIII
Bringing Lori Home

After 30 days in Vanderbilt's NICU we were finally allowed to bundle up Lori and take her home. The weeks of driving back and forth to Nashville had been expensive and exhausting, but most of all it had been a grueling routine that wore us down to numbing fatigue. We had endured the tests and surgeries, interviews and conferences, anxieties and anguish with only one goal in mind; taking Lori home.

Armed with all her life-support equipment, we triumphantly transferred Lori to our car and set off for home. Leaving Vanderbilt was like being released from prison. We were excited, but at the same time there lurked a dark concern. Here we were bringing home a baby that our own hospital had refused to accept. We had just graduated from a crash course in tube feeding, which we would have to do on alternate feedings for a long time. We were carrying a suction device, which we had been trained to use so that we could suction mucous from her nasal stints every hour, or "as needed." We had been taught what to look for in the event her kidneys began failing. We were taking home a baby that was so small we had to lap the smallest diapers over to make them fit, so tiny that we had been counseled that the best way to find clothes for her would be to go to a toy store and buy doll clothes. In addition, we had a baby that could not make the slightest sound, because of the damage done inserting a breathing tube at bith, and therefore required constant vigil.

Wrapped in a blanket and swallowed up in the smallest "I'm a Graduate of Vanderbilt's NICU" T-shirt we could find, Lori was still sporting her sixth finger as we drove out of the parking lot of Vanderbilt University Hospital. Before leaving the hospital a nurse had tied a thread tightly around the extra digit. It was explained to us that the finger would drop off in a couple of days but in the event that it did not we only had to take her to our local doctor and he would surgically remove it in his office. We had also been told before departing the hospital that Pulaski Electric System had been alerted to our needs. In the event of a power outage we would be given priority in restoration of service. They also arranged for us to be supported by a nurse from one of our local home health care operations. All these arrangements made us feel a bit more confident but not to a great extent.

Buoyed by our recent training, and the promised home nurse, we set off for home. Lori had survived a month longer than we had hoped and it looked like she had stabilized. The uncertainty was still there, but we felt we had achieved a measure of success so far.

Arriving home we deposited all of our equipment in the bedroom around Lori's crib. We had decided to place her crib in our bedroom so that we could better monitor her at night. Bottles of sterile water were stored under her bed for use when we had to suction her nose stints. Bags of tubing, large syringes, and our trusty new stethoscope were stashed beside the water. The suction pump and its plastic tubing were positioned for immediate use because we had not suctioned her nasal stints since leaving Nashville. With skill acquired from long practice at Vanderbilt Andrea cleared the white plastic tubes protruding from her nose by running the suction tubes down the stints to the point where they ended at the back of her throat.

In no time Lori was sleeping and we relaxed in our very own living room. For the first time since Lori had been born we were all home together as a family. But all too soon it was feeding time. Our sense of respite vanished as the thought came to us that for the first time we would tube feed Lori far removed from the support and supervision of a trained medical staff.

"Well," Andrea looked me directly in the eye, "it's time to feed her. You ready?"

Giving Andrea a less than enthusiastic reply we grimly adjourned to the bedroom.

In my years of police work I have faced a lot of dangerous situations that frightened me. I have tracked down burglars in buildings by listening to their footsteps, I have backed down people armed with knives, handguns, and one angry fellow who took up a double bited chopping ax. I have faced people twice my size who refused to go to jail, engaged in high speed pursuits, and wrestled with murderers, but never have I been as frightened as that first time I had to push the plunger on the milk syringe at home, alone and without medical support.

I made it through all the preparations splendidly. I measured the tube, inserted it, listened for the air insertion, and then did a bubble test for added assurance. But when I fitted the syringe of milk Andrea handed me into the plastic tube and hovered my thumb over the plunger, I broke out in a cold sweat. The sweat soaked through my shirt, it ran down my sides, and crept through my hair.

I realized that all those other things I had done before which I had believed were so dangerous had been dangerous only to me, but here, with the tube down her throat and the milk poised for insertion, I could be endangering my own daughter's life. If I was wrong, if I had made a mistake, had not really heard the air but only thought I did, or had misread the bubble test, I was hovering on the verge of drowning my infant daughter. The only way that I would know for certain was when she began to strangle from the milk entering her lungs. But by then it would be too late, I would have already killed her.

My thumb felt like it weighed a ton as I held it over the plunger. Andrea was looking at me with an anxious expression on her face. The sweat was running down my back now. I could not speak or move. I reassured myself that I had done it all correctly. I could not stand there much longer torn by indecision. I knew I had to push the plunger, and soon. The tube was inserted and Lori was trying to cry in silent wails. I must act and I must do it now.

I pushed the plunger.

The milk shot down the tubing and disappeared into Lori. She continued to struggle but did not strangle. I had done it right! It was at that point that I realized I was not breathing. I had been holding my breath the whole time.

With smiles of triumph I extracted the tube and Andrea congratulated me. I felt marvelous, I had done it, alone and unassisted. I had tube-fed my daughter without harm! Then Andrea burst my triumphant bubble.

"We get to do it again in four hours," she said wrapping up the tubing and other items for cleaning.

"That celebration didn't last long," I said, glumly deflated.

"You'll get used to it," she patted my arm as she left the room.

The truth was I never did get used to tube feeding Lori. For weeks I had to come home twice a day from work to tube feed her and at least once a night we had to get up and feed her. But no matter how tired I was or how deeply asleep I had been, just before I depressed that plunger to send the milk into her silently protesting throat I was wide-awake, and nervously perspiring. On the second day Lori was home from the hospital tube feeding took on an added, and unexpected, importance.

The day after we came home from Vanderbilt Andrea was sitting in a chair in the living room trying to coax Lori into sucking her bottle. She noticed that each time Lori sucked at the nipple of her bottle she seemed to grimace as if sucking the bottle caused her pain. She brought the discovery to my attention. She asked me to trade chairs with her because there was a light over my chair and she would be able see better.

We exchanged chairs and I went around to stand behind her. It was true, each time Lori sucked on the bottle she flinched. It was difficult enough to try to teach her to suck a bottle, but apparently we had some additional problem.

"I think she has something in her mouth that's hurting her," Andrea announced after Lori made another reluctant pull at the nipple and cringed.

"Might be," I agreed, trying to mentally come up with a logical solution to explain this most recent crisis. But I knew that Lori was a mass of contradictions and complexities, and there probably was no simple answer.

"I'm going to see if I can find it," she said, turning Lori so that she lay between Andrea's thighs, head toward her knees.

Using her thumbs, Andrea forced open Lori's little mouth and delivered us both a shock. Looking through the open mouth we were given a clear, unobstructed view up and into our daughter's sinus cavities! When Dr. Werkhaven had created her nasal passages he had gone through the roof of her mouth. After the bone had been removed and the white plastic tubes implanted, the open roof of her mouth had been sewn closed. For some reason the sutures had come lose and the roof of Lori's mouth had pulled apart leaving a gaping hole where her palette should have been. Each time she sucked at the bottle milk was filling her sinus cavities.

I felt queasy for a moment as my stomach rolled. I had seen a lot of gory things in my time, but having the unexpected disclosure of the interior of your daughter's skull in your own living room is a most unsettling experience. Andrea uttered a yelp, and looked back at me.

"What do we do?" she asked.

I had absolutely no idea.

"Let's call Werkhaven," I suggested, and we darted toward the bedroom phone.

Dialing Vanderbilt, we initiated an involved process of attempting to locate a specialist. This took some time, but finally we received a return call from a doctor we did not know. He told us that he was an otolaryngologist in residency, i.e. training. But we figured a doctor in training was better than no doctor at all.

"It may not be as bad as you think," he said after introducing himself. "If you can tell me what you see we'll walk through an examination of her."

"All right," I agreed, somewhat reluctantly.

With Andrea holding Lori in her lap as she had done before, she opened her mouth with her thumbs again at the doctor's direction.

"Can you see the tubes?" he asked.

"Yeah," I replied.

"All right, can you see the back of her throat?"

"Yeah," I maneuvered into position to see down her throat.

"Look carefully and tell me if you can see the ends of the tubes?" He spoke carefully to highlight the importance of what he was saying.

I looked down her throat and squinted. Her tongue moved around making the inspection difficult, but I finally saw what I thought were the tube ends.

"O.K.," I said, "I see them."

"Good, are they still sutured together?"

I strained to see. I could see that they were together, but sutured together?

"They're together," I told him, "but I can't say their sutured together, all I can see is that they are still together as they go into the back of her nasal passage and into her throat area."

"If they're still in place I feel safe to say that they're still sutured together," he paused for a moment. "That's the only important thing. If the tubes come undone we've got problems, but as long as they stay in place and together it doesn't matter about the rest."

"What should we do?" I asked.

"You can bring her up here if you want, but to tell you the truth if the tubes are still in place there's very little we can do. If we leave the incision alone the roof of the mouth will close up in a few weeks." He rushed to add, " I know this sounds terrible, just to leave her mouth open like it is, but actually there's no danger. It's just unsightly."

"But the milk's getting up in her head," I insisted.

"I know," I could hear him smile on the other end of the phone, "but it really will do no harm. What she's done is worried the sutures lose with her tongue. The edges of the incision are raw, but they will heal in time and it presents no danger to her otherwise. But, like I said if you want to bring her up here tonight we'll do what we can."

"No," I said slowly, resigning myself to the facts. "That's all right. If you say there's no problem we'll just stay here."

Andrea was looking at me by this point in the conversation like she seeing a person who has lost his mind.

"What you can do, if it would make you feel better about it," he offered, "is leave a message for Werkhaven and inform him about what has happened. When he's in his office next week you can bring her in and let him take a look at her himself. If there's any problems he'll find them."

"O.K.," I agreed, "I'll take her in later."

"All right," he sounded satisfied with the decision. "You keep an eye on the stints. If you think they're starting to come loose, bring her in right away. Otherwise, everything will be fine."

"O.K.," I nodded, glancing at Andrea, "I'll call his office and make an appointment."

"Great," he said, closure in his voice, "if you need me again, just call."

"Oh, we will," I assured him and said good-bye.

When I got off the phone and explained to Andrea what had been decided she just looked from Lori to me and back to Lori again. I could tell that she was confused.

"It's not a problem," she asked.

"He says it isn't," I tried to sound matter of fact. "He said that as long as the stints are in place there's nothing to worry about."

"And the milk getting into her head," her voice raised an octave. "That's no problem?"

"He says not," I also explained what he had said about the roof of the mouth slowly closing over the following weeks. I finished by relating to her that he had said we could go see Werkhaven if we wanted to reassure ourselves.

"We certainly will," she said quickly. "Won't we sweet'ums?" She addressed Lori who was cradled in her arms. "Sweet'ums" had become a nickname Andrea had hung on Lori of late. Lori, for her part, appeared completely unconcerned about the flap she had created and was beginning to doze off. Lori took most crises this way, usually far better than we did.

That night we laid Lori down in her crib and went to bed. We tried to sleep, but it certainly was difficult, knowing that our daughter lay in the dark just a few feet away with the roof of her mouth a gaping hole and her cranial sinuses exposed. It was not a comfortable way to drift off to sleep.

Eventually the roof of her mouth did close, just as the doctor had predicted. When we met with Werkhaven later that week he looked at the opening and told us the same thing the young resident had the night we discovered the opening. We felt a little better, but were still uneasy knowing her sinuses were open to her mouth. Andrea kept sneaking peeks at the hole and kept me apprised of the progress as the tissue grew together. But, as it turned out, we had much better luck with the roof of Lori's mouth than we had with the promised home health care nurse.

Andrea called me at work one day to say that the nurse had dropped by. She said that she had brought no equipment to weigh a preemie, and had asked about the stints in her nose. When Andrea explained about the coanal atresia the nurse told her that she had never heard of it before. What really worried Andrea was the nurse's reply when she had asked a question of the nurse about tube feeding and the woman told her she had never heard of anyone tube feeding an infant before.

To say the least Andrea felt the woman was less than helpful. The next time the nurse came by the house Andrea called again, saying that the woman had Andrea show her how to suction the stints and explain the process to her.

"I'm having to train her! I don't see any reason to pay good insurance money for someone who can't help us," she concluded.

I agreed and told her that if she wanted she could call the nursing facility and cancel the service. We were getting billed for it through our insurance and they were paying enough already without having to pay for educating a home health care nurse.

"We always have Weezie," I reminded her.

Weezie was short for Louise, our neighbor, and her help and advice was far better than the home health care nurse. More importantly, we trusted her. Weezie proved to be a Godsend during our years of struggle. She learned as much as we did during our ordeal, and at one point even used Lori as a research project and based a paper on her for one of her classes. As long as we had Weezie, I reasoned, we could get along. Andrea agreed, and her voice picked up a bit.

"I'll do it," she said before hanging up.

Having Lori home was certainly the beginning of a different way of life for us. First we began each day by getting out of bed and checking to see if Lori had died during the night. That sounds terrible to say, but it was the way we lived for two years. Because her kidney condition was so tenuous we never knew from day to day when the one half of her left kidney, which was the only large piece of kidney keeping her alive, might be overwhelmed by her bodily demands. If that happened she would begin dying of renal failure. Renal failure is a form of death that is not easily detected in its initial stages. We had to look carefully for the early signs each day and with each diaper change. The overall effect of such a daily routine is that you become accustomed to living daily with the possibility of death. We never knew when her body would betray her and leave us with only hours or days left to be with her.

Living life this way tends to make you appreciate each day. I began to understand the Biblical admonition; "Let the evils of the day be sufficient unto themselves." We are not guaranteed tomorrow, nor our next hour of life, not even our next breath. All we have is now, and here. This is all we can really claim as ours and all that we can say is real. Lori has taught us that today is all we have and today has to be enough. Each day that we got out of bed and found her still alive meant that we could begin the day, certain that we had made it this far, and be glad for it. Living such an existence makes you appreciate the small things in life. Just being alive is enough when you are not certain that there will be a tomorrow.

* * * * * * *

Even though she had nasal stints, and she was tiny in comparison to most infants her age, we had decided that we would make her as much a part of the family as she would have been if she were a healthy, "normal" baby. Andrea believed that we should make her feel at home, so she took soda straws and cut them into pieces. She stuck a piece of straw up each of her nostrils, and then inserted them into Little John's nose. Having accomplished this, she put Lori on her lap and directed me to take a picture of the three of them for a family portrait. We still have the photo in our family frame. That photo bears comic testament to a family bent on solidarity and inclusion.

That particular photograph accomplished something else we had never expected. Our family physician, Dr. Doug Haney, is a very nice man, but he is a very quiet person. In all the years I had known him I had never heard him laugh. On the next visit to his office for one of Lori's periodic checkups I showed the photo of the family with nose stints to his nurse, Melissa. She loved the picture and took it out into the hall to show Dr. Haney. It was then that I heard something I had never heard before: Dr. Haney loudly laughing.

By treating her as a "normal" member of the family we took her with us everywhere we went that it was proper for a child to go. When we went out, Lori went out. When we went shopping, Lori went shopping.

Some reactions to Lori were interesting. Most people, when they see a baby, come toward it, or look at it with obvious pleasure. In Lori's case we had many encounters with people who would see the baby we held in the blanket, or in the carrier, they would make for her only to draw up short and sharply direct their attention to something else as soon as they saw the nose stints.

Very few people have ever seen nose stints. We could understand that. We also began to understand that the people who did not come over and continue their inspection of the baby avoided her out of their insecure feelings or abhorrence of physical abnormality. This became our initiation into the world of the handicapped.

Even though we have come to terms with these reactions, there still are times when they hurt. Recently Andrea took Lori with her to shop for clothes. I took Little John to another store. We had not been in the store but a moment when Andrea came in leading Lori by the hand.

"What's the matter?" I asked absentmindedly, still paying attention to the book I was examining, "they out of what you wanted?"

"No," her voice carried a quiver, and made me pay more attention. Andrea was on the verge of tears. "They kept staring at Boo." Her lower lip trembled uncontrollably. "There's nothing wrong with her, but they kept staring at her like she was different or something."

"She is," I tried to keep realistic about this and yet comfort her.

"No, she's not." A tear leaked out of the corner of one eye. "You can't tell."

"Yes, you can," I insisted.

"How?" Andrea demanded. "She doesn't look different, or act different. She's just Boo."

"Yes, she does." I took her arm and she leaned against me. "She looks different and she acts different, but it's O.K. don't worry."

"Well, I'm not going back in that store if they treat Boo like that," she said, defiantly.

"You don't have to go back," I assured her.

Most of the time Andrea cannot see the difference between Lori and "normal" children because she does not look for it, but she cannot ignore the sideways glances, or disapproving stares she encounters when she is out in public with Lori. Most of the time it does not bother her, but when she has her guard down, she gets hurt. Usually I ignore it, but

I must admit that there are times when you cannot ignore what is so painfully evident.

Not long ago we were waiting in line at a checkout counter. There was a little girl in a line two aisles over. She looked at Lori standing beside me and I heard her tell her mother that she knew "that girl" because she went to school with her. The little girl was simply pleased to see someone she knew. But when the smiling mother turned to see who her daughter was pointing at, the pleasant smile vanished from her face and she quickly grabbed her daughter by the arm and turned her away. I could not hear what she said to the little girl under her breath but I had a feeling I knew what it was. The little girl turned and furtively looked at us once more, as if confused, trying to put together her mother's reaction and what she saw. In time the little girl will internalize what her mother meant and connect it with what she saw: "different people" and "bad people" are the same and they should not be acknowledged. It will not take that little girl very long to understand the meaning of "different people" and her inherent superiority to them. It is a lesson that I do not believe Lori will ever be able to learn, thank God.

We do not take Lori out with us into the public to afflict others. Quite to the contrary, we take her with us so that she can live as normal a life as possible. We believe that public exposure is extremely important to her development. But we also know that it is important for us too. We believe that should we start living our lives as if we were constrained or burdened by Lori, most probably that is the exact character that our lives will assume. Faced with awesome responsibilities, we believe if we treat them as everyday problems that is all they will be.

I am thankful many times over that we initially adopted the philosophy of including Lori in our everyday life because soon we would need the strength it would give us.

Chapter IX
Chicken Pox

There are people who will tell you that chicken pox is a childhood disease, but that it does not affect infants under three months of age. Well, let me tell you that one piece of common wisdom is universally incorrect. We are living proof.

A chicken pox epidemic had broken out all over central Tennessee while we were confined in NICU. Several children were in Vanderbilt because of complications from the disease. Andrea was concerned, but several people told her not to worry, because children under three months of age could not contract chicken pox. These same people agreed that Little John might get it but certainly not Lori.

Soon after we got her home, Lori developed red splotches all over her body. Andrea became concerned and redoubled her efforts to find out what was happening to Lori. Andrea herself began feeling ill, but she thought she was suffering side effects from her worrying over Lori's new symptoms. She called Dr. Hill, she consulted her friend Weezie, she called both grandmothers, but no one could explain the splotches on Lori, or her increasing irritability.

Next, Andrea found a small colony of splotches setting up camp on Little John's forehead. By the time I got home from work that day, she was really worried.

"I can't figure it out," she languished on the couch, her own illness sapping her strength. "Lori's still got red spots, but she seems fine. Little John's coming down with them, and all he says is that he itches. I feel like death eating a cracker, and I've got is this red spot on my nose." She pointed to the tip of her nose where an angry red spot glared back at me.

"It can't be chicken pox," she bewailed her research. "Weezie says it is, but that's a childhood illness and I'm no child. If Lori had it and itches like Little John she'd be scratching, but she isn't. I feel sick and John just scratches all the time and eats like a mule."

Andrea was getting worse, her complexion was growing pasty, and her eyes were getting red. I did not tell her but there were more red spots on her nose and others had moved onto her face. I tried to prepare her for the worst.

"It could be chicken pox, like Weeze says," I was somewhat amused, but dared not express it at that moment because Andrea was truly sick and would not appreciate the humor. "Adults can get it too."

"No, no," she persisted, rolling back and forth on the couch in her discomfort, "take Lori to Dr. Haney and let him look at her. If it's something serious we need to get to Vanderbilt right away."

"O.K.," I consoled her.

Finding a doctor after hours is not normally easy but Dr. Haney was always available for Lori, just as he was this time. When he received our page he was visiting patients at the local hospital. He called us and told me to bring Lori to the emergency room waiting area. He said he would meet me there. I packed Lori up in her little car seat/carrier and off to the hospital we went.

Once at the hospital I carried Lori down the hall and took up residence in the waiting room. When a nurse asked us what we needed we told her we were waiting on Dr. Haney. She gave us a puzzled look but left us to our vigil. In a short time Dr. Haney came down the hall, a collection of papers trapped under one arm. We shook hands and he directed us to the room on the other side of the hallway. He had me set Lori down on a couch and we took seats on either side of her.

"It'll save an emergency room bill if I see her here," he said as he set about examining her.

He felt her head, her chest, and legs. He listened to her heart, peeked in her mouth, and ran an eye over the top of her fuzzy head. Lori was undisturbed by the examination. She had had far worse. For her this was a walk in the park. She kicked her little feet, and clenched and unclenched her fingers, all eleven of them. He asked about her urine and any other symptoms she had exhibited. I explained everything I knew about her condition.

"I think it's chicken pox, but Andrea's not sure because she's been told that babies under three months can't get chicken pox," I concluded my recital.

Dr. Haney smiled and poked Lori's tummy with a finger. She wiggled at the touch and he looked up at me, still smiling.

"Well," he began, "she has chicken pox no matter how old she is, and from what you say, so does Little John. Has Andrea ever had chicken pox before?"

"Not that I know of."

"Odds are that she has them too, if she didn't have them as a child." He grew a little more serious. "Chicken pox is harder on adults than children. Tell her to come see me if she gets really sick and I'll give her something that will help."

He poked Lori with his finger again and got up.

"She seems to be fine. Children are affected less by this than adults. For them its not much more than an inconvenience." He started to leave, "but if she develops any other symptoms just give me a call."

"Thanks," I shook hands with him as he left.

Returning home I announced the news to Andrea, and Weeze, who had come over to hear the verdict. Weeze had a smile of triumph on her face as I told Andrea that Lori had chicken pox, that Little John probably did too, and that if she did not have them as a child, then it was chicken pox that was making her sick.

Andrea pondered for a time. She could not recall if she had ever had chicken pox when she was younger. She called her mother who laughed so hard I could hear it through the phone all the way across the room. No, she told Andrea, she had not had chicken pox as a child.

Adults with chicken pox are a comical experience, except for the person who has them. Pox in adults is a painful, wicked affair. Andrea was in terrible shape by the next day but true to her dedication to duty she went to work at the radio station. She worked every day she had the pox and suffered enormously for her devotion.

Lori, on the other hand, just sat around wiggling her spotted fingers and toes, all twenty-one of them and appeared relatively unaffected by the whole affair. Little John was itchy but decided that eating more food would make him feel better. It did.

****

The common cold

After we had gotten over the chicken pox and settled back into our daily routine, such as it was, Lori thrived for a couple of weeks. Her appetite grew and she began to gain weight. Her kidneys functioned superbly and she slept without incident. We were just getting comfortable with our new life when Andrea called me at work in a panic. Lori had spiked a high fever. She looked pale and would not eat. Andrea was certain that her kidneys had failed.

I dropped everything I was doing and rushed home. Andrea had Lori ready to go when I walked in the front door. I piled Lori and her paraphernalia into my investigative unit and rushed her to Dr. Haney's clinic. Andrea had called ahead so they would be prepared for our arrival. When we got there the staff ushered us directly into the examination room. Dr. Haney came in and checked her quickly. He ordered blood drawn, and told me we would have to wait for the results. In a very short time he darted back into the examination room.

"Can you take off work?" he asked seriously.

"Sure," I felt my blood pressure shoot sky high.

"I don't want you to run any stop signs or fly low," he tried to smile, but I could tell he was concerned, "but I want you to take Lori to Vanderbilt Children's hospital as fast as you can. Her blood count is very high, something's wrong." I must have paled because he quickly added. "I'm not saying that it's her kidneys, but I'd rather be safe."

He wrote something on a sheet of paper, told me to give it to the doctors at Vanderbilt and wished me well. I was off like a shot. I rushed home. Andrea was ready when I got there. We threw some things in the back of our car in case we had to stay overnight and were off. On the way Andrea suctioned Lori's stints. As she was doing this we noticed that Lori's complexion changed color. She became sort of a beige, or a pale, off white kind of color. Her breathing was regular, but the color change gave us a fright. I eased up the speed just a bit as we raced up the interstate.

Arriving at Vandy we deposited the car in the parking lot and crossed the skywalk to the clinic. At the check-in counter we informed the receptionist that we had been sent from Pulaski and the lady told us they were expecting us. She asked us to sit down and wait.

We watched Lori closely as we waited. She still had a fever and she appeared fitful. Andrea was distraught with worry, and so was I. Crowded about the open waiting area of the children's clinic were parents with children who had a variety of ailments. Most of the children were mobile and talkative, with no discernible afflictions. Some of the parents glanced nervously at our little baby with the plastic tubes coming out of her nose. In a short time a middle-aged woman came out of the examination rooms. She was not dressed in the traditional doctor's garb, but we had become accustomed to the fact that most medical staff at Vanderbilt does not dress in what could be called a traditional manner. She stepped around the couch and introduced herself, explaining that she was a pediatrician and that she wanted us to bring Lori back to the examination rooms so she could look at her.

We carried Lori into one of the many rooms lining the corridor. I deposited her on the examination table and stood back as Lori was rolled over, examined, temperature taken, and tested. The doctor was very thorough in her work, leaving nothing to chance. After her initial work was completed the doctor told us that we could take Lori back out front. She explained that there were tests to be run and it would take time to get the results.

We waited, more or less patiently, as time dragged. The nagging thought that this was the beginning of the end, that her kidneys were finally failing and that we had only days or hours left with her haunted us the whole time we waited. Finally, after what seemed like an eternity, the doctor who had examined Lori came around the counter and approached us. Another woman accompanied her. The first doctor introduced the other woman as a pediatrician. This really jolted us. Having two doctors come to talk to us cinched it as far as we were concerned. They would only send two of them to talk to us if the news was going to be really bad this time. We braced ourselves for the worst.

"We've completed our tests," the first doctor told us. "Lori's white cell count is high, her fever is up, but not too bad, and she seems to have an upset stomach. With all the test data completed we have come to the conclusion that what your daughter has is a common cold."

Andrea stared at them, first one doctor, then the other.

"Do you mean to sit there and tell me that my daughter has something common," Andrea finally said, acting dramatically indignant.

The two doctors caught the joke, knowing Lori's complex and unusual medical history. They both smiled broadly.

"Yes. Ma'am," the first doctor spoke up, trying to hide the mirth in her voice, "we are telling you that your daughter has something very common."

"Did you hear them?" She turned to me, still acting as if she had been insulted, but I could see the strain draining away behind her tear filled eyes. "They insist that our daughter has a common cold! After all we've been through," she turned her attention to Lori who lay uncaring in her carrier, "and they say you've just got a common cold! How dare they, huh, Piddle?"

The doctors enjoyed our humor for a short while, then gave us some instructions on caring for the common cold before hurrying back to the endless line of sick and injured children waiting for them in the rooms beyond.

We gathered our things together and made our way toward the parking lot. We were both relieved, but in a strange way proud. Our daughter had an ordinary cold. To any other parents such an event as this presented a real problem, but to us it was the first normal thing that had happened since the previous December when we had first been told that Lori had a urethra seal. Was it not just grand? Our daughter had a common cold, just like any other child. We had never felt so good about a cold in our lives.

Chapter X
Dilations

At the time of Lori's release from the hospital in early April, Dr. Werkhaven had told us that we had to bring her back in six weeks to have the stints removed. The nasal stints had been in place almost exactly six weeks when we returned to Vanderbilt and for their removal. Removing the stints was a minor surgical operation, which entailed cutting the sutures holding the two pieces of plastic together at the back of her throat and pulling the tubes out the front of her nose. When this simple procedure had been completed we were allowed to take her home again, but before we left the hospital Werkhaven told us that we needed to return in two weeks for an examination. He explained that the scar tissue in the newly created nasal passages has a tendency to grow closed over time, and that this would obstruct her ability to breath properly. He said that what had to be done to relieve the condition was to have the nasal passages "dilated". I had absolutely no idea what that meant but we were glad to have our daughter back in near normal condition so we agreed to bring her back in two weeks and joyfully left for home.

At the end of the second week I took a day off work, bundled Lori into her car seat/carrier, stuffed a diaper bag with all her necessary provisions and set off for Nashville. Dr. Werkhaven's office is located in a portion of the Vanderbilt Clinic that is an extension of the larger hospital complex. The office itself is a spacious, open-air affair occupying one side of a small glass enclosed garden. The space is a well-lit, efficient office, placed along side other offices housing various specialties. The waiting room consists of a large open area decorated with comfortable collection of chairs and tables. The nurses and receptionists work behind an enclosed reception area set to one side and adorned with large letters announcing that you have arrived at Otolaryngology. When I walked up to the check-in counter a young woman looked up. She appeared to be of Hispanic or Native American origin, with dark hair and eyes. She had a pleasant, round face that opened into a smile.

"May I help you?" she asked.

I held Lori up in her carrier with one hand as I balanced against the overflowing bag slung over my other shoulder. The carefully stuffed carrier Lori was strapped into made her appear even tinier than she actually was.

"Lori White," I said, an announcement as much as an introduction.

The woman's eyes softened as she leaned forward to smile into the carrier.

"Oh, isn't she sweet," she said. "Hi, Lori."

She handed me some papers to sign, took my Vanderbilt card, fed it into a machine to record our visit and begin the automatic billing process, validated my parking ticket and nodded toward the chairs scattered about the open waiting area.

"Dr. Werkhaven will be with you in a minute."

I waddled over to the chairs and sat down. Perching Lori's carrier on a low coffee table situated in front of the chair we prepared to wait. In only a short time the woman called Lori's name from where she stood, holding open a set of double doors. For the first time I could see that she was dressed as a nurse. Hefting the bag and Lori's carrier I entered the corridor beyond the doors and was shown into a spacious room dominated by a large examination table. The table looked vaguely like those used in X-ray rooms. It was long with a metal top and geometric designs formed into its finish. A bewildering array of strange machines and implements surrounded it.

The nurse took what looked like a small spine board from one of the cabinets standing against one wall and placed it on top of the examination table. I was somewhat familiar with spine boards. I had seen paramedics use them at traffic accidents to stabilize victims for transportation. From what I knew about them the intended use of spine boards is to prevent causing further damage to injured people as they are moved from one location to another. The boards are usually as long as an average person is tall, with handholds cut into the sides of the boards at intervals down their length and at each end to facilitate carrying the person strapped to the board. Every spine board I had ever seen had three or four sets of Velcro straps placed down their length to secure the person to the board.

When the nurse set the spine board on the table I thought she was preparing the room for whoever would follow us. The spine board she laid on the table was smaller than any I had ever seen before and instead of straps down the sides it was equipped with a wide flap of plastic material on each side. When she had spread out the material on either side of the board she turned to me.

"Take Lori out of her seat and put her on the board," she said matter of factly.

I hesitated. I could not imagine why Lori needed to be laid on top of the spine board. She had not been injured, or needed transportation that I could not provide. The directions seemed irrational, but I complied. When I had positioned her as directed and the nurse told me to hold her still. Now, holding Lori still was usually much easier said than done. For one thing, Lori was seldom still, and for another, she did not like having to lie on her back. In the neonatal unit the nurses had strapped Lori's hands down to keep her from ripping out her air tube. To do this they had tied gauze around her wrists and used safety pins to secure the gauze strips to the bed on either side of her body. Lori had lain in this spread-eagle type position for the better part of two weeks. Since that unpleasant experience Lori had not liked to be held down in any manner, especially not on her back.

As soon as I laid her down she began to squirm. The nurse wrapped one side of the plastic fabric over her body and I took my hands away. She quickly brought the other side of the fabric across Lori's body and secured it in place with a Velcro strip sewn into the edge of the material. Wrapped in this way Lori looked like a small papoose with only her head poking out above the fabric.

No sooner had Lori been secured than Dr. Werkhaven walked in the room. He asked how things had been going and I said, “fine.” Then he asked specifically about how well Lori had been breathing lately. I told him that from what we could tell she was doing all right. He nodded, but began to explain once again about the probability of the scar tissue closing her nasal passages over time. As he spoke he took a small, white feather from his coat pocket and held it under Lori's right nostril. The feather moved but only ever so slightly with each breath. When the feather had moved several times he shifted it to the left nostril. The feather hovered motionless under Lori's nose. Werkhaven's mouth pressed into a thin line.

"The scar tissue's closed completely on the left side," he said, putting the feather back into his pocket. "The left side's closed partially. We're going to have to dilate."

He looked up. By this time I had known Werkhaven for months and during all that time he had never looked so grim. The look scared me a little. He reached into a nearby cabinet, took out a handful of metal rods and a small tube of cream. The rods were made of what looked like stainless steel, about eighteen inches long, rounded on each end and slightly curved. As he spoke he took the tube of clear gel and began applying a portion of it to the end of the smallest gauged rod.

"What we must do is dilate each nostril to break open the scar tissue. This cream will numb some of the pain." He set the tube aside and looked to his nurse. A silent message passed between them.

"Will you hold her body," the nurse asked me as she placed her hands on either side of Lori's head.

"We've got to keep her from moving as much as possible," Werkhaven said as he leaned over the table, bringing the rod toward Lori's face.

Horrified, I held Lori's body motionless as he placed the rod into the opening of her right nostril. He inserted the rod as far as it would go. A couple of inches of the brightly shining metal disappeared into Lori's nose, then abruptly stopped. I looked up as Werkhaven steadied the rod in place with his left hand and brought his right hand up, palm open to shoulder height. With a powerful blow he struck the end of the rod sending it deep into Lori's head.

I looked in alarm at Lori. I heard a dull pop from inside her head as the steel rod broke open the accumulated scar tissue. Lori froze at the impact, opened her mouth to scream in pain, but no sound came out. She could not scream, her vocal cords were not yet healed. Although she could not make a sound she desperately tried. As her mouth formed a silent, soundless scream, I saw the back of her throat fill with bright, red blood. The blood began to rise up like a cup being filled from the bottom. The tide of shining crimson rose higher as she held the prolonged mute scream until blood ran out both sides of her mouth and down her cheeks in a flood.

"Oh, God! Oh, God! Oh, God," was all I could think. I could not believe that here I was holding my tiny daughter down so that a man could ram steel rods down her nose and break open the inside of her head until blood ran out of her mouth like a river! My mind wanted to revolt. I wanted to run away and never quit running.

The scarlet tipped rod was finally extracted from Lori's nostril and a larger one immediately inserted in its place. With less force than the first rod, the second rod was pushed back down her nose, and extracted.

When this was completed that rod was taken out and another replaced it. Each succeeding rod was a larger diameter until the last one was inserted which was as large as Lori's external nasal passage would permit. When the left nostril had been completely dilated I knew that I could take no more of this horror, but we were only half finished. Dr. Werkhaven started work on the right nostril.

Again there was a pop from inside Lori's little head, again she tried to scream, and again, the blood rolled up and out of her mouth in a maroon torrent.

The rods went in and out of her nose, growing in size just as they had done on the other nostril. My mind spun with the anguish and pain I felt for her, and for me. Then, mercifully it was over. The last rod was extracted and piled beside the others on the table. The nurse quickly unwrapped Lori and we sat her up. A suction bulb was inserted into each nostril and blood was sucked out of the bleeding passages. Lori was crying, but still made no sound. I tried to comfort her. As soon as the nurse had finished with the suction bulb I put Lori to my shoulder and began patting her back and talking to her in a soothing voice. Within a minute she had stopped crying. She was far from happy as I lay her down in her carrier but she made no complaints.

Werkhaven showed me how to suction the blood from her nose and told me to do that often on our way home. Before we left the examination room Werkhaven again conducted the examination with the feather. Under each blood caked nostril the spidery feather flopped back and forth with gusto as Lori inhaled and exhaled.

"See," he smiled, "it works."

He straightened up and started to leave.

"I'll see you in two weeks," he said as he led me into the hallway.

I recall speaking with him in as natural a voice as I could master, but as we talked so civilly my mind was racing at a furious pace. "I'll see you in two weeks" meant we had to do this again! I'd have to hold her down and he would ram those terrible rods into her head again! I wanted to ask him how long this would last, how many weeks would we come back? But I could not bring myself to ask because a part of me wanted to escape the reality that the answer would bring. I simply agreed that I'd see him in two weeks and took Lori home.

We went back in two weeks, just as we had been directed, and every two weeks thereafter for months. I never got used to the dilations, nor the pain they caused Lori. I never got used to watching Werkhaven shove steel rods down Lori's nose, and the blood rise up from her throat. Once, another doctor, seeing me suction Lori's, nose complimented me on my expert skill. I told him that in the last year I had learned more about medicine than I had ever wanted to know, but I did not tell him how I'd learned the skill I was not proud of having.

* * * * * * *

Werkhaven could do one of the hardest jobs I have ever had to witness, but he had a heart of gold. Years later, long after Lori had left his care, she was in the pediatric intensive care unit following an operation. She had to be intubated with a breathing tube due to complications that interfered with her normal breathing ability. One day we came to visit her and found that a small crisis had occurred. Lori had extubated herself while her nurse was away. She had to have the tube quickly replaced and that, even under ideal circumstances, is not an easy task.

When we first learned of this event we braced for the bad news we expected to follow, but the nurse waved our concerns away.

"Nothing to worry about," the nurse told us with a smile. "There just happened to be a doctor here and he put the tube right back in, no problem."

"Well, we are lucky, aren't we," Andrea said, looking at me with a skeptical expression etched across her face. Andrea did not necessarily believe in luck anymore, unless it was bad luck, and I could see that she was not buying this little fairy tale of a convenient doctor on the scene just when he was needed.

" Yes, we were," the nurse said as she left to attend her other patients.

Andrea walked over to Lori's bed and picked up the clipboard attached to the foot of the bed. Scanning down the papers her eyes stopped and she looked up. Tears were in her eyes as she pressed her lips into a thin line.

"What's the matter?" I asked, thinking that she had discovered some problem that we had not been told about.

She handed me the clipboard.

"That doctor that 'just happened' to be here," she said fighting back the tears. "It was Werkhaven."

I looked down at the clipboard but could not see through my own watering eyes.

"Yeah," I choked, "he just happened to be here."

"Right," Andrea snorted and walked away to collect herself.

I went by Werkhaven's office the next day and spoke to his nurse. From her I learned that every time Werkhaven found out Lori was in the hospital he made a special point of visiting her. He never mentioned the visits to us, or told us about his keeping an eye on her. Werkhaven was like that, a modest person with a great heart. God did not make a whole lot of men like Werkhaven, but then He never made a lot of any of the most precious things He created.

Chapter XI

Almost Losing Lori

When I arrived home after the first visit to Werkhaven's office for "dilations" of Lori's nasal passages I described for Andrea what the procedures involved. She blanched, horrified at the prospect of having to hold her daughter down while such vile things were done to her, and informed me in no uncertain terms that I would take Lori to all such appointments in the future. I really could not blame her. If there had been some way I could have avoided going I would have, but one of us had to do it and I knew that if Andrea was faced with no other alternative she would do it herself. Andrea had suffered through the months of carrying Lori, waiting for her to die inside her, and the indignities of all the examinations, so the least I could do was make the trips to have her nasal passages enlarged.

Every two weeks we went through the dilation ritual. Lori was packed up in her car seat/carrier, belted into my old Datsun pickup along with her diaper bag and assorted paraphernalia, and off we would go to Nashville. Despite what awaited us, Lori enjoyed the trips. Still unable to make any sound,s she would sit in her car seat and watch the world go by. She would smile and have an occasional suck at her bottle that I had become adapt at holding for her in or out of traffic.

Another skill that I acquired was the ability to suction her nose with a suction bulb, clearing the blood from her nasal passages, while driving. As a matter of fact, I got so good at suctioning her nose on the move that I could eat a cheeseburger, suck blood with the suction bulb, and drive through evening rush hour traffic in South Nashville in our manual transmission equipped old truck.

At first, I thought it was just me who had a problem with Lori's dilations until one appointment I walked up to the window with Lori nestled in her carrier. When I stopped at the reception window and proudly held the carrier up for the nurse to see Lori she grimaced, and said, "Oh, no, it's Lori."

She instantly looked guilt ridden and quickly apologized.

"Oh please," she beseeched me, "don't take it the wrong way. I mean I love Lori, she's so sweet, but I just hate to see her coming for the dilations. I hate them."

I told her that I understood, but that I thought that I was the only one who dreaded them.

"Oh. no," she gravely, shook her head, "I hate to see her suffer. She's so sweet ... I just hate to see her go through the pain."

That day when Lori was strapped into her brace, the nurse holding her head as usual, with me stabilizing her body, I consciously paid attention to Dr. Werkhaven and his nurse as the procedure unfolded. I noticed that as Werkhaven placed the stainless steel rod into Lori's nostril and gathered his strength to push it through the scar tissue, the nurse closed her eyes and turned her head to the side, unable to watch. Dr. Werkhaven grimaced with a mask of regret etched into his face as he gave the initial push on the rod sending it into Lori's head and trigging the dull popping sound deep inside her skull. At that moment I realized that he had been doing a job he detested all along, without comment or complaint, just as the nurse had done her job without protest. My admiration for both of them soared.

Just when I thought we were making progress with the dilations, we suffered a major setback. What made the tragedy even worse, was that it was a session of dilations, which triggered the event. On one of Lori's later visits I arrived at the office to find that Dr. Werkhaven had left town for a few days and another otolaryngologist was standing in for him. The new doctor completed the dilations and we left town as usual, with me driving and suctioning blood from Lori's nose as we made our way back home. The dilation session had been a late afternoon appointment. By the time we had fought our way out of Nashville traffic Lori was fast asleep in her car seat. The long drive and emotional strain was always draining. By the time we reached home I was exhausted. Andrea put Lori to bed a short time after we got in. I ate and dropped into bed early, completely exhausted. As the heavy weight of the day settled down upon me all I wanted to do was sleep.

It seems to me the worst times of my life have always cropped up just when I was least prepared to deal with them. This case was no exception. I had just dropped off to sleep when Andrea shook me awake. I could hear the desperation in her voice as she tried to get me awake. I was so tired that I had to fight to climb out of the deep well of sleep that engulfed me.

"Something's wrong with Lori," Andrea said in a shrill, shaking voice. "Oh, John, I think she's dead. John please look at her, oh, John ....."

I tried to get out of bed but fatigue dragged at my body like a huge weight, rendering me weak with an onerous, sick feeling. The long months of emotional cliff hanging had taken their toll. I felt queasy and feeble. I struggled to my feet and Andrea flipped on the bedroom light. The act of getting to my feet made me physically sick at my stomach. The room rolled in a sea of nausea and I swallowed hard. I stumbled to Lori's crib and looked inside. The first thing that struck me was that Lori had become an odd, tanish/gray color. Instantly I noted that something was wrong with her breathing. She labored with each breath as if she were smothering. Andrea was right, something was wrong, terribly wrong, but I could not make my mind function. Try as I might I could not think straight. I told Andrea to get me a wet cloth.

I stumbled to the sofa. I could not make it any further, I was sick. Andrea rushed back into the room with a damp washcloth and put it on my face.

"What should we do?" her voice trembled on the edge of panic.

"Get her ready," I forced back the bile rising in my throat, and suppressed the urge to throw up. "I'll take her to the emergency room."

While Andrea got Lori out of the crib and bundled her up for the trip across town, I threw on some clothes. In a minute we were both ready to go and I dashed out into the truck and off to the hospital. Andrea stood at the front door watching us leave. I pitied the anguished face peering out at us as we raced off into the night. I knew that Andrea was convinced that she was seeing her daughter for the last time. Although I did not want to admit it I was afraid she was right.

I talked to Lori as we raced through the night toward the hospital. I begged her to hang on, that we would be there in a minute. I remember apologizing to her for not being faster, for not checking her before I went to bed myself, for letting her down when she needed me. I took the shortest route to the hospital, raced into the parking lot nearest the emergency room entrance and entered through the pneumatic doors.

When the ER nurses saw her condition they bolted into action. Lori was placed in an examination room immediately and oxygen was applied. An on-call ER doctor was summoned. When he appeared I gave a rapid, but brief recounting her conditions to date. When he heard that she was a Vanderbilt baby he immediately ordered calls made to the hospital to alert them to her condition. Within minutes the nurse returned with an acceptance for Lori at Vanderbilt. An ambulance was called to rush her to Nashville. One of the attending nurses was assigned to ride with her as they loaded Lori into the ambulance and speed off into the night.

After the ambulance tore out of the parking lot disappearing into the darkness, there was an unearthly quiet that seemed to hold me, and the whole world, in its grip. As I stood in the driveway, the night winds swept silently and eerily over the asphalt. I slowly turned and walked back into the hospital to retrieve Lori's empty car seat. It felt wretched to hold the empty seat in my hands and know that she may never sit in it again. I thought of all the times I had carried her in it for her appointments, shopping, and visiting. A pang of guilt and grief shot through me like a bolt of black lightening and tears welled up in my eyes. I fought them back as I stood in the brightly-lit emergency room, forcing myself to wait until I was alone to let my emotions have full reign. I quickly thanked the nurses and attendants before heading back to my truck. As I left the parking lot I could not hold back the flood tide of emotions any longer. I started to cry out loud. I thought of seeing Lori wrapped in the stretcher as they hustled her into the ambulance, and wondered if that was the last time I would ever see her alive.

I chastised myself for not being faster. So I felt sick, big deal, my daughter was dying and I felt sick? Lori depended on me and when she needed me the most I had let her down, may very well have let her die. The more I began to believe in my culpability, the harder I cried. It felt as if I had killed my daughter, not with anger or vindictiveness but something, to me worse than either, with neglect. Slow, tardy, selfish neglect. If I had checked her earlier, moved faster, been better I could have saved her. In the dark cab of the truck moving through the empty streets I found myself guilty and condemned myself without mercy.

Arriving back home I quickly briefed Andrea on what had happened at the hospital. We hurriedly stuffed some of Lori's things in a bag. Again leaving Andrea to care for Little John, I set off to Vanderbilt for the second time that day, or at least that waking period because we were now into the wee hours of the morning. Dawn was not far away.

Arriving at Vanderbilt I made my way from the familiar parking lot to the unfamiliar emergency room. For all the times that we had been to Vanderbilt we had never been to the emergency room. I went to the ER admitting desk and asked for Lori. They told me she was in an examination room and asked for my Vandy card.

After providing the necessary information to get Lori officially admitted into the hospital they let me go around the corner of the hallway to see her. I found her lying on an examination table on her back, dressed only in a diaper. With each breath she would arch her back, struggling desperately to breathe. She was being given oxygen to supplement her labored breathing, but it seemed to be of minimal help.

No one was with Lori when I first saw her. I stood at the door to her room, nervously watching her and waiting for someone to come help us. After a short time two doctors came by the room. I got out of their way to let them by, but neither of them moved to help Lori. Instead they just stood and watched her struggle to breathe. One doctor used a medical term, which I was not familiar with in asking the other doctor if he had seen anything like that before. The other man chuckled and said, no.

"She's really pulling, isn't she?" He casually commented.

"Yeah." The other doctor agreed. They turned and walked down the hallway casually discussing what they had seen.

I didn't know what to do. My first reaction was to grab one of them and hit him, but I restrained my hand. They walked on down the hall and disappeared. I stood with Lori for a long time. After what seemed like an hour a nurse came by and informed me Lori was being taken to pediatric intensive care.

A group of nurses made the transfer with me tagging along behind. When we reached the 5th floor's P.I.C. Lori was wheeled through the double doors, but I was asked to remain outside. From practice I knew that parents were not admitted to P.I.C. until the patient had been "cleaned up".

I took the opportunity to lay down in an adjacent waiting room and get a little sleep. After some time I was allowed to go in and see Lori. She had been put into a bed and seemed to be much more comfortable than she had been all night. I made several inquiries of nurses and attending physicians but no one could tell me what had brought on her sudden desperate condition.

A later examination revealed the dilations Lori had been given earlier in the day had not been large enough. The scar tissue had closed up sometime shortly after the session. One nostril was completely closed down and the other had only a pinhole opening left to allow her to breath. Coupled with this nasal closure was a compounding element. Sometime during the dilation session, or very shortly afterwards, Lori had inhaled a small amount of blood. The blood had set up pneumonia. This meant that her affected lungs were not efficiently processing what little air she was getting through the pinhole in one nostril. The sum total of these conditions was that she had been slowly smothering to death.

We had come closer to losing Lori than we ever had. If Andrea had not checked her before going to bed Lori surely would have died during the night, suffocated from the combined effect of both breathing obstructions. It would have been a slow, terrible death, intensified since her vocal cords were still damaged and she could not even cry out to alert us that she was in trouble. My guilt was compounded, and shame of it kept me from telling anyone how I felt.

Lori had been in the hospital for a day or two. I had to go to class. Andrea stayed home with Little John and I made the Nashville trek alone. I stopped at the hospital to see Lori. Her bed was located at the end of the PICU unit near the exit door. As I stood over her bed watching her sleep, her nurse came by and checked her vital signs. Lori began to stir. By this time Dr. Werkhaven had replaced the nasal stints. When Lori began to wake up she unconsciously began to pull at the stints. She hated those things in her nose.

I knew that she would not go back to sleep right away after being awakened, so I asked the nurse if I could hold her and try to get her back to sleep before I had to leave. She said it would not be a problem. She helped me gather all the monitor wires and tubing connected to Lori and I sat down in a chair against the wall facing out toward the unit.

The horror of knowing that Lori had almost died and that I had been partially responsible flooded over me as I sat holding her tiny body in my arms. I began to rock her and sing to her in a hushed voice. Or, more accurately I tried to sing to her, because when I opened my mouth nothing came out. I thought it was odd, my mouth was working and I could feel my vocal cords constricting to make the sounds, but no words came past my lips. I tried harder, still nothing happened, so I continued to rock her as I contemplated this new problem. As I sat trying to understand why I was not making a sound when I tried to sing to her I became conscious of a mewing, blubbering noise. It took only a moment for me to realize that the source of the strange sounds was me. I was not singing, I was crying. And worst of all I realized that I could not stop. Tears flowed uncontrollably. The faster the tears came, the harder I rocked. No matter how hard I tried I could not get a grip on my emotions. My throat was a throbbing agony as the convulsions of weeping relentlessly racked my body. The more effort I put into trying to stop crying the harder I cried. My tears began to make Lori's little blanket damp.

I could feel Lori relax in my arms as she slept and I knew she was at peace, but I was not. My nose began to run which only add to my misery and humiliation. Eventually my gurgling noise must have attracted the attention of Lori's nurse because she headed in our direction. As she approached Lori's bed I could barely see her through a torrent of tears. When she saw what was making the noises she abruptly turned, and walked away. I was grateful for that. She had the presence of mind not to add to my embarrassment and I appreciated her thoughtfulness.

After awhile the tears subsided and all I was left with was a dripping nose and a sleeping infant in my arms. I managed to lay Lori back in her bed without waking her. Assuring myself that she was all right I patted her leg, as was my custom, and told her I loved her before darting out the exit door. Once in the hallway I blew my nose and wiped my face. For a moment I hesitated walking out in public with a red, swollen face but then I realized that I really did not care what anyone else thought. I strode out into the parking lot to get my truck and go on with my life. What I felt for my daughter was all that I cared about and what somebody else might think about how I felt was their problem, not mine.

Somewhere during all our trials and difficulties I had discovered that love is something we should never be ashamed of, neither having it for someone, nor showing it when we have it. All too often our lives become prisons in which we lock our love away in private compartments that me only visit occasionally and to which we admit very few. I had been through a wrenching experience with someone I loved deeply and the last thing I wanted to do was hide that love, and its consequences. I was not going to be afraid of love any longer. And if people were uncomfortable with that then, the Hell with what they might think. I had come to understand that it was more important to love than it was to be well thought of.

Chapter XII
A New Problem

During Lori's recovery from the nasal closure in PICU a young doctor, newly assigned to the case, mentioned that they had "found something" on one of her X-rays. He explained that a specialist from pediatric orthopedics would be coming by later that evening to discuss the discovery with us. We questioned him about the possible problem, but he was vague and noncommittal, refusing us any specifics.

We worried through the afternoon. During evening rounds another young doctor came by and told us that Dr. Green would be with us shortly. We had never heard of Dr. Green, but we acknowledged the notice and stood by Lori's bed nervously for another hour or so until the pediatric orthopedics specialist arrived.

Dr. Green is a tall, congenial, dignified man with a soft-spoken nature, which is very reassuring to his patients. His graying hair and bright eyes seemed to tell stories of a mild man not much affected by the trauma he witnesses regularly. Behind him trailed a gaggle of young men and women in white smocks, fledging specialists in pediatric orthopedics.

He introduced himself and asked how Lori was doing. We told him that she was doing about the same. He nodded and signaled for an envelope. One of the people following him handed him the envelope and from it he removed a stack of X-rays. Holding them up toward the ceiling lights of the room he scrutinized them before speaking to us.

"Apparently," he began in a calm, self-assured voice, "Lori was born with both hips displaced."

We did not know how to respond to such an announcement. What are displaced hips? Should we have known? Was it bad? What? We looked at each other and back at him. We made some sort of replay conceding that we had no knowledge of such a condition. He smiled benevolently.

"No, I'm not surprised," he said, looking back at the X-rays quickly. "And it would not have been found this time if the pediatric resident had not noticed something out of the ordinary on one of the X-rays that had been taken too low and included the hip region. If that had not happened this may not have been noticed for some time."

"What does it mean?" Andrea asked.

"The thigh bones end in what is generally described as a ball," he closed one fist to illustrate. "Normally, this ball is seated in the hip joint which holds it much like a socket." Cupping his other hand, he fitted his balled up fist into the cupped hand to demonstrate how the two fit together. "This allows movement of the legs when we walk." He moved the fist back and forth in the cupped hand mimicking a walking bone movement. "In Lori's case the thigh bones were not connected into the hip sockets when she was born." He separated his two hands, moving the balled fist outside the protective arch of the cupped hand.

"Is that bad?" Andrea pursued her original inquiry.

"It depends," Green shrugged.

"Depends on what?" Andrea asked.

"If we can successfully correct the problem."

"How will you do that?" Andrea prodded him.

"We will surgically re-implant the ball joints into the hip sockets," he said matter of factly. Andrea flinched. Directing his words to her, he said, "We don't have to worry about that right now. First we let her get over the present condition. After she is released call my office and make an appointment. We'll consider the problem at that time and decide what we need to do. They will give you my number."

Leaving us with a comforting smile, Dr. Green led his team of novice pediatric orthopedics out of the PICU. Not having an orthopedic specialist to consult, we relied on our neighbor nurse-in-training, Weeze. She explained to us what the condition implied. The bottom line was more surgery for Lori.

Twelve days after the beginning of the crisis we took home a little girl with displaced hips and new nasal stints. We had another six weeks of suctioning stints and all that implied. But the worst thing we faced was that we knew in six weeks we had to start all over again with the horrible ritual of the biweekly dilations.

On the day scheduled for our appointment we bundled Lori up in her car seat/carrier and off to Dr. Green's we went in our old truck. Once there, we were given instructions to go to X-ray before Dr. Green would see us. Leaving the office, I detected the need to change Lori's diaper. This was usually a simple operation, except when we were not at home and her mother was not with us. In my time I have changed more diapers than Custer faced Indians. I had, by this time, developed a one-handed ankle hold that was bested by none, and could change a diaper in record time, but that was at home under ideal conditions. At Vanderbilt, like every other place I'd been, there were no changing tables in the mens rest rooms.

Most womens rest rooms are equipped with a changing table and when they aren't, they use the counter area or the floor. Well, that may be an option in a womens rest room, but not in a mens room. Too many floors in mens rest rooms are hardly fit to walk on because, as a comedian once put it, too many men are not very specific in the rest room. As far as I was concerned, laying a baby on a mens rest room floor was not even to be considered as an option.

The solution I had worked out was difficult, but do-able if I was very careful. Taking the carrier/car seat and placing it on the washbasin I braced my body against it, pinning the carrier against the wall. Balancing the diaper bag on the edge of the washbasin I was able to remove the soiled diaper, wipe (since both hands were free), and put on the new diaper. It took practice to perfect, but I got plenty of practice.

Recently I discovered that all mens rest rooms at Vanderbilt are now equipped with changing tables. I was very appreciative. I told a nurse to report my compliments to whoever thought of it and authorized the installations. She said she would and admitted that none of the nursing staff had known the tables had been installed until I told them.

Having a clean baby again, I made the X-ray rounds and came back to Green's office. I noticed that, as usual, I was one of only a few men and, as usual, I was the only man in the room alone with a baby. Most babies are taken to the doctor by their mothers, grandmothers, aunts or babysitters, but seldom by their fathers. Husband's usually just tag along on doctor visits like excess baggage, porters whose only use seems to be lagging behind the main entourage bearing diaper bags.

When our son was an infant Andrea worked for a radio station out of town and I used to have to take him for his checkups. This always occurred during the middle of a workday and I would attend the checkups by taking a break from work. I would show up at the doctor's office loaded down with a diaper bag in one hand and the carrier with Little John strapped inside in the other. In addition, I had a walkie-talkie in my back pocket, a badge, clipped to my belt, and a holster with a .38 stuck in it.

I was quite a sight adorned with all my equipment plus Little John to sit among the gaggle of mothers and infants. After several checkups I became one of the "girls", as it were, and appeared to be generally accepted as one of the group. By the time Lori came along, being the only man in the waiting room was no big deal, unless someone began staring at me. Usually the men paid me little heed, it was the women who stared.

After being shown into an examination room, Dr. Green and his attendant trainees filed into the small space after me. Dr. Green had me place Lori on the examination table. He took her legs and bent them at the knees, flexed them one at a time, and worked them as if she were riding a bicycle. Then he brought her legs up and apart in a wishbone fashion.

Completing this examination he then turned to the x-rays. Snapping them onto the view boxes mounted against the wall, he peered intently at them, snapped off the light behind the box and turned to me.

"It's as we suspected," he began, "the hips are not connected. It appears that they were not connected originally, so they have not been pulled out of socket or dislocated after birth by some other condition."

"She had a distended stomach," I explained and he nodded.

"What we're going to have to do is implant the ball joints into the sockets. We will do this manually, then put her in a body cast. She will have to stay in the cast for six weeks. That should correct the problem."

I grimaced at the mention of implantation. Green caught the flinch and inquired about it.

"My wife," I offered. "We've had so many operations and hospitalizations. My wife ... had a hard time during the months they told us Lori would not live to be born. But she did, then the surgeries started ... she's just had a bad time and now we have to do this ... I don't know, I just hate to break the news to her."

"I understand," he thought for a moment. "It's something we really need to do, but I'll see you in two weeks. During that time I'll check with her other doctors and see what my plans might mean to her other conditions. In the meantime, talk to your wife. If I can answer any questions please call."

With that he left, trailing his trainees behind him like a mother duck.

When I got home I told Andrea what Green had said. She took the news with expected reservations. Her friend Weeze came over and explained how serious displaced hips could be and that there was no real alternative to the surgery.

The two weeks went by quickly, and Lori and I trucked back to Nashville. Once in the examination room Dr. Green came in and sat down beside me. He never looked at Lori, but directed his attention at me.

"How's your wife?" his first words took me off balance, I expected him to ask about Lori.

"She's ... she's all right," I stammered.

"How is she taking the up-coming surgery? Is she prepared for it?" He was gravely serious.

"She's adjusting to the idea," I appraised.

"Good," he nodded. "I know she's been through a lot, and that having another surgery is a imposition, but it's something we must do."

"She understands that," I assured him.

He paused for a moment, then launched into a briefing as to when and where we were to report to the hospital with Lori to be checked in for surgery as well as a recitation of the prohibitions against eating or drinking after midnight the morning of the surgery. Then, with a reassuring smile, he led his covey of trainees out of the room. Lori and I were left alone. He had not touched Lori during the appointment. His only concern during the meeting was our emotional well being. Green cared about the whole family, not just Lori's physical health. He had used the appointment to secure assurance that we would not be too stressed by the procedure. I was impressed, and told Lori so. She just wiggled in her carrier and smiled.

Andrea was distressed to hear that the surgery was still on, but she was not surprised. The days passed uneventfully and the morning arrived for Lori's admission into Vanderbilt for the hip surgery. We could not feed her from midnight the previous night until we got her to the hospital. Her sucking sounds were pitiful as she tried to communicate her desire for food. Andrea rocked her and talked to her as I drove through the early morning darkness.

Arriving at Vanderbilt we made our way through admitting procedures and were directed to a preparation room. The pediatric prep-room is equipped with a row of small beds on each side of the room creating an aisle down the middle. Several of the beds had parents readying their children for surgery. The children ranged in age from infancy to preteens. Soon a nurse came by and asked us to dress Lori in a miniature hospital gown. Even though it was the smallest size they had it seemed to swallow her little body in folds of cloth. The nurse had to put Lori's ID bracelet on her ankle because her wrists were too small.

We spent the time before surgery talking to Lori and trying to make her feel comfortable. She was ravenously hungry and kept making her sucking sounds, which we had welcomed as one of her food signs. When that failed she ran a finger down the side of her throat, a more emphatic food sign. Dr. Green came to our bed. Predictably, the first thing he wanted to know was how we were doing?

"Fine," Andrea tried to smile, but her nervousness showed through the thin veneer of her disguise.

"This shouldn't take too long," Green tried to console her anxiety. "One thing I must stress," he said, changing the subject abruptly, "when Lori comes out of surgery she'll have a complete body cast from her chest to her ankles. We have to do this to insure that the hips are held in the proper position. The cast is hot and uncomfortable. If you cover her with sheets or blankets, you have to be careful not to place too many on her and cause her to overheat. But the most important thing is that she will lie on a Bradford Frame most of the time. You'll see one in the room when she comes out of surgery. It is very important that you remember to turn her every two hours. That is imperative because if she is allowed to remain in one position for too long she could develop sores inside the cast. If that happens we would have to remove the cast to treat the sores. This could prove very detrimental to her recovery process. We would have to reset the hips and recast her. That would cause her a good deal of pain and discomfort."

"How do we move her?" Andrea was fully attentive to his directions.

"Turn her from side to side, front to back," he demonstrated with his hand, turning it in positions as he spoke. "With the cast you can place her on her stomach, her back, and either side. Try to rotate her position so that she does not stay in the same position very long. At night when she's asleep you can let her lie in one position longer than you can during the day, but if you get up during the night I suggest you turn her before you go back to bed." He smiled reassuringly, "She'll be fine. I'll have someone come by to teach you how to handle her when she gets to her room. Any other questions I can help you with?"

"I guess not." Andrea said, tentatively.

"They'll be along to get her in just a few minutes," he said departing. "I've got to go get ready. I'll see you after surgery."

He strode off down the aisle between the beds, his long legs making short work of the room. Andrea held Lori and cuddled her until the nurse came.

"It's time," she said, smiling at us. "Are you ready?" She asked Lori, who squirmed in response. "Here we go." The nurse said, as if she were telling Lori they were going out to play.

She wheeled the bed out of position and down the aisle toward the door at the other end of the room. Tears welled up in Andrea's eyes as she watched Lori being taken away. No matter how many times Lori had been taken to surgery we never got used to giving her up to strangers who found it necessary to cause her short term suffering in order to circumvent long term maladies.

"Let's go get something to eat," I suggested, trying to break the mood.

"Piddle can't eat," Andrea's voice cracked and a lone tear rolled down her cheek. "And she's so hungry."

"I know," I put my arm around her and guided her out of the room. "But she will eat as soon as they wake her up."

"And I'm going to give her anything she wants," Andrea said, her lower lip quivering with her brave effort to keep from crying.

"Sure you will." I patted her shoulder as I turned her toward the door.

Since Andrea smoked, we made our way outside to the designated smoking area. Andrea kept looking up at the red brick wall of the hospital.

"It's so hard to bring her here when she looks so well and let them cut on her," she finally said.

"I know," I agreed.

"It was different when she was in the hospital," she turned her red-rimmed eyes to me. "It was life or death. We didn't have any choice, but she's been doing so well. She was happy, and now we take her in and they cut on her and she's miserable again. It's like we're doing it to her. She'll hate us when she grows up," she began to cry softly.

"No," I corrected her, "she won't think we did it to her. We didn't, and besides there's no choice here either. We've got to get her hips fixed."

"I know," she dropped her head. "I know, but I worry about it just the same."

I tried to reason with her but I knew what she meant. Lori did seem healthy in every other way, and now we felt she was taking a step backwards. We felt we were losing, rather than gaining ground. These long months of struggle had seemed to be coming to an end and here we were facing yet another challenge.

We went back inside, ate and wandered around for a while before making our way to the waiting room in the second floor verandah. I hated the surgical waiting area because time dragged in that place. You could sit there and watch people coming and going below on the main floor. I tried to read a textbook for a class I was taking but couldn't concentrate. Andrea thumbed through magazines listlessly, watching the nursing station and jumping with each announcement for a family to come forward. After what seemed an eternity the announcement came for "The Lori White family" and we jumped to the information desk.

An older woman, a volunteer, sat behind the raised counter equipped with a surgical schedule and a telephone.

"Are you the White family?" she asked as we stepped up to the counter.

"Yes," Andrea answered quickly.

"Your daughter is out of surgery," she announced dispassionately. "She's being taken to Pediatric Intensive Care on five South."

"Pediatric Intensive Care?" Andrea asked, shocked.

"Yes, ma'am," the lady nodded.

Andrea started to ask why but realized the woman probably did not know.

"They said Dr. Green will meet with you on the 3rd floor. There's a waiting area just where you get off the elevators." She started to tell us how to get to the elevators but we told her we were well acquainted with them and headed off in that direction before she could reply.

This unforeseen turn of events concerned us deeply. What could have gone wrong? We were not supposed to meet Green on the 3rd floor, we were supposed to be called to Lori's room. And what was this about PICU? What had gone so wrong that it necessitated Lori's transfers to PICU?

The bank of elevators was interminably slow as we waited for a car to descend to our floor. When one opened, we darted inside and hit the 3rd floor button. Andrea rocked back and forth as the car ascended. When the doors open she shot out into the hallway. There were several gray room dividers set about in an area directly across from the elevator doors. Which way were we to turn, we wondered.

Members of another family were in conference with what appeared to be two doctors as they huddled in one of the cubicles. Andrea and I paced the area in front of the elevators until Green came around a corner and approached us. Not waiting to get into a cubical, Dr. Green addressed our concerns immediately.

"The operation went very well," he said decisively. "The hips have been put into their sockets and we've cast them in place."

"Everything went well?" Andrea repeated the information as if savoring it.

"Oh, yes," Green beamed. "We had to cut the tendons and muscles in the inner thighs." He made indications at his own thighs with a slicing motion of his hand as he spoke. "We discovered that they were too short to allow us to reset the hips. If we had not cut them," he added quickly, "they would have pulled the ball joints back out of their sockets as soon as we cast her. There's no reason to be concerned. The incisions will heal nicely while she is still in the cast. There should be no problems."

"Why is she in PICU?" Andrea pressed her apprehensions.

"There was some difficulty with her breathing when we went into recovery," he said.

"Difficulty in breathing?" her alarm was increasing.

"Yes," he nodded, "but I'm sure it's not serious. She just isn't registering oxygen levels where they feel comfortable with her breathing on her own."

"There's nothing connected with the operation?" Andrea pursued the avenue.

"No," he frowned dramatically. "Absolutely not. The surgery went fine and we set her hips without complications. I had one doctor hold each leg after I had set them back into their sockets. They held them exactly in place until we had finished the casting. Everything looks fine, as far as the hips are concerned. The breathing is another problem, but I feel confident it is only a momentary setback."

"Can we see her now?" Andrea was still anxious, nervously wringing her hands.

"You can check up on the 5th floor, South, PICU," he indicated. "I'm not certain they're ready yet, but they will tell you when you get up there."

We thanked him and set off for PICU. At first we had trouble finding the room because, unlike NICU, it was not cloistered off with scrubs required for entry. PICU was a set of rooms behind wide doors that had beds along both walls. The patients were placed in the beds as they became available with nurses working the whole room. There were fewer patients per room in PICU than NICU, the beds were larger and took up more space.

We attracted the attention of one of the nurses and told her we were looking for Lori White. She motioned us in and indicated a bed across the room. The bed was against the far wall and atop it was a set of boxes that we took to be the Bradford Frame. Lying on top of the boxes and crossbars was little Lori in her new body cast.

We were shocked at the sight. She was intubated with a respiration tube and was covered from her upper chest to her ankles with a beige cast, which held her legs apart and bent at the knees. An opening had been left in the cast at her groin in order to allow a diaper to be inserted. The diaper would have to be carefully maintained because it was imperative that the cast is kept dry and that we not allow urine or any other fluids to seep into the cast. We had been told that liquids would weaken the cast and necessitate its removal and replacement.

An assistant from Dr. Green's office taught us how to position Lori at night while we slept so that she did not need a diaper. We would lay her on her back or stomach and drape a strip of gauze material from between her labia to a diaper laid out beneath her in a plastic pan. When she urinates the gauze strip will absorb the urine and allow it to drain down the length of the gauze into the diaper without letting any of the liquid run into the cast. If we got up during the night we could turn her over on her opposite side, reattach the gauze and go back to sleep. The system actually worked very well. Defecation was simply allowed to drop into the diaper and pan like urine.

The Bradford Frame was designed much like a cot. It was made of two wooden struts down each side between which there was a cloth band at each end leaving the middle open. We were told we could use anything to set the ends of the frame upon when we got home but that the most practical and readily available were dresser drawers set on end. Dresser drawers provided the right height and were maneuverable. Their most important feature was their availability, almost everyone already possessed enough dresser drawers to set up a Bradford Frame. This saves the trouble of building boxes or searching around town for orange crates or the like. We solved the problem of mounting the frame by using a set of freestanding stereo speakers.

Andrea checked Lori's appearance, read her chart, and inquired from the nurse about her condition. The nurse could add very little to what we already knew, Lori was not coming out of the anesthesia very well. For some reason she was not processing oxygen well enough to breath on her own. Obviously, her breathing was suppressed, but exactly why this had happened, no one knew. The only thing they kept telling us was that nothing had gone wrong during surgery to account for the condition.

Going back to Lori Andrea fawned over her for a few minutes, talking to her and assuring her that her mother was with her. Then she turned to me, sadness dragging at her eyelids.

"She doesn't have a pillow," she said, almost crying. "She'd be more comfortable if she had a pillow."

"I'm sure they have one around here somewhere," I offered, knowing that it wasn't just Lori that was in need of comforting.

"No," Andrea stuck out her lower lip. "She needs her own pillow. Can't we go buy Piddle her own pillow?"

"Sure," I told her, and put my arm around her waist as we left. "Besides she needs to rest now."

On the way out Andrea announced to the nurse that we were going to get Lori a pillow. The nurse looked sort of confused for a moment, then shrugged and nodded. We made our way to the car and began driving around looking for a place to buy a pillow. A few blocks from the hospital we found one of the more "up scale" department stores in West Nashville at the Green Hills Shopping Center. Making our way through expensive sweaters and slacks we went downstairs to household goods.

A saleswoman glided effortlessly around the stacks of merchandise to where we were standing and asked if she could be of assistance. Andrea told her that we were looking for a pillow. The woman looked us up and down, disdain wrinkling her nose, and told us the pillows were, "over there." She led the way, glancing back at us as we wove a path through the aisles. We had learned to dress for comfort when we were attending Vanderbilt affairs, so we had not worn our better clothes. In addition, it had been a long day. I knew we must have looked more like we belonged in a bargain basement shop than in this “up scale” store.

Andrea had caught the woman's initial “down the nose” appraisal of us. She turned and gave me a conspiratorial expressions as we neared the pillow display. My wife was definitely up to something. The saleswoman led us to the cheaper pillows. Andrea looked them over, shook her head, and asked the woman if they had anything else a little bit better, because the pillow was for our daughter.

The woman seemed somewhat thrown off by the request but she moved up the line to the better quality pillows. Andrea felt of several pillows and kept moving up the price scale. Offering one pillow to me to feel its softness she leaned close and whispered,

"I'm going to use the hundred dollar bill, O.K.?" I nodded ascent, and immediately knew what she was going to do.

I had given her an emergency hundred-dollar bill some time before so she would always have money if she needed it. She had protested when I had given it to her, but now she was digging in her purse surreptitiously as she switched her attention from one pillow to another.

After a few moments of feigned indecision she handed the saleswoman the most expensive pillow of the lot. The woman looked a bit surprised at her choice. Ringing up the sale she asked,

"Cash or charge?"

"Cash," Andrea said, producing the hundred-dollar bill with a slight flourish. "It's the smallest I have," she smiled as the saleswoman did a double take.

With the pillow packaged and under her arm, Andrea beamed at the confused woman and thanked her for all her assistance. As we walked down the aisles toward the stairs I heard a single word escape from Andrea's clenched, still smiling teeth, "Bitch."

Returning to Vanderbilt we placed Lori on her new, expensive pillow. Thus began days of perpetual consistency. Every time we came to see Lori she was laying on top her pillow, on her back. Occasionally a respiratory therapist would come by and administer mist treatments to aid her breathing. Essentially, Lori's condition remained as unchanged as her position.

I did not notice it at first but Andrea began pointing out that Lori was always lying on her back when we came to visit her, even though we had been told to turn her every two hours. She began asking the nurses if Lori had been turned, but never received a satisfactory answer. Andrea read Lori's chart but could find no indication that reported her being turned.

I could not believe that she had been left unturned for days on end. I assumed that we had always arrived about the same times of day and therefore we had always been present at the intervals when she was lying on her back. But as the days went by I too began to believe that Andrea might be right.

After several days of Lori's residency in PICU Andrea called me at work. The emotion in her voice made her vocal cords quiver as she spoke.

"I just called PICU and talked to Lori's nurse," she said shakily.

"And?" The emotion in her voice froze my heart, I had the terrible feeling that something had happened to Lori.

"John, she hasn't been turned since she's been in PICU!" She broke down crying. "I just knew it, I knew it! I called and asked her nurse. She admitted it. She said they didn't know how to handle Bradford Frame cases, they never have them in PICU. John, she's lain there for days! We've got to do something!"

"I will," I said, thinking at hyper speed, "I will."

"What?" Andrea wept. "What can we do?"

"I'll call Dr. Green." It dawned on me that he should know what would be the best thing to do. It was his case after all.

"You're right!" She seemed to brighten somewhat. "He'll know what to do."

"Certainly," I tried to sound positive and shore her up. "He's right there at Vanderbilt and he can check it out and see what the problem is. I'll call right now."

"Call me back when you hear something," she said before hanging up.

"I will," I guaranteed her.

I dialed Dr. Green's office. A receptionist answered. When I asked for Dr. Green she informed me that he was out of the office at the moment. I debated whether to leave a message or have him call me back. I opted for a message. Quickly I filled her in on what Andrea had been told by the PICU nurse, that Lori had not been turned since she had been placed in PICU, and we were concerned. I verified that in all that time she had been on the ward, that every time we had seen her she had been on her back. Openly concerned, she told me that she would give my message to Dr. Green as soon as he could be located.

It was getting late in the afternoon and I knew that soon Dr. Green would be leaving his office for the day. I feared that if I did not get in touch with him today that it would be another twenty-four hours before I might contact him. As I was considering calling again, my intercom rang announcing that Dr. Green was on line one. I quickly punched in the line.

"Dr. Green," I asked.

"Yes," he sounded unusually somber. "I got your message, and I'm sorry that I have not been able to return your call sooner. I went down to PICU as soon as my secretary called me." He paused. "Your wife is right, they have not turned Lori since she was put on the ward. I have corrected the situation, and I'm very sorry this happened."

"Is she all right?" I asked, fearful of the answer.

"Yes," his voice picked up a bit, "she seems to be. I can not detect any problems."

"Thank goodness." I exhaled.

"Again," his voice took on that serious edge, "you have my personal apologies. If I'd had any indication something like this had happened I would have checked sooner."

"Oh, no," I almost cut him off. "You have no need to apologize. I'm grateful you checked on her and got things straightened out."

"I don't think there'll be any more problems like this," he said confidently.

I thanked him again for all he had done for us and hung up. I immediately called Andrea and told her what Green had said. She was excited, but troubled. I repeated that he said his exam had found nothing wrong with her. I tried to comfort her with the fact that within the hour I would get off work and we would drive up to see for ourselves. Andrea accepted that for the time being, but I knew that nothing would settle her mind until she had seen Lori for herself. When it came to our children Andrea takes no one's word for anything. She always wants to see for herself before she could be at ease.

When the time came I left work, shed my badge and pistol, picked up Andrea and sped off to Nashville. Andrea alternated between a nervous excitement over seeing Lori and the fear that we would not find her in good shape.

When we arrived at Vandy we discovered that the PICU unit was shut down. We could not gain entry, nor could we find a nurse to tell us what had happened. Andrea was becoming alarmed, she began to believe that something had happened to Lori and that they had closed off the unit because of it. I told her that was nonsense, but I privately worried that she might be right.

Desperate, Andrea finally said "closed door be damned" and barged into the nearest room. A nurse quickly confronted her and told her that we could not come in.

"I want to see my daughter. Where's my daughter?" she demanded, unmoving in the face of the challenging nurse.

"She's been moved to the peds floor," she pointed north, indicating the pediatric ward on the other side of the building.

"Moved?" Andrea challenged her. "She wasn't supposed to have been discharged from PICU. Everyone said she hadn't recuperated enough to be moved. Why's she on the peds floor?"

"She was moved out of PICU," was all the nurse would say. She then told us in a very firm tone that we would have to leave the unit.

During our conversation with the nurse in PICU, I noticed there was a dark urgency about the room, as if something important was going on and no one had time to talk to us. Having been in many situations where I was not wanted (a common feeling for policemen) I sensed that this was what was happening now. We had become lepers. Nurses would not look at us, everyone hurried past us, and no one spoke to us.

Leaving the PICU we walked around the hallway to the other side of the hospital. Andrea and I tried to figure out what had happened. Lori would not be released to a ward if she was still in danger, but we had not been told she had improved enough to be moved any time soon. Arriving on Five North we walked down the hall to the patient wall chart. All peds patients are listed on huge plastic charts on the walls near the nurses' station. The chart lists the patient's name, their room number, and their nurse for that shift. Scanning down the chart we saw "Lori White", her room number, and nurse's name. She had, indeed, been transferred.

We went down the hall and into her room. A nurse and young doctor were attending Lori when we stepped through the door. They turned and offered us the first smiles we had seen since entering the hospital.

"This must be mom and dad," the nurse said cheerfully.

We confirmed that we were, and introduced ourselves. They in turn introduced themselves. When the nurse told us who she was she added that she was Lori's nurse for the shift.

"Yes, I noticed on the chart," Andrea said giving scant notice to the nurse as she closely inspected Lori. "I'd wished Mandy *(Not her real name)* was her nurse, she was her nurse last time we were up here and she knows Lori's history so well."

That was all that was said for the time being. The two finished their work and left the room. Andrea and I stood on either side of Lori's bed and scrutinized her condition. The Bradford frame was erected properly and Lori was fast asleep, lying on her stomach. We looked at each other. Things had certainly changed. Just at that moment Mandy walked through the door and began taking Lori's vital signs and making a notation in her chart.

"Hi," Andrea greeted her as she came in the room.

"Oh, hi," she smiled. Mandy was a slender young woman in her early twenties with long dark hair and large glasses. She was a pleasant person with a perpetual smile.

"I was kind of disappointed when we saw that you weren't Lori's nurse," Andrea told her as she went about her duties.

"I am," Mandy said. "I've been switched."

"Switched?" Andrea looked at me and back to her. "Why?"

"I don't know." Mandy continued her work.

Things were getting very strange and Andrea and I both sensed the difference. Andrea made small talk for a few minutes as Mandy finished her work. When Mandy was ready to leave Andrea pointedly engaged her.

"I feel that something's wrong," she said, and I noticed Mandy glance nervously about the room. "What's up? Did I get someone in trouble?" Mandy made a noncommittal reply, but Andrea persisted. "All I wanted was to keep Lori from getting bedsores, I didn't mean to cause any trouble. What happened?"

Mandy admitted that she did not know everything but she conceded there had been a shakeup following our call.

"Dr. Green went down to PICU and pulled her chart. Lori hadn't been turned since she had been on the unit. Then he went to the head of nursing and got her down to the unit. That's when everything started happening."

"What happened?" Andrea pressed her for more information.

"They closed the unit, shipped Lori up here ...," Mandy hesitated, apparently trying to pick out the right words, "heads rolled."

"Heads rolled?" Andrea repeated, but Mandy was not about to press her luck any further.

Too much trouble had plagued pediatrics that day and Mandy was not about to contribute any more ammunition to the firefight, especially if it might fly back to wound her. She made an excuse and ducked out the door.

Andrea felt uneasy for some time, feeling that she had caused trouble in the unit that had helped our daughter so many times. I tried to explain that there was no reason to feel guilty, there had been a slip-up, she was only looking after Lori's best interests, and it had been me that called Green, not her.

We found out later that none of the nurses in the PICU unit knew how to handle a baby in a spica cast. They did not know she had to be turned every two hours. As a matter of fact, some did not even know how to "petal" a cast. Petaling a cast is a skill we learned from a nurse on the peds ward. It involves covering the groin, leg, and chest openings of the cast with strips of a material commonly called moleskin. Moleskin is an adhesive backed, light brownish material that is very soft to the touch, hence the name "mole skin." Overlapping squares of moleskin placed around the edge of the cast openings makes the area look like it is decorated with flower petals, thus the origin of the term. Petalling the cast keeps the edges of the rough plaster from chafing the infant. It also keeps the exposed plaster edges dry. All-in-all petalling made attending Lori's needs more comfortable for everyone involved.

We were on the peds ward only three days before we were able to take Lori home with us. We discovered that the open leg posture that she had been cast into was perfect for carrying her around with us. All we had to do was set her on our hip, one leg in front and one behind. In this position we could easily take her anywhere we wanted. In time we became so used to the cast and the Bradford frame that caring for Lori was a breeze.

At a later checkup Dr. Green was pleased to find that we were taking Lori with us everywhere we went, and that we carried her around the house while we did our daily chores.

"Many parents of children with spica casts are afraid to touch them," he said. "When they get them home they just let them lie there. That's why we stress the turning, we try to get people to pick up their children and move them around. What you're doing is wonderful. Lori should have no problems with the cast."

As was our luck in general his prediction was absolutely wrong. Lori had been in the cast about a month when I came home from work one night to find our neighbor Weeze and Andrea working with Lori on the couch. They had taken clear plastic tape and wrapped it around the right leg of her cast at the hip juncture.

"What is going on?" I asked, dropping down to a knee beside them on the floor.

"Lori's cast broke," Weeze said, pointing at a crack clearly visible through the tape that circumnavigated the hip and leg juncture.

"Great," I sighed, "now what?"

No one answered. We had been warned about the problem of sores developing inside the cast but no one had mentioned what to do in the event the cast broke. Securing the cast as best we could, and making a point of not laying Lori on her right side during the night we anxiously waited until the next morning. As soon as practical I called Dr. Green's office and apprised him of what had happened to the cast. He directed me to bring Lori to Vandy immediately, the cast had to be repaired as soon as possible.

Arriving at his office, we were ushered into an examination room. This particular room was longer than the usual rooms. It was equipped with two long, low tables, some devices that looked like small electrical saws, various supports, and appliances that appeared to be braces.

Dr. Green came in and examined the clumsily taped cast. He evaluated the crack running around the right leg joint from several different vantage points, and, moving the leg with his fingers, he completed his appraisal of the damage. Standing up, he told me what I expected.

"We've got to replace the cast."

"I was afraid of that," I said, recalling his admonition to keep down the likelihood of having to replace the cast.

"It's not that bad," he consoled me. "We'll take off this one and put on a new one."

"But what could have caused it," I asked, feeling somewhat better about the prospect of having to recast Lori. "Andrea said that she didn't hit it, or bump it. It just broke when she went to pick her up."

"Moisture," he announced confidently, "moisture somehow got inside the cast, most probably urine leaking down into that side over a period of time. The cast absorbed it and became weak at that point."

He set about preparing to take the cast off and I gave my attention to Lori. She did not like to lie unattended for any length of time and by the time Dr. Green had finished his inspection she was squirming in protest. I talked to her and told her everything was all right and that we were going to fix her old cast. I knew she did not understand a word of what I was saying, but it calmed her just to have someone talk to her. Reassuring her helped my spirits a bit as well.

Dr. Green sent over a middle-aged black man with a small device that looked like a portable circular saw. The attendant told me that he was going to cut the cast off. He said I could help by holding Lori's right leg in place when he got the cast off. Another orderly came by and prepared to help hold the left leg.

As he began cutting the cast I cringed, thinking of how close that saw must be coming to Lori's skin. I knew there was not much room between the cast and her body. The attendant noticed my reaction and smiled.

"It won't hurt her," he said, taking the saw out of the groove it was making in the cast and running it over his hand. "See. It'll cut the cast but it's designed not to cut flesh."

I was astounded. I had never seen such an apparatus. The whirling blade could cut the thickest plaster, but when it encountered skin it brushed harmlessly over it. I found it fascinating to watch. Deftly the technician sliced the cast down one side of Lori's body and then down the other. In only a few moments the cast fell apart in two halves.

Lori's naked body was exposed. The sight of her was shocking. She still had the stain of antiseptic swabbing all over her legs and midriff, along with plaster dust, cotton bits, and other debris. She was a mess. I thought I could seize the opportunity and clean her up a bit. I held her in place with one hand as I reached to the sink located nearby and wet a paper towel with the other. While I was doing this she was wiggling and trying to move around. Holding her as steady as possible I started to clean her by running the damp towel down her right leg. As I started down the leg with the towel Lori froze, her face distorted with pain. She could not make any noise due to her damaged vocal cords, but the appearance of crying was unmistakable. I pulled the paper towel away immediately to see what had happened. When I did a piece of her skin came off with the towel leaving an ugly, red hole in her upper thigh.

I had rubbed her skin off!

Lori's skin had become fragile as tissue paper while encased inside the cast for so many weeks. The idea had not occurred to me, and although the piece of skin that had rubbed off was less than the size of a dime, the hole was deep, and from her reactions, very painful. Lori has a high pain threshold and for her to "cry" so much the pain had to be excruciating.

I felt horrible. Apologizing profusely, I tried to soothe her. By the time the team came back with Dr. Green to start recasting her, she had settled down and seemed to be eased.

Collecting myself, I held the right leg in the same position that it had originally been placed during surgery while the other attendant held the left leg. Dr. Green and his intern doctors proceeded with the rewrapping and recasting. They skillfully created a duplicate of the original cast, with groin opening and a chest high upper body section. In short order their work was completed. When the cast was dry and met with Dr. Greene's approval, we were allowed to leave. If only everything in life could be so easily repaired, I thought.

Chapter XIII
The First Kidney Removal

Lori was removed from her body cast in December 1990. Dr. Green was pleased with the progress of the development of the ball joints that had stayed in their proper placements. The incisions that had been made on the inside of each thigh to relieve the stress on the joints were completely healed by the time the cast was removed.

All the while, Dr. Hill had continued to monitor Lori's kidneys. The upper right kidney, which had been so large when she was first born, had shrunk in time, but it was still a mass of destroyed tissue atop a very tiny piece of healthy tissue. The lower half of her left kidney, which had been destroyed before birth, had shrunk to a small, knobby lobe at the bottom of the healthy upper half as Hill had expected.

Dr. Hill's major concern was that the ureter on the upper right kidney was allowing reflux to wash back and forth between the kidney and the bladder. From birth, Lori was on a daily dose of an antibiotic called Septra. Abruptly, Dr. Hill changed to a different renal antibiotic to, as he put it, "Give her kidneys something different to look at for awhile." These antibiotics were designed to suppress urinary tract infections that were a constant threat in Lori's condition.

Lori also grew physically during this time. She ate well, slept well, and seemed to be thriving. In addition, she had developed a set of communication hand signs to tell us when she was hungry and happy, as well as other messages, and could scoot around in her walker fairly well.

In late summer of 1991, Dr. Hill began tests in preparation for her first kidney surgery scheduled for January of 1992.

During those presurgery tests he discovered an unprecedented phenomenon. The tests showed that the destroyed upper half of her right kidney had developed a covering of living tissue. And even more astounding the upper half of the kidney gave test indications that it was working.

Dr. Hill rejected the results of the test outright because destroyed kidney tissue does not regenerate working kidney tissue, it was impossibility. In his considered opinion what the test had discovered was a reflux condition masquerading as kidney function. Dismissing the test results related to the upper pole of the right kidney, he scheduled surgery to remove the lower pole of the left kidney. The day of surgery arrived all too soon.

Andrea stayed up late the night before to feed Lori at the eleventh hour, but by five a.m. that food had been long forgotten and Lori was very unhappy. Bedeviling her mother all the way to Nashville during the hour and a half drive Lori repeatedly made her food signs. The silent pleading signs tore at Andrea's heart as we drove through the cold darkness and she cried as Lori pressed her need with energetically desperate finger signs to her mouth.

"Oh, John," Andrea whimpered, tears running down her cheeks, "She's starving."

"I know," I said, concentrating hard on the road so that I would not see the urgent food signs. "I know. We'll be there soon."

But I knew that once we were at the hospital we still had check-in to complete and pre-op to get through, and Lori would become more and more ardent in her demands for food, just as Andrea would become more heartbroken.

Added to this grief was the knowledge that we were bringing a seemingly perfectly healthy child to the hospital to have surgery. Which meant that in only in a few days we would bring home a sick and recovering baby again. Though it was illogi cal, emotionally we could not escape the feeling that we were somehow culpable, like conspiring partners in a crime against our helpless child.

Trying desperately to avoid the guilty feelings that threatened to overtake me I drove determinedly through the cold January morning. The tension felt as though ice water was trickling through the ventricles of my heart. We reached Vanderbilt in the graying light of dawn and immediately began the admission process, a series of questions (mostly about money), papers to be signed (also about money), and directions to follow. The pre-op ritual began with dressing Lori in a hospital gown, and ended with snapping the I.D. bracelet on her ankle. We tried in vain to ignore her food signs and imploring eyes that searched our faces for the reason why we had not satisfied her gnawing hunger.

Dr. Hill came to meet with us once Lori was ready. Being his usual confident self, he spoke to Lori and then turned to us.

"We're ready," he announced with a wide, affable smile. "They'll be here in a minute to take her in. I've got to go get ready. This shouldn't be more than a couple of hours. We're going to excise the lower portion of the left kidney. At the same time I'm going to resite the upper pole ureter to a higher placement on the bladder."

"I'll close the ureter site from the lower pole and that should take care of our work on the left side. If she makes it through without complications she should be able to go home in a couple of days."

"But we always have complications," Andrea abruptly cut in. "Every time, we're supposed to be able to go home in a couple of days we end up spending ten or twelve days in PICU."

"I know," Hill nodded, but did not abandon his optimistic demeanor. "We're going to try some new things this time. An anesthesiologist is going to come by and talk to you before Lori goes in. Tell him what you can about her consequences to anesthesia in the past." His manner was always cordial but brisk. "I've got to go get ready. I'll be out when we're finished and let you know what happened."

Flashing a wide smile he was off, making short work of the ward in energetic strides toward the surgery doors. We spent the last few minutes with Lori talking and playing with her, knowing she could not understand that soon she would not feel like playing or laughing. Our primary concern was centered on the fact that she could not understand what was about to happen to her or why. Andrea continued to worry that Lori would grow up to hate her. I too wondered at times if Lori would begin to associate our bringing her to the big red brick building and to the pain she would experience here. But at the same time we knew we had no real choice in the matter. We could only keep on loving her and making the time between surgeries as good as possible in hopes that she could eventually forget the painful experiences.

As we were talking to Lori a young, heavyset man walked up to us and announced that he was the anesthesiologist we had been promised. Before every surgery we talked to the anesthesiologist assigned to the case. They all had the same lines to recite; although the surgery Lori was about to enter into was not necessarily dangerous, all surgery possesses the potential for injury or death resulting from the procedures. We had the right to refuse, etc.

They always produced papers for us to sign acknowledging that we were aware of the risks and that we consented to taking those risks. But what choice do you really have at this point? Not sign and let Lori die? He talked, I nodded, he talked, I signed, and then we got down to the real business.

The anesthesiologist asked about Lori's earlier surgeries: her difficulty in recovering, the ability to breath proficiently on her own. He asked about her oxy-sats (oxygen saturation levels). Andrea could recite them from memory, day by day. He made some notes and then announced:

"We'll use a smaller tube on her this time and start cutting back on the anesthesia earlier than usual. That may make a difference." He scribbled more notes on Lori's chart before taking his leave.

Immediately on the heels of the anesthesiologist came a nurse in green scrubs to announce that they were ready for Lori. We kissed her good-bye and watched them take her away. A lump formed in my throat and my eyes were wet. I knew that the anesthesiologist was right, there was a chance that I was seeing her alive for the last time as she was wheeled away. I wanted to prolong the minute, make a last contact, say something important, meaningful, but I just stood there like all the other parents who have their children taken to surgery and wordlessly watched her go.

When she disappeared into surgery we were left standing in a place where we no longer belonged. Around us were parents with children, all of them much older than our little girl, who was busy preparing for their turn. They did not need a couple of misty-eyed people standing around staring at a closed door to make them feel worse. We left and began the old game of "let's pretend we're normal and that everything's fine" that we had learned to play when Lori was taken into surgery.

Andrea and I wandered down to the cafeteria, picked at some food we really did not want, made the rounds of the nearby Vanderbilt campus bookstore, and consulted our watches, a lot. Our insides were a knot. As we roamed the campus sidewalks I began looking at the young people we met. They were all dressed in typical college garb, some riding bicycles, most walking. They all had backpacks full of books slung over their shoulders and wore the intense look of committed college students. Most conversed about music, parties and concerts. As we walked I became acutely aware of the couples.

The pairs of immersed lovers walked slower than the single students, strolling along with arms wrapped about one another or holding hands, typical coupling signals. I began to wonder about them and their futures. At the moment they were planning their lives, dreaming of the careers they would have, the lives they would enjoy, eagerly anticipating the adventures they felt awaited them, confident that all would go well for them. But I knew of other futures, other possibilities, horrible possibilities that could await them around the dark corners of their lives. I knew the reality of unintended futures where couples leaned on each other in support, desperately clinging together in anguish, and I wondered what the future really held for them. I knew that some would live out their dreams, but I also knew that one or two couples that we passed would end up like us. Where would their strength come from? I looked at the young women and wondered if they had the courage Andrea had.

I looked at the young men and wondered the same thing. What would be their choices when life became a trial? Would they keep the fervent promises they had made in the heat of passion, or would they crack beneath the weight? Life waited to test each and every one of them in ways that they could not possibly imagine at the moment, and each one of them would have to pass the test, individually, alone, or fail. But failing life's tests, unlike college, doesn't just produce a low grade. In life's classroom the moments spent in candlelight and breathless desire would melt into dim days of indecision and uncertainty without the benefit of passing a recognizable line of demarcation to announce when the change had occurred.

If someone had asked me if I wanted a child with multiple health problems and life-threatening aliments I would have said "no!" But now I would not take anything in the world for Lori, and would give up anything for her, including my next breath if it came to that. We had answered our questions, faced our tests and demons, and we had prevailed, so far. But what of them, I wondered.

Leaving the students and my thoughts behind we reentered the waiting room and sat until our call to the desk came. We were directed to meet with Dr. Hill outside the surgery room. In a few minutes Dr. Hill and another, younger, doctor came into the hallway. Both were still dressed in their green operating scrubs. Dr. Hill introduced the other doctor, whose name we immediately forgot, as we waited impatiently for Hill to relate the results of the surgery.

"Everything went perfectly," he beamed, exuberantly. "The lower pole was just as we thought, small and shrunken. It came off easily. I re-sited the ureter higher on the bladder. There is one thing though," he hesitated, "you remember the tests that indicated that the upper right kidney was working?"

We nodded and said that we recalled the test.

"While we were in there we took a look at it. There is tissue covering the right kidney, just like the tests showed, and it does appear that the kidney is working."

Andrea and I looked at him for a moment as if we had not heard him. Lori had grown tissue when she should not have grown tissue and the dead kidney was working? To us it sounded like he was saying pigs flew and that everyone knew they did.

"What we want," he went on, ignoring our slack jawed expressions, "is your permission to conduct one more test before she leaves the hospital. It would require our putting her to sleep. We would need to wait until Monday morning to do the test and keep her in overnight to observe her in case an infection set up or some other complications arose. We would inject material into her kidney," he indicated his own back on the right side, "and let her lie there while it was processed through the kidney to get a better picture of what is happening."

We looked at one another, intuitively knowing that we would consent to the test even before we turned back to him and nodded.

"But," Andrea began, confusion laced her voice with a ragged uncertainty, "if this right kidney is enclosed in living tissue, what about the dead part? Do you go in and take it out, or what?"

"Oh," Dr. Hill shrugged off the question, "that's not something to be concerned about right now. It's working and that's all we're really interested in. We can wait until she's a teenager to begin thinking about doing something with the interior, unless she develops infections or other complications at some point ...."

We had stopped listening. Andrea looked at me in dumbfounded shock.

"What did you say?" she blurted out, quickly turning her attention back to him.

"In the event that she develops infections or we find...," he started to repeat the last part of his statement but Andrea cut him off.

"No, no," she waved her hand, beginning to move up and down on the balls of her feet in an excited little dance. "Before that, when did you say that you might start to think about doing something?"

"Oh, not until she's at least a teenager ...," he began and Andrea abruptly turned away from him.

"He did say it!" Her voice cracked as she gleefully grasped my hand.

"Yes, he did." I was all smiles too, he had said that they would not do anything until she was a teenager!

"Oh," he suddenly realized what we were talking about and flashed a small, embarrassed smile. "Has no one told you? Lori's doing fine. With the amount of kidney tissue she has working, and now with this added assist from the upper right pole, there's no reason she shouldn't survive a relatively normal life span."

Tears swelled up in Andrea's eyes.

"I'm so sorry," Dr. Hill's voice lost its cheerful tone and dropped an octave. "I thought you both knew, Lori's been out of danger for some time."

And that is how we learned that our daughter was not expected to die. There was no fanfare, no special meeting or dramatic announcement, just us standing in that drab hospital hallway listening to an after surgery report.

Regaining our composure, we told Dr. Hill that we would consent to the test. After receiving permission for the test, he finished the briefing by describing how he had also operated on Lori's bladder, lapping it over, stapling it to reinforce the thin walls. She had a small incision in her lower abdomen but that particular surgery was not considered serious. We thanked him for his gratifying announcement and walked off to see if we could visit Lori in PICU. As we walked neither of us talked about what we had just learned for a few minutes. I think that we each were trying to come to grips with its implications. No more reluctantly climbing out of bed each morning and peering into her crib to see if Lori had died during the night. No more smelling diapers to see if her kidneys had decided to shut down and death hovered nearby. No more waking in the middle of the night and creeping to her crib to listen to her breathe just to reassure yourself that she was still alive. With this simple pronouncement from her doctor we did not have to do any of those things any more, with the passing of a mere sentence those times were over.

Amid our joy a small voice inside my head kept telling me that we would never resume life as we had known it. That the reprieve from impending death for our daughter did not mean that things would "go back to normal". We had turned that corner long, long ago. The news buoyed my spirits though, and I glanced over at Andrea as we walked. She beamed like a schoolgirl with a new boyfriend. There was a spark in her eye that had not been there in a long time. For just a moment she became the young woman that I had dated and fallen in love with so many years ago. We held hands as we walked, just like the students had done.

"Did you hea?," she giggled, trying to suppress her glee.

I nodded.

"Not 'til she's a teenager!" She dropped her voice, so as not to disturb other patients. "Lori's going to be a teenager!"

When we got to PICU we discovered that Lori was not yet "ready" for us, which meant, of course, that they had not finished cleaning her up. Most surgical procedures require a little cleaning up of the patient before the family is allowed to see them. All the tapes, tubes, disinfectants, needles, and patches are sometimes disturbing to family members and so patients are cleaned up before being allowed visitors, whether they are conscious or not. This rule is especially true in the case of infants. There is a heightened emotional element where they are involved.

We waited in a designated area down the hall from PICU. The interior room was crowded with people so Andrea and I waited outside in the hallway. As we were biding our time the anesthesiologist we had spoken to before surgery came along. He seemed in high spirits as he approached us.

"Well," Andrea challenged him, "is Lori intubated again?"

"No," he smiled, triumphantly.

"No?" Andrea asked.

"Nope," he appeared proud of himself, and justly so if his news was factual. "We've determined that Lori's opening to her trachea is smaller than normal. In the past when a normal sized tube was used this caused the area to swell, impeding her ability to breath normally, thereby causing the post-op breathing problems. We also decided to back down on the amount of anesthesia, and started taking her off of it before the surgery was complete."

Andrea was all smiles at the news.

"We feel that the combination of pain killers and anesthesia may have an undesirable synergistic effect. So far the strategies have proven successful. She's recovering nicely, with no complications."

"Are you going to make a note of this in her records so that in the future other doctors can duplicate what you did today?" she asked anxiously.

"Oh, certainly," he guaranteed her.

Having delivered his news he made his exit, saying that he had some work to do and we went back to waiting.

The news was a blessing. For the first time Lori would not have to be kept in intensive care for days on end while her ability to breath on her own slowly returned. It was ironic that we had agreed to stay over the weekend for the extra test because this would have been the first time that we would be able to go home in a normal term. But all else aside, Lori was recovering nicely and that was all we cared about.

After a long time waiting in the hallway we were allowed in to see Lori. She lay sleeping in her bed, just like other children, all her indicators registering in normal ranges. Andrea was thrilled and spoke enthusiastically in hushed tones of how proud she was that we had finally overcome the long stays in intensive care.

"We've got to remember what he told us about how they did this," she whispered urgently. "So in the future we can make them do the same thing and get her back to normal as soon as possible."

Andrea had learned not to trust doctor's notes in medical records.

Chapter XIV
Recovery

For the first time in her life Lori was released from PICU after a single night of observation. She was placed in a standard room. Although this should have been a wonderful time it really was the point at which Andrea's ordeal began. Lori did not, had never, and probably would never, abide being put in a bed and left there. All she wanted was up and out of the bed. She fidgeted and fretted, rolled and grabbed anything close to her. She even exhibited something we had not seen before, a temper! She pushed away her food, slapped at a bottle of milk offered to her (and chocolate milk at that!), and cried, behavior which was absolutely un-Lori.

Andrea walked her, played with her, tried to entertain her, and by midmorning was completely worn-out. The thought of going through a whole weekend of this torture was completely out of the question. Andrea had only made it through half of Friday morning and already she was exhausted. At Vanderbilt while a child stays on the Peds ward, nurses do very little to help with the child's non-medical care. There are simply too many children and too few nurses. Andrea's only respite was an occasional visit by a nurse to check vital signs or monitors. While the nurse was in attendance Andrea could duck out of the room to go get coffee, or a bite to eat. She took full advantage of these interruptions in the routine, but they were infrequent and far too brief. Even under normal conditions Lori's regular hospital stay left a noticeable change in Andrea. Fatigue clawed at her, she was irritable and temperamental, her face sagged and her spirits dragged. To add to the difficulties, Lori was older and much more active now than she had been in the past. By the time Dr. Hill made his rounds in the late afternoon Andrea was physically and mentally impoverished.

I had worked that day and drove up to the hospital in the late afternoon. When Dr. Hill came in the room he gave Lori a once over and reviewed her chart. She had no post-op fever, and she was eating, drinking, and producing urine, which indicated that the excised kidney had not been affected by the surgery. Dr. Hill's chief concern going into surgery was that the left kidney would shut down following the operation. In his experience, he had found that some kidneys cease functioning for a period time following surgery. In Lori's case this could have been disastrous because the left kidney contained the most productive mass of both her kidneys systems. If the left half of her kidney terminated operations following the surgery the consequences could have been disastrous. But instead of faltering, the half of a kidney on her left side kept on working despite the fact that its lower half had been cut away.

Lori was equipped with drain tubes galore. Beside a catheter to relieve her bladder she had two other drain tubes ducting blood and other body fluids away from her internal organs. The seeping fluids emptied into plastic bags in a blended collection of pinks, reds, and yellows. All these tubes emerged from her diaper and were supposed to be attached to her bed rail, but in Lori's case they stayed hooked into the pockets of Andrea's jeans as she followed Lori around the hallway in her walker.

Our baby had developed a light-footed maneuverability in her walker that belied the fact that without it she could not take a single step on her own. The walker gave Lori independence and freedom, and a bit of control over her life. Although the tubes and collection bags presented some difficulties for Andrea, she carried them around behind a wandering Lori without comment because she knew that it was the only way to keep Lori happy.

Lori spent so much time rolling around the hallways of Vanderbilt that to this day she loves to wander through hallways. When she encounters a hallway she will smile and clap her hands. We also believe that it is the reason she is infatuated with department store aisles. The corridors of Vanderbilt seem to be have been impressed upon Lori's mind as the definitive symbol of freedom, and she still remembers that wonderful sensation after all these years.

When Dr. Hill came to her room that afternoon Andrea was forced to pull Lori out of her walker and put her to bed for his examination. Lori rolled, and tried to pull herself up by the bed rails. She made mewing sounds and fell into a silent crying jag.

Such activity would be painful enough considering she had a new incision about five inches long in her left side, and another at the base of her stomach, a catheter and two tubes protruding from her body in various places, but she also had an IV (intravenous tube) known as a "cut down", or central line in her upper chest. This incision had been necessitated because of the difficulty the nurses had putting needles into her small, elusive veins. A surgeon had cut into her upper chest, opening up the flesh so that he could implant an IV needle directly into the artery leading away from her heart. The process is quick and easy and the IV is much more durable than those installed in hands, feet, arms or the top of the head which have to be relocated after several days or hours, according to the abuse they receive. Fluids were inducted directly into her system by this central line system. When not in use, the tube was capped and covered with a bandage. Lori acted as if it did not exist, but every time she pulled up on the bed rail, I flinched.

Andrea told Dr. Hill about her problems keeping Lori quiet and occupied. She bemoaned the prospect of having to keep up this level of attention over the entire weekend so that they could do their tests the following Monday. Hill stood in thought for a moment, looked at Lori with an appraising eye, then turned to us.

"Do you think you could learn how to care for a central line?" he asked, looking from one of us to the other.

"If we learned how to tube feed her," Andrea reasoned, "we can learn how to do anything. Why?"

"I was just thinking ...," he looked back at Lori who was trying to chin up on her bed rail again, and flashed him a wide, toothless grin at her accomplishment. "She has no post-op complications ... If you let the nurses teach you how to care for the central line we could let you go home for the weekend and bring her back in Monday for the test."

Andrea jumped straight up in the air at the proposal. "John will learn," she thrilled. "Pleeeeease let us go. John can do it, can't you, Hon?"

"Here we go again," I thought, but I knew my response had only one possible reply. I nodded.

"Yeah, sure."

"See!" She twirled around on Hill. "He'll do it. Can we go?"

Hill smiled broadly.

"Sure," then he cautioned, "but you'll have to keep a very close eye on her all weekend. At the first sign of a fever you've got to get her back up here immediately. O.K.?"

"O.K.," Andrea calmed down to show her sincerity. "Anything you say, just let us go home, please."

"Before I leave I'll instruct Lori's nurse to come in and show you how to clean the central line, and sign a release so that you can go home in the morning, IF," he stressed the word, "she doesn't have a fever tonight."

Andrea showered him with appreciation and praise as he left, then grabbed me by the arm and hugged me.

"We're going home tomorrow," she said between clenched teeth, then turned solemnly to Lori who was peeking out over her bed rail and covetously eyeing the hallway outside the open door. "And you, little miss priss, you better not have a fever tonight, you understand?"

Lori smiled a wide, gum lined grin, but I thought it had to do more with what she saw outside the door than it did with the instructions her mother was giving her. A nurse came around that evening to train me on how to clean Lori's central line. First she explained the process, then handed me a syringe and told me to go ahead and do the procedure while she watched. The tubing was capped with a plastic plug to keep it clear of accidental introduction of air or foreign matter into Lori's arterial system. Cleaning the central line requires uncovering the tubing and revealing the incision in her chest. Sutures held the plastic tube in place in her skin. Care had to be given not to dislodge or pull on those stitches when uncapping the central line. As the cap is removed from the tube a syringe of saline is held at the ready. Once the cap is off, the syringe is inserted into the end of the plastic tube and a steady pressure is applied to the syringe to inject the saline. My first attempt was tenuous. The thought that I was injecting liquid directly into my daughter's main artery gave me pause. I concentrated on keeping my hand steady as I pushed the saline into her system.

Lori fidgeted and looked around, bored by having to lie still for the cleaning procedure. When the plunger was at its terminus I withdrew it and recapped the tube as the nurse had instructed me.

"You did very well," she praised me while I breathed a sigh of relief. "You would make a good nurse."

"Thanks," I said, laying the syringe aside and wiping my palms on my pants (they were damp from the tension). "But I know more about medicine now than I ever wanted to know."

She smiled, gathered the materials together and left. Andrea was all smiles, anticipating our release.

That night I spent time at home with Little John while Andrea stayed with Lori. The next morning I drove back to Nashville to find Lori prowling the hallways in her walker and bugging the nurses at their central station.

Lori loves computers. From the first moment she became mobile she would go to our computer and watch her mother or me work at the keyboard. We reflected on this and came to the conclusion that she might remember the key strikes she had heard in the womb before she was born.

At first the nurses allowed her to stay but they learned quickly that Lori also loved to punch the keyboard to make the key-sound. That was not healthy for either the computer or for the programs inside. Soon they were helping Andrea drag Lori out of their station, but they did it with tenderness and compassion.

Before we left the hospital a nurse went over the central line cleaning once more as she aided me in cleaning the tube. Satisfied that I was competent, they told us to be back Monday morning at 6 a.m. (no food or drink after midnight, naturally). They removed the catheter but left the drain tubes in place. These we must also service at home.

Tubes dangling and central line taped, we set off for a weekend at home. As inconvenient as it was, it was better than staying in the hospital and maintaining separate lives 75 miles apart.

The weekend was troublesome, servicing the collection bags and keeping Lori from tangling them in her walker as she scooted around the house, but Andrea's ingenuity came to the fore and she figured out a way to mount them on the walker. Sunday after church, and under the close scrutiny of soon-to-be-nurse Weeze, I cleaned the central line just as I had been trained. Weeze said that she had never seen it done better. I felt proud that I had been able to go through the process without help or advice. Despite my reluctance I was turning into a good nurse.

After a weekend of checking for fevers, our worries were realized on Sunday afternoon when Lori grew warm to the touch and appeared to become listless. Andrea was convinced that we had not cleaned the central line adequately and that Lori's fever was indicative of a condition associated with our neglect in proper line maintenance. We called the hospital and told them that we would be on our way with one hot infant. They said they would be ready.

Arriving back on the Peds ward we were assigned a room. Dr. Hill did not come by on Sunday. The nurses began administering medication in an attempt to dispel the fever. Andrea told them that she felt it was our fault, that we had not properly cleaned the central line. The nurses all agreed that was highly unlikely. It was the consensus of opinion that Lori was experiencing a postoperative fever associated with an infection. Such fevers were commonplace. That she had not had one already was unusual.

One of the drugs that they gave Lori Sunday night to reduce the fever was a pinkish liquid that she refused to swallow. She would clamp her little mouth tightly shut and let it run down either side of her compressed lips when the nurse tried to administer it. Andrea, always the observant mother, noticed that Lori's reactions were abnormal. Never one to readily take medications, Lori was seldom so adamant about any other preparation in the past. One of Andrea's guiding principles involving her children was when in doubt find out for yourself. While the nurse was out of the room Andrea tipped the dispenser cup to her lips and dipped her tongue into the medication. She gagged and shivered at the horrid taste of the concoction.

When the nurse came back into the room Andrea was waiting for her.

"Have you ever tasted this medicine?" she asked, holding the cup out toward the nurse.

"No," The nurse shied away from the offering.

"Try it." Andrea held the cup at arm's length.

The nurse hesitated.

"Try it," Andrea demanded, putting a harder edge of insistence on her voice.

The nurse reluctantly accepted the cup and tipped it to her lips.

"Gad, that's awful," she grimaced, dropping the cup from her lips and making a face as she experienced the after taste of the offending medication.

"What is it?" Andrea asked.

"It's ...," the nurse spit, "it's tablets we grind up in water."

"And you've never tasted it?" Andrea demanded, hands on hips.

"No," the nurse stuck out her tongue as if to air it out.

"Maybe you should next time," Andrea drove her point home.

"Point well taken," the nurse nodded, as she made her exit. The medicine was changed to something more palatable and Lori readily accepted the new prescription. The fever was broken within an hour.

The next morning Dr. Hill arrived. He had looked over Lori's charts and spoken to the nurses before he came to our room. It was his opinion that she had suffered a postoperative infection. From the blood tests performed during the night the antibiotics he had ordered were working admirably in fighting off the infection. He was ready for the test.

"Did they tell you about me making the nurse drink the medicine?" Andrea asked before he left to prepare for the examination.

"I heard," he laughed.

Andrea's forced taste testing apparently was the news of the ward.

Lori was taken to surgery for her test directly from her room. Again, we wandered the building trying to divert our attention while the test was conducted. We returned to her room and waited until a nurse came to tell us that Lori was in recovery and that Dr. Hill would be with us soon.

Hill came out in his scrubs, accompanied by another, younger doctor, evidently in training with Hill. Dr. Hill was high-spirited and there was a twinkle in his eye. He liked giving good news and obviously had a load to deliver.

"We've finished the test," he began. "The test showed that the upper pole on the right kidney is processing urine at a normal rate."

We stood there for a moment trying to grasp what he had just said. A dead kidney had spontaneously generated living tissue. That was marvelous enough but now he was saying that same dead kidney was working just like a healthy kidney.

"You mean its working just like a normal kidney?" Andrea rephrased his statement, trying to better understand it.

"Yes," he said with a wide grin. "It's rate of function is normal. We watched it process the test fluid perfectly."

"But how can it do that?" Andrea shook her head. "You told us that the upper right kidney was destroyed, that it was just old urine and cysts, that it would never be any good."

He nodded in agreement with her restatement of his original diagnosis.

"Yes," he said when she finished, "that's right."

"Then how?"

"I don't know," he shook his head. "But I'm not going to question it. As long as it works that's perfectly all right with me. We'll watch it and see if any problems develop, otherwise I'm going to leave it alone and let it work."

Neither Andrea nor I knew exactly what to say, then Andrea asked,

"But what about the dead tissue inside, is there some way you can go in and remove it?"

He shook his head.

"Well," she persisted, concern edged her voice, "isn't that ... unhealthy? I mean isn't there a problem leaving dead tissue inside her?"

"That's why we need to keep an eye on it," he agreed that there was reason to be concerned. "But right now I'm not going to do anything."

"But what about in the future?" Andrea pressed the issue. "What can happen to it?"

The other doctor, who had remained silent during the exchange, was becoming visibly agitated as the conversation pursued this line of thought.

"It might heal itself," he blurted out, sarcasm dripping from each word.

Hill cut his eyes toward the younger man like a scythe slicing through tender wheat. It was the only time I ever saw him upset, but he contained his angry flare and turned back to us with reassuring warmth and sincerity.

"We'll just watch it and see what happens," he said, as he prepared to leave. "I'll have my nurse call and make an appointment for next week. After that, bring her in every few months. We'll monitor the kidney. For now, that's about all we can do. Just be thankful that it's happened."

"Oh, we are," Andrea told him as he led his disgruntled assistant away.

After Hill had gone we went back and waited for Lori to return. When they brought her into the room she was asleep. We stood around her bed looking at her. What miracles were we seeing, I wondered as we stood beside her bed looking down at her tiny body. What great and wondrous things were happening before our very eyes? God had raised this nearly dead child and made her live. Why? How?

A passage from the Bible came to mind as I stood there that I recalled reading in my childhood. The passage was from Revelation and it dealt with a miracle. The dead shall lie in the streets for three days and the whole world will see them, and on the third day they shall arise. I remember being confounded by this passage when I first read it, and wondering, as a child wonders, how the whole world would see and how the dead could come back to life. Now as an adult I wondered the same thing, but this time the awe was compounded and the mystery much deeper.

With these questions crowding our minds we looked down at our little girl as she slept. She was so tiny to be such a great miracle. She was truly God's child and we were just caretakers entrusted with her until He wanted her back. I thought of the high priests of the temple of Jerusalem whose duty it was to care for the Holy of Holiest and how they must have felt about their hallowed function, that I was like that now, entrusted with one of God's miracles.

But then I realized that I was not like them at all. Those priests had been entrusted with the guardianship of mere artifacts. The miracles had occurred to Moses, the guardians came later. No, I was not like them, God had not given me a thing to care for, he had given me a precious child to nurture and tend. I recalled the admonition in the New Testament concerning those who would harm one of these little ones, that it is better that a millstone be hung around his neck and he be cast into the sea. I realized that caring for God's little ones was the greatest responsibility anyone ever has in life.

Standing there I recalled all the dead baby cases I had worked in my career. I remembered the beaten infant who took so long to die in her crib while her killer gave her water to drink to stop her crying. I recalled the little four-year-old boy shot in the face by his father as he backed away from him across his bedroom, trying to escape. I brought to mind the newborn that rolled away from her mother during the night to become trapped and die between the waterbed mattress and the wood railing, the SIDS cases I had worked, the neglect, and abuse I had seen for so many years. One by one they all come to visit me while I stood watching over my little girl.

Was I given this special child to make up for all the horror and suffering I had seen? For years the dead children had haunted me, the injustice of it all, the sorrow, anger, and mental anguish had plagued me like a black dog panting at my heels. In some incomprehensible way, was God setting the balance aright? And if so, why me? How was I special enough to deserve these miracles? And why so many miracles?

Perhaps it was because I had ignored all the first ones; the surgical team that disbursed but not left the hospital when Little John was born. I took that miracle for granted and ignored it. The ureter bypassing the bladder to save Lori. I had walked through miraculous occurrences and had not recognized them for what they were. Now I had this miracle, this undeniable, unavoidable miracle that I could not walk away from so easily. God had stepped in personally to make the dead live, and at that moment that very miracle was keeping my daughter alive right before my eyes.

In the beginning of this experience I had told God I would accept what he decided without reservation. Now it was my job to live with His decision and not question His judgment. This was becoming harder to do than I had thought. The questions lingered around the edges of my conscious mind; what does he want in return? What do I owe? How do I repay him adequately for all these wonderful miracles I have received?

I had no ready answer, all I could think of was the old counsel, "Deo Volente", God's will be done. It was.

Chapter XV
Teaching Lori To Walk

One evening, as I was getting ready to leave, Andrea walked me down to the hospital's central lobby. As usual, she would be staying at the hospital with Lori and while I was headed home to be with Little John. Leaving the elevator at the ground floor we walked out into the wide, open enclosure of the central entrance to the main hospital. As we came into the outer fringes of the waiting area I noticed a distraught group of Pulaski folks congregated off to our left. In the center of the mass of humanity was a couple that we knew. Andrea and I walked over to say hello and see what had happened.

One of the group informed us that the young son of the couple was seriously ill and they had been sent to Vanderbilt for emergency surgery. Their son was only a couple of years older than Little John. It sounded very serious.

I made my way through the crowd and got my first clear view of them. It seemed that the wife couldn't be still as she made phone calls, talking ceaselessly as she desperately sought for something to occupy her mind. The husband sat slumped in a chair some distance away, head down, obviously in great distress. Even though friends and relatives surrounded him, he was sadly, utterly alone. My heart ached for him. I thought how strange it was, here he had more people with him in this one moment than had ever visited us with Lori the entire time we had been at Vanderbilt. I thought back on all the times that Andrea and I had had to make life and death choices, and not once did we have a tenth of the friends around us that these people had. Yet for all of that we had never felt lonely or alone.

I knew then that I would not trade places with them for all their social position. I felt more sorry for them, than for their son. I knew of nothing I could say that would relieve the silent suffering I saw in the destitute husband, nor in the perpetual motion of his wife who was seeking escape in activity. An ocean separated us from even communicating with one another. To simply converse with them meant that they must listen to what I could tell them, but the spiritual bleakness which sucked the air from the place in which they were testified that there was absolutely no entry into the dark world where they resided at that point in their lives.

As Andrea and I passed through the crowd, I scattered encouraging comments like seed cast upon rocky soil. We were not part of the support "congregation." Someone in the group asked us why we were at Vandy. When I told them that Lori was there a few was surprised to learn that we had an ill child. Since we were not part of their social circle, our miraculous journey was completely lost to them. We wished them well and left.

When Andrea and I were outside the glass front of the main entrance I looked back. I could still see the press of well-wishers milling about the fearful couple. I recalled one of the few times that anyone had come to see us while we had been at Vandy. Lori was just a few months old at the time. Our pastor and her daughter dropped in for an unannounced visit. She could stay for only a short time but before she left she asked if we might have a prayer for Lori. She had us gather around Lori's bed and hold hands in a circle, which enclosed her tiny body. Lori, so small on her white sheets, slept in a bed, which seemed huge by comparison. We stood around her, hands clasped and heads bowed. It is hard to describe what an immense comfort that simple ritual brought us. For a moment I wished that the couple in the waiting room could experience the blessed consolation our unpretentious little ritual had given us, but I knew it could not. Giving her a kiss, I left Andrea in the covered entranceway and went home to Little John.

* * * * * * *

As Lori continued her rapid recovery from the kidney surgery Andrea decided that she needed to try to teach her to walk. Andrea put a lot of time and effort into the project, but with her job at the radio station and her normal home duties, there was too little time left to make any real progress.

Sitting on the living room floor one day as she worked with Lori, Andrea suddenly made an announcement.

"I'm going to quit the station," she said, looking up at me with a troubled expression.

"O.K.," I agreed, but knew she was not completely at ease with the decision.

"I hate to, they've been so nice to me," she looked back at Lori. "But I've got to do something with her. The grandmothers just love on her all day long and bow and scrape to her every wish. If I don't do something she'll never learn how to walk or talk."

"Don't worry," I reasoned, "they won't think anything bad about you. Everybody at the station knows what you've been going through. They'll understand."

"I know, but I had to take so much time off, and they were nice enough to let me keep on working," she was torn by loyalty to her boss and her duty to her child.

I knew Andrea was a fiercely loyal employee. She believed that all good employees should never take advantage of their bosses or their bosses' good intentions. She felt that when someone did a kindness to her she must repay it a hundred fold. But I also knew that Lori's delayed maturation was tearing at her. She felt that she had not done enough to support her daughter when she needed it most.

"Don't worry about it," I told her. "Do what you think you have to do. If you're really worried about Lori take the time off and teach her what she needs. You're a great broadcaster. Everyone knows how good you are. You can always find another job, but you only have one daughter."

I assured her that wouldn't be a problem, but I could see that the decision was a painful one. The next day she told me that she had made up her mind. She would take off what time it took to teach Lori how to walk, then go back if they would rehire her. Her only problem was that she would not be bringing in any money to the household and we would have to live off what I made. I assured her that would be no problem, but knowing how she prided herself on being able to contribute her share to the family, I knew she would feel as if she was a drain on the family's economy. It took a lot of effort for her to overcome her pride and self-respect to cease making a financial contribution. But she did it because Lori's needs outweighed her personal pride.

Thus began the ordeal of Lori's training. Day after day Andrea sat in the floor trying to get Lori to simply get up on her hands and knees, creeping style. After months of falling onto her stomach, Lori finally mastered the skill.

Next, Lori learned how to crawl. This was both funny and heartbreaking. Lori would perch on her little arms and legs while Andrea would try to inch one knee forward. The only problem was that when Andrea moved a knee forward Lori would not move an accompanying arm. The result of the effort was that Lori would pitch forward onto her face, splat. Andrea would pick her up, steady her in the crawling position and start the process all over again. Every time Lori fell Andrea would flinch, but she made herself pick her back up and begin again.

This repetition of moving and falling went on for weeks. One day I came home to find the training still in the "move and plop" phase. After one of the countless times that I had watched Lori pitch forward onto her nose, Andrea looked up with tears in her eyes.

"She's going to hate me when she grows up and remembers what I've done to her," she said, picking Lori up from her most recent fall.

"No, she won't," I tried to comfort her.

"Yes, she will," Andrea said, tears falling onto Lori's narrow back.

Although the endless process crushed Andrea's heart, she made herself push Lori to try again. I began to have doubts that Lori would ever learn to crawl, then one day I came home and Andrea was sitting victoriously on the couch.

"Watch," she called as I came through the door.

She took Lori out of her walker and placed her on the floor. At first Lori stayed as she had been placed, swaying a little as if unsteady in the stance.

"Watch now," Andrea beamed. "Go on Lori crawl, show daddy, crawl like mommy taught you."

On command a little arm moved forward followed by a skinny knee, then the other side inched forward where she promptly pitched forward onto her nose. It was not much but it qualified as an official crawl in our book.

"See, she did it!" Andrea crowed with delight. "She can crawl."

"Well," I said, a knot coming up in my throat, "it's not what I would call an Olympic crawl, but I guess it'll do."

We danced around the room, careful not to step on a bewildered little lump on the carpet who could not figure out why her adults were acting so silly. As we celebrated Lori lay watching us, absently rubbing her nose.

As the days passed Lori became stronger and more skilled at moving about on her own. Crawling around the house gave her a certain independence that appeared to please her, and it was not long before she was underfoot everywhere. The kitchen linoleum gave her some problems at first. When she hit the slick surface her hands flew out in opposite directions, as did her legs, and she would fall flat on her stomach. Then she would scramble back up onto all fours, and off she would go.

After Lori mastered the crawling skill, Andrea began working on teaching her to stand. Holding Lori by her hands she would raise her to her feet and hold her upright. Lori would bend her knees in an attempt to get on all fours and return to the familiar mode of locomotion. Lori had little patience with her education. All she wanted to do was go. Having to stay in one place and practice standing was not what she considered fun.

Months of holding Lori upright finally resulted in another command performance. Coming home from work one day I found Lori standing in front of the couch, holding on to the cushions, wavering back and forth ever so slightly. Andrea sat on the couch smiling like a Cheshire cat (Andrea is the only person I know who can strut sitting down).

"Well," I said, walking around to stand over the swaying little lady, "and what do we think we're doing?"

Lori looked up silently and smiled.

"Just something I picked up, Dad," Andrea mimicked Lori's reply in a little girl's falsetto voice.

About that time Lori lost her balance and sat down hard on her diapered bottom. My heart seemed to fly out of my chest and I reached for her out of reflex.

"Let her do it," Andrea shot an arm out between Lori and me. "Come on, Piddle, get up."

Lori looked up to where her mother patted the couch. She rolled over onto her hands and knees and headed west, away from the couch. I reached down and picked her up. She squirmed in my grasp, wanting down so she could go exploring. I tried to stand her next to the couch, but she instantly dropped onto her all fours and tried to make an escape.

"Let her go," Andrea finally told me. "She's tired. We've been working on standing all afternoon and she's pretty bored by now. I just wanted her to show Daddy what she could do."

I was proud of what Lori had accomplished but I was even more proud of what Andrea had achieved. After almost six months of daily work she had managed to teach Lori to crawl and now to stand. Her perseverance was admirable, her dedication exemplary. Few parents would set aside their personal lives and career to teach their child to walk but Andrea was sticking to her guns, and her work was bearing fruit.

One concession Andrea had to make when she quit her job to teach Lori to walk was that she would not quit college. After Lori was born I had talked Andrea into going back to college to work on her degree. I did this in an attempt to divert her attention from the constantly draining pressure of losing her father then waiting for Lori to die (and to save my computer from utter destruction). Andrea had taken only a couple of classes before we were married, and did very well. She could succeed at college work and deserved the opportunity. Before Lori had the half kidney removed Andrea had finally started back to school at Martin Methodist College, making some headway toward her A.A. degree.

When she told me that she wanted to quit work to concentrate on helping Lori learn how to walk, I never protested. As a matter of fact, I firmly believed it was the correct decision, but when she mentioned quitting school I adamantly objected. She had helped me through the initial years of doctoral classes and I had promised myself that I would support her in an education.

While Lori struggled to learn how to walk by day, Andrea attended college classes at night, maintaining an admirable GPA in the process. We all seemed to be on a path to somewhere and were working hard to get there. Many people never try to improve themselves by going to college or taking on a project, deciding that they do not have time for it. Actually, we have time to do whatever we want to do, and Andrea is living proof of that fact. She juggled a hectic day keeping our house in order, spending hours patiently working with Lori and yet managing to get in enough study time to pull almost straight A's in her classes. Yes, it took help from me and others, at times, but the main burden was Andrea's and she excelled.

Winter passed and Lori began moving the length of the couch on her shaky little legs, mostly with only a tenuous grip on the cushions. She rarely tripped or stumbled. It was not too long before she was reaching for chairs and other items to aid her in expanding her territory. Andrea taught Lori to walk by holding her hand. With only weeks of handholding Lori could walk by holding a single finger. We felt that she had gotten to the point where she could walk alone but she did not seem interested in attempting a solo trip.

About this same time we learned of another problem that had previously been undetected. Most people's hip joints are connected to their thighbones from the ball joint by a 100-degree bend in the leg bone structure. This sets the legs apart and at an angle that aids walking. In Lori's case the bones immediately proceeding from the ball joint bent at only 7 degrees, almost straight. Dr. Green had discovered this condition in one of his follow-up examinations. In the spring of 1993 we had an appointment with him to explore the options. The one option that seemed most likely was that the bones would be broken and reset with metal pins at the appropriate 100-degree angle. As our appointment drew closer we became anxious about the prospect of Lori going back into a body cast.

Andrea was particularly apprehensive about another operation. On the day of the appointment, very uncharacteristically, Andrea wanted to go with us. I gladly agreed and we all appeared at Green's office. Following the routine X-rays we were put into an examination room to await him. Lori was unhappy about being closed up in the examination room and began fidgeting. Andrea opened the door and Lori clapped her hands in excitement. Holding out a finger Andrea invited her to go outside.

"Come on Piddle," she said as Lori grabbed hold of the extended finger.

Taking the room in only a couple of strides Lori made it to the door. Just outside the door was a chair that Andrea let her hold onto. During the ensuing year since Dr. Green had seen Lori she had grown over five inches in height. When he came around the corner, an envelope of X-rays tucked under one arm, he did not recognize her at first. He smiled and nodded at her as he continued on his way. Abruptly, he stopped on the opposite side of the hallway and turned around. He studied the child standing, holding onto the chair for a minute, looked up at Andrea and then noticed me sitting just inside the examination room. He squinted at Lori for a moment and then in an unbelieving tone spoke her name.

"Lori?"

Lori turned and looked at him, a wide grin spread across her face. Andrea held out a finger, and Lori grasped it instantly. Leading Lori across the hallway, Andrea led her up to where Green stood, clearly amazed. He leaned against the wall as he stared at Lori walking proudly across the hallway.

"Please Dr. Green," Andrea mimicked in a child like voice when they had stopped before the taller man, "don't operate on me. I can walk just fine."

"It's truly amazing," he said, his eyes locked on the little girl in front of him.

He lifted his gaze to me. I had stepped out of the room and stood just outside the doorway.

"And you thought she'd never walk," he said in amazement, looking back at her.

Actually I had never had any such thought, but I wondered if he might have at some point. Whatever his original opinion he was visibly astonished at her progress. I walked over to join them.

"Andrea taught her to walk," I told him as he continued to scrutinize Lori with an unbelieving eye. "It took a long time but she managed to get her going."

"And did a good job of it," he added, still studying Lori who, by this time, was trying to get her mother to move along and go somewhere more interesting.

He stood looking at her for a time and then seemed to make some inner decision.

"I don't need to see her for another year," he said with a wide smile.

Andrea mimicked a thank you from Lori and led her off down the hall. I saw Green watch her go, studying her walk as she went. There was a visible glow of satisfaction that radiated from him as he watched Lori go.

Unaided walking occurred, like most things in our life, when least expected and under the most unanticipated circumstances. We had suspected for some time that Lori could walk alone if only she would try, but we could never get her to try. Once, when her attention was diverted, she took a couple of steps on her own, but we couldn't get her to duplicate the feat again.

Holding to a finger Lori walked everywhere we went with no trouble whatever. She loved to go in stores with us, clapping her hands and making happy noises. One day we had her seated in a shopping cart while we made some household purchases at our local Wal-Mart. Andrea had moved away from the cart to inspect something that had attracted her interest in the next aisle. Lori began pulling on my shirt. She had started doing this as a signal that she wanted down. I ignored her at first, concentrating on the shopping list. Letting Lori down required holding out a finger and letting her walk with me. At the moment I was busy and did not need the distraction.

She kept pulling at my shirt and making insistent growling sounds, she even kicked me once in a most delicate place just to emphasize her point. Her persistence was becoming annoying. I turned to her and she held up her arms. The message was explicit, she wanted out of that cart and she wanted out now.

"O.K.," I said in exasperation. "I'll let you down, then what are you going to do? You can't walk, so get down." I lifted her out of the seat and set her on her feet.

Thinking that she would grab onto the side of the cart and stand there I was shocked when she immediately tottered off down the aisle clapping her hands with excitement. At first I just stood there, looking after her. She came to the juncture of two aisles and stopped. Looking first one way and then the other, she smiled and began clapping her hands loudly. I finally found my voice.

"Andrea," I called, "come here, quick."

Other shoppers stopped their activities and looked our way expecting to see something unusual. All they saw was a father standing by a shopping cart and his daughter wandering off down the aisle. As commonplace an event as can be seen in any shopping mall.

"What?" Andrea sounded a little irritated as she turned around, an item in her hand, to see what her husband felt was so important that he had interrupted her concentration.

"Look," was all I could say, pointing toward Lori as she wandered farther down the isle, clapping as she went.

"God!" Andrea gasped and rushed to my side. "When did she do that?"

"Just now." I said, staring at the little girl disappearing down the aisle.

People turned around again at Andrea's exclamation, but still saw nothing so novel as to excite such a declaration, they turned back to their original concerns.

"How?" Andrea asked, open-mouthed.

"She just wanted down, so I set her down and she took off." I explained.

"Well," Andrea smiled, "don't you think you ought to go get her before she gets lost?"

"Oh, yeah." I suddenly came to my senses and rushed off after Lori as she darted around a corner and out of sight.

And that is how Lori learned to walk alone. As with most monumentous things in her life it happened without fanfare or acclaim. It was something that she just did one day, like any other day.

The process had taken nearly a year. From age two until age three Lori had labored to learn the skill of walking. It had been a long hard journey, but we were delighted. Our pleasure at her achievement was not long-lived when we realized that her increased mobility brought about many more headaches. We contented ourselves with the idea that we were making headway and that was what really counted. We felt we were "over the hump". As with most things in our life, we were completely wrong. There were more unexpected and unknown hurdles awaiting us just down the road.

Chapter XVI

Lori's Teeth, Lori's Eyes

Since Lori's first days with us, when we could actually see her face, we noticed that she had, what we believed to be, a condition known as lazy eye. The condition runs in her mother's family. Andrea had had the condition as a child, as did her mother. Andrea's eye had been mended when she was very young, but her mother's had not. Ursula had grown up as a child in Nazi Germany. At that time medical attention was being directed to the war effort and not to a little girl with a wandering eye. Because Ursula's eye was not corrected while she was still young, she had been told that there was no cure.

Lazy eye is a condition that usually affects one eye, causing it to draw inward. The muscles that operate the eye are weak and do not work efficiently. In Lori's case it was her left eye that was affected. We noticed that the eye appeared to "roam" at times, independent of the other eye. We did not mention it to any of her doctors earlier in her medical history because we had to deal with much more serious problems. But now she was three years old and we began to discuss the problem of her apparent lazy eye and decided to make an appointment to have it checked.

I called Vanderbilt and was given an appointment with Dr. Johnson, an optomological-physiologist (M.D. & Ph.D.). Dr. Johnson's office was located in Vanderbilt's East wing, one of the few places in the large hospital we had never been before. Waiting in his outer office I watched an array of children of various ages waiting for his services. The children had an assortment of ailments which ranged from those I could not detect to conditions where there was obvious blindness in one eye or the other. I felt sorry for the blinded children. Blind adults are a sad enough sight to me, but blind children are especially heartbreaking.

Lori was a bundle of energy that particular day. She would not sit still nor stay in one place. I spent most of the time waiting for Dr. Johnson by chasing her around the waiting room as she flexed her new-found walking skills to the limit. Finally we were directed into an examination room and told that the doctor would be with us shortly. Dr. Johnson was a soft-spoken, studious looking, middle-aged man with a pleasant disposition. He sat down opposite us in the examination room and asked about my concerns.

I explained about Lori's lazy eye and its attendant family history. I briefly outlined her medical history as a way of excusing our not having brought her to him before. He nodded as I spoke and when I was finished he picked up a device that looked like a flashlight. He asked if I would hold her so that he might look into her eyes.

Having a quick look into Lori's eyes turned out to be a task that was much easier said than done. Lori twisted and turned as he attempted to look into her eyes. In desperation she spun around and grabbed my shirt, hanging on in an effort to keep him to her back and away from her face. He thought for a second as he pondered her new position.

"Do you think she would stay like that," he pointed to her back, "over your shoulder? If so I will try to get a look from behind you."

I told him I thought she would because she liked to lie up over my shoulder, it was a comfortable, safety-associated position for her. I patted her back as he slipped around behind me. I felt her move a couple of times and finally she seemed to push at him. Dr. Johnson came back to stand in front of me.

"I couldn't get a good look at both eyes," he began, putting away his instruments. "She's slightly nearsighted in her right eye, but she would not let me look at her left eye at all."

He thought for a moment.

"Does she have any other surgeries scheduled soon?" he finally asked.

"No," I tried to recall her surgical schedule. "She probably will have more, but I don't know when that might be."

"I just didn't want to put you to the trouble and expense of putting her in outpatient surgery just so that I could examine her left eye. If there is any reason that she has to come in during the next few months have her doctor call me and I'll try to rearrange my schedule to slip over and take a quick look. It shouldn't take long, but I will need to have her knocked out because she won't let me look in her eye while she's awake," he smiled at her as he put away his tools.

I told him that I would keep the problem in mind and alert him at the next opportunity.

"But," he cautioned, "don't wait too long."

"Yeah, I know we have to have this taken care of while she's young or the surgery won't correct the lazy-eye," I said.

"No," he shook his head, his face losing its humor, "that's not the reason. She doesn't have lazy eye. When a child has lazy eye the muscles usually pull the eye toward the center. Lori's left eye roves in both directions. She definitely doesn't have lazy-eye, but I need to perform a complete examination before I speculate about what is wrong with it."

I thanked him and walked into the waiting room. As I gathered up Lori's diaper bag, I felt a foreboding brewing in the back of my mind. Leaving the office I started down the hallway toward the parking lot. All this time we had assumed Lori had lazy eye. But then, nothing else we had counted on had turned out the way we expected, so why should this?

At home I told Andrea of the Dr. Johnson's opinion about Lori not having lazy eye and his recommendation for a more extensive assessment. Andrea began worrying immediately. She did not see any sense in wasting time, she might as well dive right into worrying at once. In the days that followed she came up with explanations that ranged from a brain tumor (all headaches, to Andrea, are potential brain tumors) to blindness in the left eye. I told her not to worry, nothing of the sort was going to happen.

There are no halfway measures with me. When I am wrong, I am usually wrong in a large way, and this time proved to be no exception.

* * * * * * *

A couple of months after the initial examination by Dr. Johnson, Andrea brought Lori to me one day and pried open her mouth. For some time she had been noticing that Lori was not eating properly and acted as if something was bothering her. While she had been feeding her that day Andrea noticed that Lori's front teeth had almost disappeared. Lori hates anyone poking around in her mouth and no this occasion she was no less accommodating to our inspection. She pulled her head to one side, closed her mouth, and pushed at us with her hands.

Although my examination of her teeth was brief it was undeniable that the front teeth did appear to have rotted away in the past few days. I knew children's baby teeth decayed in a lot of cases, and had seen several children with rotten teeth, but I had never seen teeth disappear so quickly. I made an appointment with a local dentist to examine her teeth. But as soon as he heard her medical history, having tried unsuccessfully to look in her mouth, he immediately referred us to dentists at Vanderbilt.

The specialists at Vanderbilt x-rayed her mouth as she lay on my chest so that I could hold her head still. The dentists poked around in her mouth as best they could, and then, leaving a nurse to distract Lori, they conferred with me in the hallway.

They pointed out a condition that we had been aware of for some time, Lori's lower jaw had grown at a much faster rate than her upper jaw. Hence her lower teeth did not match up with her upper teeth. This condition caused her lower jaw to protrude, giving her a noticeable under bite. But, the dentists quickly noted, this had nothing to do with her present dental condition. From what they could tell the enamel on Lori's teeth was literally melting away, leaving the interior of the teeth exposed and causing them to quickly decay. I had never heard of such a condition. They said that it was not that unusual and speculated that most probably it was a combination of some birth defect and the great numbers of antibiotics she had been given over the past three years.

They concluded that she needed immediate medical attention, but her condition was beyond their abilities. They referred me to a Dr. Taylor in Hendersonville, Tennessee. More doctors, I thought, but at least we were getting to see a new city for a change. I was thankful for small favors by this point.

Dr. Taylor was an affable middle-aged man of medium height. He tried to examine her teeth as had his previous colleagues, but she was as equally uncooperative with him as she had been with them. Letting her relax he spoke with me.

"It appears that the Vanderbilt doctors' assessment is correct. She has lost a good deal of the enamel on her teeth, which has brought about their rapid deterioration. We've got to intervene soon," he spoke quickly but not in a rapid staccato pace. "I suggest that we make arrangements to put her in out patient surgery at Vanderbilt as soon as possible."

"O.K.," I agreed.

"I'll have my receptionist check the operating schedule and set up the date," he rose to leave. "Leave her your number. She'll call you when all the arrangements are made."

"Thanks," I said as he was leaving.

Driving back to Pulaski, I mentally explored the implications of what I had learned. Lori's teeth were literally melting away. More than half her front teeth had disappeared in just the last week. At that rate they would rot into her gum line in another week, or two at the latest. Dr. Taylor had not sounded alarmed but the urgency of his assessment had not escaped my attention.

Returning home I explained these newest discoveries to Andrea. She was upset by the prospect of yet another surgery and completely unconvinced that we could pull it off in one day. She reminded me that we had been promised this before and it had never happened. I reminded her that the last time we had surgery Lori had not spent a long time in PICU because they had discovered what caused her breathing difficulties. If we made a point of telling the staff in out patient surgery about her intubation difficulties we might not have to stay in PICU for several days. Andrea finally agreed that it was worth a try but she was still unconvinced that it would actually happen that way.

Remembering Dr. Johnson's need to examine Lori while she was unconscious, I called his office and coordinated the scheduling with Dr. Taylor. Confirmation came that the two offices had agreed upon a day and time, and that both men would be able to complete their work in back to back rotations.

A couple of days later I had to take Lori to Vanderbilt's outpatient surgical wing for her pre-admission examination. A wonderful nurse attended us. The wife of a Metro Nashville police officer, she and I shared cop stories as Lori's vitals were taken, and she was weighed and measured.

Early on the morning of the surgery we readied Lori for travel and made the trip with Lori pulling at her mother's arm and making her incessant food signs. They say that you can get used to anything but a rock in your shoe. To that brief list I would also add that you could never get used to your child's unattended hunger.

Andrea was on the verge of tears as we pulled into Vanderbilt parking lot. Going to the third floor of the East wing we began processing. Even though we had been to the wing only a few days earlier, we had to fill out a lengthy medical history on Lori. I must admit that I was facetious with my answers as the questioning dragged out. Under the section requesting a brief medical history, I wrote, "refer to volumes 1 through 6, Vanderbilt medical records." In the space that inquired about Lori's diet, I wrote, "She will eat anything that doesn't eat her first."

As I was considering the next silly notation I heard a familiar voice. Looking up I saw a nurse enter that I instantly recognized. Her name was Carol Rogers. She was a long time Pulaski resident whom I had not seen in several years. Her father, a remarkable man, had been my minister for a time. I knew that her husband of many years had run out on her and that she was single-handedly raising her children. She was a humorous, warm, caring woman, and I was thrilled that she was on the floor.

"They're mine," she informed the woman behind the reception desk as she rounded the counter to greet us.

"I'm Charge Nurse today and I'll assign who I want," she said, taking the papers from the receptionist and turning to us. "I take care of the Pulaski people." She flashed a sincere, welcoming smile.

"Carol," I said, motioning toward my wife, "You remember Andrea." Andrea nodded as Carol said, “Hi.”

"And this is Lori." I held Lori by the hand as she struggled to free herself from my grasp so that she could wander off down one of the many hallways.

"Hi, Lori." Carol bent down to speak to her.

"She doesn't speak," I offered when Lori's only reply was to stare back at Carol.

"Well, that's all right," she said standing erect and motioning us through the double doors. "You don't have to talk to get what you want, do you Hon?"

Down the long brightly-lit corridor we walked, following Carol. On each side of the hallway were small cubicles equipped with beds. Patients were assigned to the cubicles where they changed into surgical gowns, had their vital signs taken, and attended all other needs prior to surgery. Patients were taken directly from the cubicles into surgery, according to the scheduled availability of the individual operating theaters.

We were shown to our own cubical. Carol told us to undress Lori and put her in a gown. She left to attend to other duties as we attempted to comply with her request. Getting Lori undressed and into her gown was not a difficult task, but when the change was completed Lori wanted out of her bed so that she could wander around the halls as she was accustomed to doing on the peds ward. We agreed to let her out of the bed so that she could move about the room because we knew the impossibility of trying to keep her in the bed until her turn came for surgery. But this was not enough for the little lady and she immediately began trying to escape to the freedom beyond the door. In an attempt to block Lori's access to the much-desired corridor I had positioned myself in the doorway just as Carol returned.

"What's wrong, Hon?" she leaned down and asked Lori as she entered the room.

"She wants out," I explained, shifting from one side of the door to the other to keep Lori from darting past me.

"Let her out," Carol said, nodding toward the door.

"She wants to walk up and down the hall," I said. "We don't want her interfering with anything. She'll just get in your way."

"She won't get in anybody's way," Carol insisted. "You let her go." Carol stood by Lori and held out her hand. Lori instantly latched onto the offered hand with a wide, snaggle tooth smile and Carol walked her out into the hallway. Once she was out Lori let go of Carol's hand and looked around at the hallway. She crinkled up her eyes, smiled and clapped her hands in approval. A nurse came by and looked down at her. She spoke to Lori, patted her on the head and walked on. Soon another nurse came by and acknowledged Lori.

"See," Carol said, making notations in her charts as she sat just outside our door, "she's no problem."

Becoming bored with standing still Lori soon began roaming the halls, first one way, then the other. In short order she found the nurse's station and began trying to peek over the counter. The counter was much taller than she and all Lori managed to do was pull herself up on tiptoes. I started to pull her away but a nurse warded me off.

"She's not bothering anyone," the nurse told me, then turned to Lori and asked her name.

At this point Carol's assistant came up and took Lori with her. Some minutes later I found the assistant sitting in the hall playing with Lori like a child herself. She was a middle aged, sad-faced woman who wore the weight of years on her shoulders like a heavy coat. But with Lori she smiled easily, her sad wrinkles turning into a wreath of happiness. The woman seemed wholly content to occupy her time playing with this child who only wanted to walk the halls. In some unspoken covenant Lori and Carol's assistant appeared to be kindred spirits lost in a world of their own.

While I stood watching the nurse at play with Lori Carol came by our room. As she made more notations on Lori's charts I pointed out the affinity between the assistant and Lori.

"She was married to a man who abused her. Then she tried to get a child of her own after she left him," Carol said. "She wanted to adopt one. He had problems too, like Lori, but the adoption fell through and she wasn't allowed to adopt him. It broke her heart to give him up. Since then she likes to play with our special children."

I turned back as the nurse squatted in the floor and tried to get Lori to take a small red ball she had found somewhere. I could see the joy in the nurse's eyes as she played and I knew that Lori was giving this woman something that no one else could. Between them existed a silent harmony. I had seen Lori touch other people, but usually it was a sympathetic reaction she engendered, not one of such unbounded joy. For the first time I saw Lori give what only she was able to give to a person who desperately needed what she had to offer. For the first time I watched Lori help someone by just being herself and offering up her unique gift to a thirsty soul. Before I started crying I left them to their play.

Later, Lori was as difficult as ever while a nurse tried to take her vital signs. She squirmed on the bed, pushed at us when we held her, and tried every trick she knew to get out the door. When given toys she threw them and when spoken to she ignored the speaker. She engaged her limited arsenal of weapons at her disposal to get herself out of bed.

When the anesthesiologist came around Andrea made a point of detailing the procedures that had been successful in Lori's last operation. She made notes as Andrea recited the procedures. After listening to the familiar warnings we signed all the required documents and waited our turn in surgery. Lori finally got to walk the halls with her new friend and clapped her hands in appreciation.

After a half-hour the anesthesiologist returned. She came to our room and Andrea found me where I was walking Lori in the corridor. We were past the nurse's station and I started back, holding Lori's hand as we walked. When we rounded the corner toward our room we met Andrea and the anesthesiologist standing just outside the door of our cubical.

"All she wants to do is walk," I explained, as the doctor smiled down at Lori.

"Do you want to walk with me?" she held out her hand.

Not hesitating an instant, Lori dropped my hand and grasped the doctor's extended hand. And without so much as a backwards glance Lori walked off with her down the hallway, past the nurse's station and into the corridor leading into surgery. As the woman and Lori disappeared behind the double doors adorned with a sign announcing that this room was not to be entered by the general public, I noticed that Lori's exit had an audience. All the nurses had stopped what they were doing to watch this little girl walk hand in hand with her doctor into surgery. One or two nurses shook their heads, and I detected moisture rising in a couple of eyes.

"I've never seen the like," one nurse murmured.

"I wish that boy that cried all the way to surgery awhile ago could see this," Carol said, and I became aware of her standing beside me.

"I've never seen one walk to surgery before," another nurse said to Carol.

Andrea stood by Carol, tears welling up in her eyes as she watched her daughter go merrily off and round the corner into surgery.

"Let's go get something to eat," I said, trying to divert Andrea's mind from what was going to happen in a few minutes.

"How can I go eat when she's going into surgery," Andrea said, tears beginning to leak down her cheeks.

"Your daughter," I croaked out the words, "just waltzed off with a stranger, happy as she could be. I don't think she's in any great danger, and if she is, she's the last person you could convince of it."

"He's right. She'll be fine," Carol shooed us away. "Go get something to eat and by the time you get back maybe we'll have word for you."

We ate at the in-house McDonald's that had been added to the main hospital complex since our last surgery and quickly returned. When we arrived Carol said she had nothing to report and suggested that we go back to our room and try to get some rest. We went to Lori's room and waited. After an hour Dr. Taylor emerged from the operating room.

Taylor looked tired as he approached us with some documents tucked under his arm. He came to our door and began briefing us on the progress of his work.

"I cut out four of her upper front teeth, the ones that had deteriorated so badly," he began, motioning to his own mouth as an illustration. "Then we did eight root canals, and put on ten caps. Eight of the caps are silver, only the first two on each side of the extracted teeth are white."

Andrea asked about how Lori did during surgery and Taylor said that she had done very well.

"Dr. Johnson is examining her now," Taylor said, preparing to leave.

We made arrangements for a follow-up appointment the next week and Dr. Taylor was gone. We had little time to discuss our new knowledge when Dr. Johnson appeared at our door.

"I've completed the examination," he announced, but I could tell that something was amiss, he was not as cheerful as he had been in his office. "Lori has retinal scarring of the left eye. Apparently there are two distinct sets of retinal scars. One appears to have occurred before birth. The retina detached before birth and then reattached. The second scarring occurred sometime after birth, but I have no way of telling exactly when. When the retina reattached it formed the second set of scar tissue." He paused, "I can't say if she's blind in her left eye or not, she may very well be, but she may have some limited vision. The only way that we will be able to determine that is by testing her."

"We're going to have to bring her back for the tests or will she have to stay here?" Andrea asked.

"No," he shook his head. "You can do it at home. The test is relatively simple. Go to your local pharmacy and buy an eye patch kit. Place the eye patch over her right eye. If she starts crying and won't move, or just sits down in the floor, she's completely blind in her left eye. If she doesn't and is able to walk around then she has partial vision in the left eye."

"How long do we patch her eye?" Andrea asked.

"All day, if she exhibits sight in it," Johnson said. "After she's been up for about an hour patch the eye. Leave it patched all day. You can remove it an hour before bed time if you wish, but what we've got to do is make her brain begin paying attention to that eye. Right now the vision is so bad that her brain is ignoring her left eye, that's why it wanders around like it does. If we can get the brain to start paying attention to what the left eye sees I think we can salvage it."

"How long would that take?" Andrea inquired.

"I don't know, months," Johnson offered hesitantly. "Call me and let me know how she does. Then we can see what our next step should be, but we won't know until you can patch that eye. If you have any problems, call me," he said as he was leaving.

We stood rooted to the floor, stunned. We had not anticipated that our daughter might be blind in one eye. It was a possibility that had never really occurred to us. I sat down and thought about this. To me, blindness is one of the worst things that can befall a human being. My next thought was, if she is blind in her left eye, what are we going to do if something happens to the right eye? She would be totally blind. In such a simple way a new horror had entered into our lives.

Carol came by our room. Andrea told her the news and she seemed dejected at the recent discovery.

"She's been through so much already," Carol lamented, almost to herself.

"When can we see her?" Andrea asked, sitting upright for the first time since hearing the news.

"I'll go check," Carol spun around and darted out of the room.

Carol was gone only a few minutes when her smiling face reappeared at our door.

"You can go back now," she said, flashing a wide grin. "They weren't ready but I told them they had better let you guys come on back, you've seen all there is to see in recovery, so they're letting you back early. They were concerned that she wasn't cleaned up yet, but I told them you had seen worse." She led our way through the pneumatic doors into surgical recovery.

The East Wing recovery room for outpatient surgery is an L-shaped room with a nurse's station that runs along the North wall. Patients rolled out of surgery are lined up against the south wall. Each bed station has all the equipment necessary to handle one patient. Each location includes a track in the ceiling that holds a curtain in the event privacy is needed. Along the front of the nurse's station is a row of rocking chairs. Lori was about half way up the room, just before the bend of the L. The first thing I noticed were her little shoes pinned to the foot of her bed. A picture of our little girl walking into surgery flashed in my mind. She was semiconscious when we came up to her. Dried blood was caked around her mouth. Her lips were swollen so badly they rolled outward. Lori resembled a lot of people I had attended over the years who had been beaten severely in a fistfight. When she saw us she began to wiggle and cry. I knew what would calm her, but I doubted that they would allow it in recovery. Andrea was not so timid.

"Could we let her off the bed?" she asked the young, attractive woman who had just approached us to announce that she was Lori's nurse.

"Well," she appeared reluctant to agree. "I suppose ... who's going to hold her?" she asked as she dragged a rocking chair over to the side of Lori's bed.

"Her daddy will hold her," Andrea stepped aside and made a grand gesture toward me standing behind her. "She's a daddy's girl."

I moved around and sat down in the chair. The nurse worked the monitoring wires and I.V. tubing around Lori's bed so as not to tangle them during the transfer. Slipping an arm under her, the nurse lifted Lori into my arms and I placed her over my left shoulder. Lori nestled into her comfortable, customary position wiggling against me. She instantly stopped crying and began looking around. For the first time I looked into her left eye and knew that most probably she saw nothing from it. The left eye wandered away to the side, but the right eye stayed locked on me. She appeared to be pleading with me to get her out of this place where they hurt her so badly. A deep, hoarse sound rattled up from her throat that I knew must be swollen from intubation. The mewing sound was a beseeching wail, in deep base tones, so unlike her normal voice. The rolling guttural sound never formed any words per se, but she spoke clearly to me with her sad eye searching my face for some hoped for sign of relief. Then her face fell forward onto my shoulder and she began squirming again.

I knew what would calm her, but I was apprehensive about trying it. I looked around the room and found her nurse busily engaged with duties elsewhere. I decided that the only thing they could do was scold me so, lifting her carefully over my lap, I set Lori's slender feet on the tile floor. Her face lit up instantly, she looked quickly around, and started to smile, but the movement brought pain to her mouth and she flinched. I thought she was going to cry but she directed her attention to movement at the next bed and only managed a whining grunt.

Standing, Lori felt much better and seemed fully awake. When the nurse returned she did a double take seeing Lori standing between my knees. Lori looked up at her and instinctively made a movement to avoid the woman. I held her firmly so that she could not escape. Lori pushed at me, but I persisted, and she stopped struggling. The nurse stood looking at her for a moment, then smiled. She could see the immediate improvement in Lori's condition since she had been set on the floor. She made no mention of the unorthodox method of our recovery process.

"Do you think she could drink anything, Sprite, or 7 Up?" She bent forward and asked.

"She doesn't like the bubbles," Andrea said from behind me where she had taken up her post so that she could have the best view of Lori. "But she might drink some juice."

"It has to be clear liquid," the nurse shook her head.

"Water, then," Andrea said.

"Water it is," she was off in a flash.

Lori continued to look around her, occasionally looking back at me and whining. She wanted to leave this awful place. I told her several times that we would go soon, but first she would have to drink some water. In a minute the nurse had returned with a plastic glass full of ice and water. She held the plastic cup down to Lori who immediately gave the glass a smack with her right hand as she turned her head away. The frigid water and fragments of ice showered over my chest and down into my lap. It was a breathtaking experience. The nurse grabbed towels and Andrea snapped them out of her hand as she dabbed at the chilly trail down my chest.

"No," Andrea said as she blotted at the spots, "Lori, don't do that to daddy. That's not nice."

Lori looked away, unmoved by Andrea chiding. I asked the nurse if I could have the glass. I knew that Lori associated her pain with these strangers. If I gave her the water there was a chance she would take it. I held the glass in front of her so she could see it. At first she hesitated, then dipped her face forward and locked her swollen lips over the rim of the glass. She took a sizable drink of water, then stood erect and pushed the glass gently away from her. She had had enough water for the time being and was interested in seeing what other people were up to at the moment.

"Good girl," the nurse said, but Lori pointedly ignored her, keeping her head turned in the opposite direction. "Keep trying to get her to take some water. She's dry after all the time in surgery and it's best if we can replenish her body fluids.

The nurse left us to ourselves. Lori took a couple more drinks, but finally pushed the glass away with enough force to spill some more onto the floor. She began pulling and pushing, trying to get lose from my hands so that she could go walking around. I knew better than to allow that, but I also knew that she had fully recovered without having to spend time in the intensive care unit. The techniques had worked again!

As Lori became more insistent on her freedom our nurse came by and took one last round of vital signs. She began unplugging the monitor wires and removing the I.V. site. The tape dots used to keep the monitor clips in place are painful to remove and it is best that they be stripped off as quickly as possible. We had once had the terrible duty of trying to take off several of these attachments days after surgery when they had enough time to become firmly glued to Lori's skin. Andrea does not like to do it, but I know that the pain is only temporary and that it is better to do it as quickly, and as soon as possible. I swiftly ripped the monitor spots off Lori's chest and underarms. She cried out at the sudden, sharp pain, but was promptly comforted. Soon the unpleasantness was forgotten as she became intrigued with the preparations being made to release her from recovery. Lori always had a much higher pain tolerance than most people I know. Where other children cried and whimpered long after the pain had stopped Lori only cries during the actual painful event. As soon as the immediate pain has stopped so does her reaction to it. I had often wondered if her years of exposure to pain had developed some sort of immunity to its longer-lasting effects. Whatever the reason, she was dry-eyed and watchful as all the other equipment was detached from her and her recovery area was closed down.

The only part of leaving recovery that Lori did not care much for was that I had to put her back into the bed to be moved. She fidgeted at first but when the bed started to move she stopped wiggling and looked about to see what was happening. Andrea walked along on the other side of the bed and talked to her as we rolled down the hallway, back to our original room.

After the recovery nurse had departed Carol came to check on us. Lori was making unhappy noises, wanting down. I was trying to keep her in the room, concerned that not all the anesthetics had worn off and she might fall. Lori's temper was beginning to display itself once again when Carol arrived.

"What's wrong, hon?" Carol asked as Lori pushed at me to get past and into the hall.

"She's cranky," Andrea told her.

"I guess so," Carol said, standing upright. "If you had just undergone that much oral surgery without any pain killers you'd be short tempered too."

"No pain killers?" I asked.

I knew that there had been a plan to hold down painkillers to prevent an adverse reaction with her breathing, but I had no idea that they had not given her any at all.

"None," Carol said, shaking her head. "She's had all her teeth messed with one way or the other without one drop of anything. They didn't want it to interfere with her breathing. Do you think she would take some Tylenol if I got some?"

"Probably not without a fight," Andrea smiled. "But we need to give her something. Bring it on."

Carol ducked out of the room and came back with a dose of red liquid in a small plastic cup. Lori saw it as she entered the room and began pushing at me when I went to pick her up. Lori's experience with red liquids had not been very pleasant and she reacted predictably. Holding her on my lap we forced open her sore mouth and poured the red liquid in. She pushed part of it out of her mouth with her tongue, but some of it she swallowed, then made a horrid face. Gathering up a handful of tissue we wiped red spittle and spillage off her, me, and the floor. The Tylenol began to diminish the pain quickly, if not her mood, and after a half-hour Lori was her old self again.

As we were preparing to leave I reminded Andrea that she had to get an excuse signed for her class that evening, a humiliating requirement placed on her by a myopic English instructor who apparently was more accustomed to teaching children than adults. When Carol came back to our room with the final preparations for our departure I prodded Andrea.

"Ask her," I said, nodding toward Carol.

"No, just forget it," Andrea was too embarrassed to make the request.

"What?" Carol became intrigued at the coded exchange.

"No," Andrea insisted.

"What?" Carol raised her voice as if to elevate the question to a higher level.

"If you don't I will," I challenged her.

"Oh, all right," Andrea said, looking at Carol with a resigned, sheepish expression on her face.

She explained her teacher's requirement for missing class, she must bring back a note from the doctor justifying her absence. By the time we got back to Pulaski the class would be in progress and she would be counted absent if she did not produce a note. Andrea was genuinely mortified at having to make such a request.

"You are kidding?" Carol accentuated each word to underline her disbelief.

Andrea shook her head.

"No, she's serious," I confirmed.

"You wait right here," Carol said, darting out the door, "I'll get you a note."

She was gone for a short time and came back with *the* absence note of all time. She had typed it on official, water marked, gold embossed Vanderbilt stationary! The note described in minute, detailed medical terms all the procedures that had been performed on Lori that day and the necessity of the attendance of her parents. At the bottom Carol had signed her name over a definitive listing of all her degrees, credentials, and her administrative titles. It was one of the most impressive documents I had ever seen.

"There you go," Carol said handing over the paper to Andrea, "see if that don't do the job, and if she doesn't like that one I'll get one signed by every doctor on staff."

We did not have to ask for another note. Carol's letter did the job perfectly. As it turned out, the teacher was more embarrassed receiving the note than Andrea had been asking for it.

Once again we were released from the hospital with no side trip to the intensive care unit. We were elated as we drove home. Lori's teeth were a vast improvement over her previous condition. She was happier than we had seen her in months. Apparently she had been in great pain, and for how long we could only guess. One unexpected side effect of the surgery surfaced the next day. I was sitting in my chair watching the news after work and I heard an odd sound. It sounded like metal clicking against metal. I listened intently for some time but could not identify the sound or its source. The odd noise seemed to move around. First I would hear it on one side of the room and then on another. Finally I heard it directly behind me. I turned around in my chair to find Lori standing behind me, clicking her new teeth together. Apparently she had discovered that her metal teeth could make a new sound if she moved her jaw up and down, clicking upper and lower teeth together. The new teeth met just enough along the sides of her jaws to make a noise and she was intently exploring this new ability she had. Lori noticed me looking at her. She stopped snapping her teeth and broke into a wide grin. The two white-capped teeth gleamed on either side of the space where she used to have four front teeth. The impression she made was classic.

"Vampire teeth!" I said to her. It was the cutest smile I had even seen.

* * * * * * *

The problem of Lori's teeth resolved, we were left with the question of her eye. Just as we had been directed we got the eye patch and put it over her right eye. As soon as it was in place, she tore it off. We tried taping it to her skin but she ripped that off as well. Andrea even tried to stop her from removing the patch by putting socks over her hands, but that only slowed her down at bit.

Finally, I called Dr. Johnson for advice. He said he could cast her arms in plaster, but he felt that was too drastic. His other suggestion was that we put cardboard tubes over her arms so she couldn't bend her arms and reach the patch.

We made the tubes out of cardboard as instructed, then taped the tubes around her arms. Once her arms were secured we patched the eye. Lori cried when we succeeded at patching her good eye. We were afraid that she was completely blind in the left eye, but she managed to maneuver around a chair to come toward me. We noticed, however, that the left eye seemed to be "searching", moving wildly about in its socket. In addition, she whined and cried almost constantly while her good eye was covered.

That broke my heart. When sweat developed on Lori's forehead and ran down onto the patch the tape became unglued and the patch dropped off her face. I let the patch fall away without trying to replace it. Lori smiled at me when her good eye was uncovered. We gave serious thought to giving up the whole eye patch business.

We conferred with Lori's doctors, specialists and teachers, but no one could help us. Acutely aware of her developmental deficits, we saw two choices; try to save the eye at the expense of Lori's mind, or save her mind at the expense of her eye. We finally chose to leave off the patch.

Three years later Andrea succeeded in getting Lori's cooperation with the eye patch. We discovered that Lori had much more vision in her left eye than anyone had ever supposed. With the good eye patched Lori was able to move freely about, avoid objects in her path and respond to her mother's call by going directly to her.

A woman who has a severely handicapped child once told Andrea that God gives special children to special people.

I disagree. I think that God gives special children to perfectly ordinary people, and it is the pressure of the decisions and conditions that they face on a daily basis that makes the parents special. Like diamonds, parents of special children are only ordinary pieces of coal that the constant pressure of life with a handicapped child turns into precious gems. The pressures of decision-making on such a grand and continual scale will either crush the people involved or harden them into crystals of priceless durability. The only problem is there is no way to tell which way anyone will go and, sadly, many parents are crushed by the experience. Too many parents of handicapped children get divorced. They separate for a variety of reasons, but having to make heartbreaking decisions, like to one we made with Lori's eye, are usually associated with the disintegration of the relationships. I can understand it, but I'm still saddened by it.

Chapter XVII

Just Another Train

During a checkup on Lori's kidneys when she was four years old, Dr. Hill thoughtfully watched Lori for a moment as she ambled about the examination room.

"Why does she act like that?" he asked.

"I don't know," I replied, curious at his inquiry. "She's developmentally delayed. We guessed that it had to do with her long stay in NICU, and all the hospitalizations she's had."

"Nothing related to her kidneys has anything to do with that," he shook his head pensively. "I tell you what," he said, as if he had made some cryptic decision, "I'll call a friend I have at Vanderbilt and get her an appointment for an assessment at the developmental center."

I did not know what to make of his sudden concern. I knew that Lori was far behind other children her age, but she had been through so much for so long that Andrea and I had assumed that her development had simply been delayed.

"O.K.," I agreed, and Hill set off to contact his friend.

Hill's associate was not available that day so he sent us home with a promise that he would make contact as soon as practicable, and that his nurse would call us with the appointment. Needless to say, when I arrived home Andrea was less than enthusiastic about a session with the child development people. She was concerned, as was I, about what they might find. We had never spoken our fears out loud before, but each of us had harbored an apprehension that Lori might be mentally impaired in some way. Her significant deficit in manual, mental and verbal skills was clearly obvious, but without a diagnosis we did not have to face the reality that she might be mentally handicapped.

On June 18, 1994 we were scheduled to have Lori assessed by the multidisciplinary child development team at

Vanderbilt Clinic. By the time we arrived for the session neither Andrea nor I held any illusions about the probable outcome of the assessment. Once we began watching Lori's actions with the idea in mind that she could be mentally handicapped, the signs were all too vivid; the inability to speak or make intelligible sounds, the stunted motor skills, the repetitive hand motions, we knew there could be only one conclusion.

When we arrived at the assessment unit we were shown into a room with a long, two-way mirror on one wall. Initially, two women came in and spoke with us. The taller of the two informed us that she would take Lori into the next room and assess her motor skills while the other woman would adjourn with Andrea into another room to run through some questions with her.

When everyone departed I was left alone behind the two-way mirror. I watched the woman and two assistants put Lori through her paces. They conducted play therapy with a doll on the floor to assess her reactions. They offered her food and toys. Lori took none of them, nor did she reach for anything they offered. Her attention drifted quickly. She crawled away from the women, pulled herself to her feet beside a chair, and began to look around the room on her own, ignoring the presence of the people around her and their attempts to gain her attention.

About this time the shorter woman came down the hall with Andrea following along in tow. As they passed me Andrea mouthed the words, "I don't know what they're doing. They're asking about us."

Depositing Andrea in a nearby room, the interviewer returned to me. I had been a cop long enough to know that this was a simple "divide and question" technique. In theory, if you interview two people separately their compared answers will produce a more objective truth than if you interview them together where one person's answers can influence the other's responses. A separate interview also reduces reluctance in one or the other partner, making the interviews more candid. Also, it is assumed that mothers know more about children than fathers, so I assumed that they believed the interview with the mother would be more significant in developing an accurate picture of Lori and her home environment.

The woman came in with a greeting smile and sat down across from me. She began a series of questions, mostly about our personal relationship and home life, rather than about Lori. We had been through this before when Lori was in NICU. I answered the questions while watching Lori's examination in the other room.

"You're trying to find out about us because you have bad news for us and you want to see how we will take it," I thought, as the woman continued to make her inquiries.

"What do you expect from this examination?" she asked, breaking the established flow of her questions.

"What?" I asked, my mind did not immediately grasp the sudden change in direction.

"What do you expect us to tell you?" she reworded the question.

"What's wrong with her?" I said, returning my attention to Lori in the other room.

"Is that all?" she asked, coldly I thought, as if she were assessing the expectations I might have about the purchase of a new car.

"Why?" I said, challenging her.

"Why?" she repeated.

"Yes, why?" I said. "Why is she like that? Was it something we did ... something we didn't do ... what?"

I expected her to ask why I wanted to know that, but she did not. I was relieved. I really did not want to tell her about the night in the crib, about my fear that I was responsible for her mental damage, about her laying on the table in Vanderbilt as the two doctors made wry comments about her struggle to breath and that I had let it slide, had not intervened, had not grabbed one of them by the throat and demanded they help, right then, right there. She did not ask. I did not tell. I would hold the secret until they discovered the cause. I promised myself I would confess, if they discovered I was at fault, but only then.

The day wore on into more questions, tests by interrogations, games with double meanings. Lori tired quickly and hand signed her impatience. I became tired and mentally floated away. Andrea became tired but refused to show it, she even pretended to eat at lunch. Lunch time was spent in the now familiar hospital cafeteria, struggling with food we did not want before hurrying back to the test center, to wait for the results we were not sure we wanted either.

After we returned to the assessment center the team assembled for their conference with us to present their findings. They began slowly, making positive comments as I am certain they had been trained to do. I had seen this approach many times before, had even used it myself in countless situations. Now I simply endured it, waiting for the real results I knew would come after the initial flattery had softened up our reception. Finally it was said, thrown into the discussion as if it were a matter of fact already established; Lori was mentally retarded, profoundly so, though they were quick to add that a lot depended upon her future training and education. They pointed out that nothing could be for certain at this stage in her life, a lot rested on how she responded to training, how teachers and educators treated her. A lot of psychological terms were applied to her condition but I must admit I didn't hear all of them, a deep depression was edging its way into my mind.

The next day I returned to work and a coworker approached me, casually asking what the test results were.

"About what we expected," I told him, "she's profoundly mentally retarded."

"Now, don't you yell at her," he suddenly erupted into a fierce concentration of grim seriousness, almost yelling at me in his agitation as he assumed an aggressive posture. I was startled by his unexpected outburst.

"We're not going to yell at her," I tried to smile to show our benign intentions, but his face remained tense and ardent.

"Well, just don't yell at her, it's not her fault," he insisted, I could not fathom what precipitated such an emotional blitz from an otherwise unflappable person. Something in his past, perhaps?

Through my experiences with Lori I have discovered that we all have hidden feelings regarding illness and handicaps. Whatever my coworker's motivations, Lori's mental retardation touched a tender spot within him. It made me realize that Andrea and I had been experiencing a lot of unusual reactions from people since Lori's birth.

Back when Lori had surgery to reconnect her displaced hips, her body was covered in a cast from the upper chest to her ankles. Although she was easy to carry around the house, we found this mode of carrying her very tiring when we had to go out for any extended periods of time.

The biggest problem we had was transporting her once outside the car. We initially solved the problem by using her brother's little red wagon. We would pile pillows in the wagon and place Lori on top of them. It was comfortable for her, but awkward for us, especially in stores, and it drew a lot of undesired attention. We had tried to find a baby carriage for the task, but they were too small to accommodate the body cast comfortably.

Finally we found one in a shopping mall in Florence, Alabama. We had brought Lori into the upscale store perched on her red wagon. Andrea quickly found a carriage on display that met every requirement. A saleswoman came by just as we were completing our inspection and we told her that we wanted to buy the carriage.

"We'll take this one," Andrea said.

"Certainly," the lady smiled brightly, as she began looking about the store, "I'll have one of the boys get one down from the warehouse you."

"Is it assembled?" Andrea asked.

"No," the saleswoman casually replied.

"Uh, no," Andrea insisted, "we want this one."

"I'm afraid you can't have that one," the woman graciously declined the demand, "this is a display model."

"But we need <u>this</u> one," Andrea persisted.

"I'm afraid you don't understand, we only sell unassembled units," she resisted our demand with a waning smile.

"No," Andrea persevered, as she pulled the little red wagon from behind the floor display where it had been hidden from the saleswoman's view, "I'm afraid you don't understand, I need this one .... now."

"Yes, ma'am!" The woman quickly agreed, upon seeing Lori atop the pillows piled onto the little wagon. "Come right this way."

On our way to the cash register the saleswoman called to her supervisor, "They're taking the assembled model."

With Lori wiggling on her pillows we were processed promptly at the register. I quickly deposited the wagon back at our car while Andrea got Lori arranged in her new carriage. Even with its larger size we still had to fill the carriage with pillows and let Lori ride on top with her feet sticking out the front.

Body casts are notoriously hot, so we did not cover Lori when at all possible. We would simply insert a diaper into the opening at the leg juncture and let it go at that. With Lori so arranged we decided that the day was young and that we would take her for a stroll through the mall to do some shopping. I was pushing the carriage when a woman suddenly appeared out of nowhere, shoved her carriage in front of ours, blocking our progress.

"What's wrong with that baby?" she demanded in a fierce, challenging voice, staring accusatorily into my eyes.

She was a complete stranger, but I could tell by the way she looked me directly in the eyes with her straight-backed defiant stance that she was certain that I was responsible for the baby's condition. Andrea flushed bright red with anger.

"She was born with displaced hips," I offered calmly. "She's had surgery to repair them."

"Among other things," Andrea said in a disturbingly quiet voice, "if it's any of your business."

Realizing that she had challenged the parents of a birth defective baby, the woman was suddenly embarrassed and tried to make some conciliatory remark as she pulled back her carriage to allow us to pass.

The parents of handicapped children are forced to see the world differently than "normal" people. Our slant on life is a bit different compared to most people, just as our values take different forms. Where the parent's of a normal child are displeased with their offspring's inability to master a musical instrument, or exhibit great physical skills, the parents of retarded children prize the simplest ability. Their children's progress is measured in inches rather than feet. And they do not set lofty goals and insist that their children meet them.

After Lori's assessment at Vanderbilt, we had to reassess our goals. Where other parents long for college for their child, we developed a hope that she would eventually learn enough life skills to live in a group home and have some sort of life of her own. Where other parents lead hectic lives centered around sports, scouts, and social events, we continue to try to get Lori to simply feed herself. Where other parents wish for athletic prowess we labored to teach basic potty skills.

As other parents vie for inclusion of their children into the main streams of their social set we work toward simpler ambitions. We learned to appreciate each day for itself and to ignore the fears of tomorrow. The mentally retarded live in the world of the constant "now." Lori has no concept of later. There is now and there is nothing, it is as simple as that. We have learned to live without dreams, to place no faith in plans for the future, and we have learned to try not to worry about what the future might bring, but accept each day as it comes.

As parents of a mentally retarded child, we have learned to forget about preconceived notions of other people, places, or things. Lori has no use for such silly things, and neither do we. In the role of the great teacher Lori has taught us to more fully appreciate the biblical admonition, "...sufficient unto the day is the evil thereof."

Chapter XVIII
The Miracle Of The End Of A Miracle

By the time she was five Lori's health seemed to be better than ever. As we had been instructed, every six months we took her to Dr. Hill for kidney checkups. During these visits, he determined the left kidney had grown to normal size and our lives settled happily into an uneventful sameness.

Then one day, during a checkup in the fall of 1995, Dr. Hill made a disturbing, and wholly unexpected discovery. After reviewing the ultrasounds we had taken at Vanderbilt before visiting his office, he came into the examination room with a serious frown etched on his face.

"The upper right kidney is swelling," he said flatly.

"Uh ... what does that mean?" I asked, baffled by the news and uncertain how to react.

"For one thing, it's pressing on the lower portion of the kidney that we were hoping to save." He led me into the hallway to the display light mounted against the wall. Lori's films were already shining ghostly within the bright lights emanating from the metallic box on the wall.

"See," he outlined an area on the black and gray film with the tip of his pen, "this is the lower portion last time. Growing nicely, just as we wanted, but here," he switched to the next photo, "you can see that the area has been reduced. What is happening is that the upper pole is swelling and compressing the healthy tissue. We have to do something, and soon."

"When do you want to do the operation?" I asked, intuitively knowing that the phrase "do something" translated into operation.

"As soon as possible," he announced, searching a scheduling sheet in his office. "I don't want to wait."

He offered the earliest date his schedule would allow. I agreed and he immediately had his nurse call Vanderbilt to reserve a time for the surgery. The surgery was to be performed in the outpatient surgical wing, Surgical East, as before but this time we would have to stay for several days to monitor Lori's postoperative progress.

As I drove home that evening I wondered at the unbelievable turn of events. Just when we had thought things were going so well this had to happen. I thought of the hospital stay, the constant driving back and forth, of Andrea having to stay with Lori through the long days and nights of her recuperation.

"We are reliving the past," I thought.

Then it hit me. I was staring another miracle in the face and did not recognize it for what it was. After all I had been through I still did not have the sensitivity to identify a miracle in the making!

I reviewed Lori's amazing medical history. She had been born with only one half of the left kidney in functional condition. The upper right kidney was damaged beyond repair with only a very tiny piece of functioning tissue remaining intact on the right side. Then, as the doctors were preparing to take the lower half of the left kidney, they discovered the upper right kidney was functioning, even though it should not. The upper right kidney worked perfectly for five years, long enough for the left kidney to grow to normal size, thus being capable of handling Lori's needs on its own. That right kidney, which was supposed to be dead, had been pressed into service for as long as it was needed. In terms of her kidneys, the dead had been raised and worked just long enough to keep Lori alive. That having been completed the kidney returned to the dead where it belonged.

I was amazed. I no longer thought about the inconvenience the surgery would present. I looked at little Lori nodding in her seat as we drove through the hills of Southern Tennessee and I knew for a fact that I was personally witnessing another miracle. I recalled the story of Moses, when he had seen the burning bush, saying that he must turn aside and see this marvel. All he went to see was a bush that burned but was not consumed, here I was sitting next to a little girl, my little girl, that had within her a dying kidney which had already been dead for five years, but had been brought back to life just long enough to save her.

Lori's angelic face nodded and bobbed with the rhythm of the road, blissfully asleep, completely unaware of the spectacular events transpiring within her. Her absolute innocence, her benign acceptance of life as it came to her was living testimony of her candidacy for the vehicle of such an astonishing miracle. She had lived a miracle from the time before she was born, and this was just another turn along the way.

For a moment I regretted that the surgery would mean more pain and suffering for her. I wished there was some way I could relieve her of this or endure it myself , but I knew that this too was something between her and God. Between them was a bond that I was not a part of and it was not up to me to wish one way or the other. Lori would bear her pain, as God had equipped her to do, and I would bear mine as He meant me to do. Her little head nodded with the sunlight raking across one cheek like a kiss from above and I felt like weeping. All my life I had wanted to be present at the moment of a miracle. I longed for some way to transport myself back to the time of Christ and experience what it must have been like to be so close to God during such an important time. Here I was riding in an old beat-up pickup truck along Interstate 65, edging into the hills just North of Giles County, Tennessee, on an ordinary day, and I was being given my life's wish, and in a much larger and grandiose way than I could ever have dreamed of in the past. I was present at the time and the place of a great miracle, and, a little child was leading me to it. The greatest part of it was that the child was my own daughter. Who else should lead a man to a miracle? It was all so right. It was all so marvelous.

Rolling off the hills and dropping into the valleys near Lynnville, Tennessee, I thought about John the Baptist who declared the coming of a miracle but was not to participate in it himself. I felt a little like that John must have felt, personally insignificant in comparison to the event which he knew was happening all around him, yet at the same time I had an enthralling sense of participation in something cosmically momentous. God had known of my wish to see a miracle, and he had granted it in a way no one could have predicted. A smile came to my face as I left the Interstate headed toward home. I remembered the old Jewish admonition; beware what you wish for, you may get it.

When we reached home Andrea was waiting. She slumped against the porch railing as she saw us get out of the truck. By now she had become adept at reading my face. She required only the bare essentials to be appraised of what was to come. She had been through enough to know the rest.

* * * * * * *

Once again the day for surgery arrived and we drove a hungry little girl through the early morning darkness to a surgery she did not know was coming. Again, Andrea cried all the way to Vanderbilt for Lori's suffering.

As we were led into the unit toward our assigned cubical we met Nurse Carol. She stopped and talked with us for a moment, pointed out our assigned room and said that she would be with us shortly.

Lori was her usual hard case, she refused to stay in her room. She pushed, strained, and complained until she was allowed out into the hallways. As soon as we allowed Lori her freedom she was a completely happy child. She walked up and down the halls, stopping every so often to look around at people, the lights in the ceiling, or movement occurring around her. At odd intervals she applauded her approval.

Andrea and I took turns walking her up and down the corridors. We peeked in other people's rooms, watched passersby in the halls, and visited the nurses' station several times. Lori tried to peek over the nurses' station but the counter was still too tall for her to see over its top edge. We explored the recesses of the ward from west to east and back again. When her doctors came for their pre-op assessments and conferences we had to force Lori back into her room to undergo unwanted inspections and probing. They failed at taking her blood pressure, as usual, and she would not hold still for anyone to listen to her heart. For a child with zero vocabulary and limited intelligence she had no trouble expressing herself

Carol hovered nearby, lending comments, insight, and comfort when she could, but usually she just smiled and supported Lori in whatever Lori wanted to do. Dr. Hill came to see us before surgery to tell us what could be expected. He was as confident as ever and highly optimistic about the surgery. Lori tolerated him only a little while and then was off to explore the hallways.

The anesthesiologist on this trip was a tall woman in her mid-thirties who was demure and rather plain beneath her green scrubs and hair net. She recited the customary precautions against surgical procedures, which we knew from memory, obtained our signatures on the proper papers, tapped Lori's back, listened to her heart, and read her charts. One more time Andrea reiterated the procedures that had proven successful in the past to keep Lori out of intensive care. The woman nodded her comprehension and said that she would try her best to replicate previous successes.

A short time after the anesthesiologist left, Nurse Carol came to our room with a small cup of liquid she wanted Lori to drink. We had our reservations about this but Carol succeeded where most had failed and Lori drank the red fluid with very little protest. In moments Lori was staggering as she tried to walk the halls. We finally had to be put in her bed. For once she would be rolled into surgery like everyone else rather than leading the parade on foot.

Andrea and I stood watching her being rolled away until the doors closed behind her. Once again, a lump caught in my throat and tears began to pull at the corners of my eyes. I was never going to get used to this no matter how many times we did it.

Seeing us standing there, Carol said,

"Go get yourselves something eat. This one's going to take time and there's no use in you hanging around here." She waved her hands at us. "Go," she commanded, and we complied.

We walked across the hospital complex and got food that served only to fill up time. We went back to the room to await the call that Lori was in recovery. After a couple of hours, Dr. Hill came out, all smiles and optimism.

"Well," he began as he slipped into the room, "everything went just great. The kidney was swelled as we had expected. It had pressed the lower pole down but we think it might rebound now that the pressure has been relieved."

Andrea asked about Lori and Hill grinned.

"She's great," he beamed. "They have her in recovery and she should be ready in a few minutes." He shifted his surgical box and x-rays to his other hand as he talked. "I'll be by tonight and see how she's doing." He nodded at Andrea because he knew she would be staying with Lori through the night.

"The usual time and place," Andrea tried to act flippant, but without being able to pull it off very well. "I'll be there."

Time dragged by. Andrea paced the room, I slouched in a chair. Suddenly she turned on her heels, snatched up her purse and dug out some money.

"Here," she thrust a dollar bill at me, "go to the main hospital, take the Children's Hospital elevator down to the basement floor. There's a Snapple machine there. She likes pink lemonade. If they're out of that, just get anything."

Andrea's sudden outburst had caught me of guard, but I set off on this most suddenly urgent journey without asking questions. Just as she had described I found the Snapple machine. We were in luck, the pink lemonade was there. I quickly returned with it, still not certain why I had been dispatched in such haste. Andrea impatiently stalked the room, she was upset.

"What's wrong?" she shot the question at the wall, rather than anyone in particular.

"I don't know," I answered, even though I knew she had not really spoken to me.

Andrea paced and became more agitated as the minutes dragged past. Finally the anesthesiologist came to our room. I could tell by her walk that she was not bringing good news. Andrea confronted her at the door.

"What's wrong?" she demanded.

"We're just taking our time," the woman began.

"Lori's not breathing on her own is she?" Andrea challenged her openly.

"Well, things are not preceding as expected...," the woman began and Andrea cut her off.

"I want to see her. Can I go in?" She was physically approaching the woman who took a step backwards at her advance.

"We need just a little bit longer, uh .. she's not cleaned up from surgery and ..."

"Has she got needles sticking in her head?" Andrea sliced into the other woman's explanation.

"No!" The doctor seemed shocked at such a suggestion, and at the same time confused by the sudden assault.

"Well," Andrea shot back. "What has she got that's so bad? I've seen everything else that you people have ever done to her in the past and that was the worst, so if my daughter doesn't have needles sticking out of her head then I'd like to see her ... NOW." Andrea took another step toward the woman.

Carol had been standing just outside the door, to the right of the bewildered doctor. She took the opening Andrea had presented.

"I told you, they've seen it all. There's nothing you can hide from them. They know what is best for Lori. Let them in, they can help." I knew Carol was walking a thin line for a nurse to dare tell a doctor what to do.

"O.K.," the woman finally nodded, but before she could finish her statement Andrea pushed past her and was out into the hall headed toward recovery.

"Grab my purse," Andrea called back over her shoulder as she led the procession down the hallway.

I had to run to keep up. I caught the end of the line just as they entered the automatic doors of the recovery room. We quickly negotiated the compartment to where Lori lay at the far end of the L-shaped room. As we entered the interior of recovery the doctor called out to the staff a warning, "The Whites are here, I've authorized it!" Other parents turned to look and nurses stopped what they were doing to see the odd parade storm through their well-ordered space.

A male nurse we had never seen before was attending Lori. He smiled and introduced himself as we approached but Andrea was paying no attention to social formalities.

"What's her oxy-sats?" she snapped as she sought out the monitor on the wall to gather her own information. "Has she woke up at all?" she asked the nurse before he could answer her fist question.

He looked from Andrea to the anesthesiologist whom he believed to be in charge. She shrugged and motioned toward Andrea as if relinquishing her authority in the matter.

"Does she still have pain killers in her?" Andrea snapped at the anesthesiologist before the nurse could do anything more than shake his head, no.

"Well ..." the anesthesiologist started to say, "we have a little ..."

"Can you block them?" Andrea interjected quickly and to the point.

"Yes," the anesthesiologist replied.

"Then do it," Andrea turned her attention to the nurse.

He looked from Andrea back to the doctor. The doctor quickly ordered an injection of a blocking agent and he set off to get it. In a moment he was back inserting a syringe in Lori's IV. As he was doing that the doctor quietly withdrew, I suspected she was getting out of the line of fire.

"What can she have?" Andrea asked, as the nurse was withdrawing the syringe from the plastic tubing.

"Chips and sips," he was learning to reply faster.

"Of what?" Andrea fired back.

"Clear liquids," he said, almost defensively.

"Get me a large syringe," she ordered him and turned to me. "Give me the bottle out of my bag."

As I retrieved the bottle of Snapple the nurse came back with two large syringes. The syringes were capped in individual plastic cases.

"These are ...," he started to say as he handed the syringe cases to me. Andrea cut him off.

"He knows what they are and how to handle them," Andrea shot at him, and then to me on the side. "Get it ready."

"Won't you say that this is a clear liquid?" Andrea demanded, shoving the bottle of pink lemonade Snapple within inches of the nurse's shocked face.

"Looks ... looks clear to me," he stammered and took a step backwards.

"Right," Andrea barked, passing the bottle to me. "Give her some to drink."

In the background I could hear the nurse trying to tell us how much liquid Lori should be given. I heard his voice fade away as I popped the cap on one of the cases and filled the syringe with Snapple. I did not have to look back to know that Andrea had probably withered him with one of her piercing looks. Raising Lori's head slightly I placed the syringe tip to her lips and pressed on the plunger ever so lightly. A thin line of Snapple flowed out and onto her lips. I stopped. Lori's tongue flicked out and took it. I delivered a few more drops. Drop by drop she drank the offered liquid and began to stir, ever so slightly. Soon she had taken several cc's of the liquid and her movements became more pronounced. I stepped back and Andrea took my place by Lori's head. She began to sing a little song she made up and sang to Lori whenever she was in pain or trouble.

"Lori is a pretty girl, Lori is a honey," Andrea chanted singsong fashion over and over. Soon a foot moved under the covers, then another. In a minute Lori stirred and a small hand reached out and grasped her mother's fingers.

"There's my little girl," Andrea thrilled to the sudden touch.

Lori opened her eyes and looked around. For an instant there was no reaction, then her face creased with pain and she began to cry. All the analgesics in her body had been neutralized and she was in terrible pain.

"It's O.K., I'm right here," Andrea tried to console her daughter as she withered in agony.

Lori could not be confronted. She hurt horridly from a combination of the fresh incision and amputated kidney. Andrea patted her hands as Lori made quick hand signs, grasped at the bedding and rolled to get away from the pain, but no matter what she did, there was no escape. Andrea turned to me with the most heartbreaking mask of sorrow I have ever seen. She knew that Lori's pain was her doing. She had requested that the analgesics be removed so that Lori's breathing could be stabilized. This was necessary but now she was awake and in dreadful agony. Andrea turned back to Lori, still trying to comfort her.

Lori tugged at Andrea's hand, silently pleading with her to stop the suffering. She pushed away when no help was immediately forthcoming. Lori rolled her head and looked around the room. Tears flowed freely from her eyes and her mouth opened in a long, noiseless cry. No matter how excruciating her anguish Lori never screamed or cried out in a loud voice. Now she sobbed, sucking air between moans. Her body was racked by quiet wails of desperation.

"Mama," Lori called out in a loud, clear voice.

Andrea was jolted as if struck by a bolt of electricity. She turned to me, wide-eyed and open-mouthed.

"Did you hear that," she said, just before tears rolled down her cheeks and she began to cry.

"I told you she could say mama when she had to," I said, choking back my own emotion.

Many times when I had brought Lori for examinations at Vanderbilt and Andrea had stayed home with Little John I had heard Lori call for her mother when everything else failed. Usually this had occurred when I had to hold her under an X-ray machine for prolonged exposures. Lori hates to be held still, and in the heat of her resistance she would call out for her mother in a clear, distinct voice.

The nurse stood back, astounded by the fact that Andrea had accomplished in fifteen minutes what they had failed to do in over an hour. He called for the anesthesiologist. She appeared promptly and examined Lori.

"She's awake," he told the doctor as she completed a brisk examination of Lori's condition.

"Yes," she smiled, standing back from the bed. "She certainly is. You really know what you're doing," she said to Andrea who was still holding Lori's hand on the opposite side of the bed.

"I told you," Andrea said matter-of-factly, and turned her attention back to Lori who was still pleading for help in her own ways. "Could she get some Tylenol now?"

"Oh, yes," the doctor said, turning to the nurse, "I don't see why not."

She rapidly gave instructions to the nurse for Tylenol. He disappeared and instantly reappeared with the prescription contained in a syringe which he injected into Lori's IV. In a few moments Lori was calmer, though still a bit restless.

Within half an hour we were released from recovery and were rolling Lori down the corridor toward the peds ward across the hospital causeway. Nurse Carol had met us in the hallway as we collected our things from the original room to transfer to the hospital. Andrea briefed her as she gathered up our belongings.

"I told the anesthesiologist to just be honest with you two," Carol said as she stood in the doorway. "She didn't know what to do and I told her before she came in to see you that the one thing she had better not do is lie to you. You two have seen it all, there's no reason to hide the truth from you. I told her, "you lie to them and they'll know it. Just tell them the truth, they can handle it." One of the hardest things I have to do around here is to get doctors to trust parents. Parents know what is best for their children, all we have to do is listen to them."

"I had her up and awake in five minutes," Andrea beamed.

"That's what I told her," Carol grinned. "Just listen to you, you two know Lori better than anybody."

As we hurried down the hallway after our daughter, Carol threw us one more smile and a wave before disappearing. Several months later I would recall Carol's kind and compassionate benevolence in a most painful way.

The following year, on a drab and nippy November day, Carol's nephew walked into his high school armed with a .22 caliber rifle and cold-bloodedly shot two teachers at point blank range as they stood outside their classrooms. After mortally wounding one teacher and seriously wounding another he shot at another teacher, missed, and instantly killed a sixteen-year-old girl walking down the hall to class.

The horrible, senseless murders would shock our county and state, and gain national attention. Weeks after the terrible events at Richland High School I walked into the Giles County Courthouse unaware that a hearing in the case was in progress. The hallway outside the courtroom was filled with people during a recess in the hearing. Amid the crowd of witnesses, spectators, families, and survivors I saw Carol, standing alone and downcast amid the sea of people. I walked over to where she stood slump shouldered and greeted her.

"Carol," I said, trying to be encouraging at a time when I knew she needed support, "I haven't seen you in a long time."

"I didn't think you'd want to let anyone know that you knew me," she said as tears brimmed in her eyes.

I felt my heart break. I was a very good friend with the husband of the teacher her nephew had killed. He is a wonderful man whom I respect and care for immensely, but here stood the woman who had worked so hard for my desperately ill daughter saying that she was afraid I would be ashamed to let people know that I knew her. I stepped up to her and put my arm around her shoulders as she began to cry.

"I don't care what anyone thinks," I said loud enough for several people to hear standing near us. "You're my friend, I would never abandon you."

She hugged me back and we stood there for a moment. Some of the people stared at us as we stood locked in an embrace. I fought for control of my emotions as I stepped back from her and looked into her tears streaked face.

"If you need anything just call me," I said.

She smiled and said that she would. I looked out over the crowd. I saw looks of open wonder in many eyes. Here I was a policeman comforting a relative of the accused. I could read the questions in their faces. Some frowned contemptuously, others appeared uncomfortable with my presence. The courtroom turns us all into adversaries, pitted against one another. The battlefield of the courtroom is where I have spent a good deal of my adult life. I understand it completely, but I also understand that there are truths beyond the ability of the courtroom to contain or comprehend in its adversarial world. This was one of those times. I left Carol in the midst of her family, but I took her with me in my heart.

Lori's recovery from the kidney operation was swift. She was operated on shortly after nine a.m. on Wednesday. Before I left to take Little John to school Friday morning at seven a.m. Andrea called to tell me to come and get them. After making quick provisions at work, I drove to Nashville and found them waiting outside in the patient delivery area with their suitcase packed and a balloon bouquet fluttering in the breeze. Lori still had a large swelling on the right side of her body where the kidney had been removed but otherwise she appeared to be in fine shape. We put her into the van and she clapped at the idea of traveling away from the hospital where she had been trapped for the last two days.

Within a week or so the swelling receded and Lori was left with matching scars on each side of her waist. Since glue had been used to close the wounds instead of stitches, the scars are small, simple lines etched into her flesh. Everything seemed fine until a checkup in the early spring of 1996 revealed a problem, the remaining kidney on the right side was not draining. The ultrasounds showed a large mass with no conduit for the urine to flow into her bladder. Dr. Hill scheduled surgery for the next week.

Andrea and I were distressed at this sudden turn of events. Lori did not act as if she were suffering a shut down of her right kidney. She was happy and active. Her color was good, as was her appetite and her urine output. But the ultrasound pictures could not lie.

Yet again we rushed through the pre-dawn darkness to surgery with a hungry, unhappy little lady strapped in the back seat. We filled out all the papers, changed her into a surgical gown and saw her off to surgery as we had done all too many times. We trudged across Vanderbilt hospital to eat another horrid breakfast neither of us wanted. Getting back to the room we checked on any messages and found there had been none. It was actually too soon for any messages, but we always checked, just in case, because we had learned that early messages from surgery were the worst sort of news. Thankful that there was no word we sat down in our room and the phone rang instantly. It was a nurse from surgery.

"Dr. Hill is coming out to speak with you," she said.

"About what?" I asked as my heart froze and a lump seized my throat.

"He's coming out to talk to you," she repeated and hung up.

I sat there holding the phone, looking at it as if it would tell me more than I had heard if I would only wait.

"What was it?" Andrea asked, slipping to the edge of her chair as the flesh of her face drew tight against the bone.

"A nurse from surgery," I said, putting the phone back on the cradle, "Dr. Hill's coming out to talk to us."

"Oh, no," Andrea gasped, her face going white.

"No," I waved off her concern, " now, it could be anything."

"It has to be bad news," Andrea insisted. "He's never come out so early, and you know if he comes out he isn't going to scrub up again if it isn't something terribly wrong."

"Not necessarily," I said, trying to keep my voice level and restrain the emotion I felt building behind it. "It could be anything."

We waited nervously as time slowed to a crawl. A nurse came by the room and Andrea told her about the phone call.

"That doesn't sound good," the nurse said before she thought better of it.

Propelled by her unguarded comment the nurse hastily disappeared and we waited alone. Just about the time we felt our nerves would snap Dr. Hill briskly stepped around the corner of the corridor, making a swift approach to our room, carrying his surgical box and a large manila envelope under his arm. There was a flicker in his eye, but not his usual cheerful smile. He deposited the box on a table built onto the wall and opened the envelope.

"Let's review the kidney, shall we?" he flipped an ultrasound film onto the florescent view box on the room's wall and snapped on the light.

The light flickered and came alive. The varying shapes in gray appeared stacked one atop another in two rows. I had seen these films many times in his office but Andrea stepped closer and looked intently at the pictures.

"You recall that we had viewed this area here," he circled one picture of a large dark shape with his pencil.

"Yes," I said, and Andrea stared more seriously at the designated photo.

"Well," Hill smiled, "that was what we were concerned about all right, but here," he shifted his pencil down to the next photo on the sheet, "is her right kidney. See the ureter here," he traced a medium gray line from the dark shape downward and to the right, which connected into an area of darker gray, "as it flows into the bladder?"

"Yeah," I said, following his pencil as it snaked across the picture from one point to the other.

"That's her right kidney we're looking at, and its ureter, not this," he points back to the original picture.

"I don't understand," I said, looking from one picture to the other. "What happened?"

"We were looking in the wrong place." Hill smiled now, wide and boyishly as only he can do at such times.

"But how?" I asked, completely confused by this time.

"This," he said pointing back at the first picture, "is a cyst. We believe it was formed from the residue left behind by the upper pole we excised last winter."

"A cyst," Andrea said behind me, still leaning into the picture intently.

"A cyst," Hill smiled warmly.

"What do we do about that?" I asked.

"We've put a drain tube in her back," Dr. Hill said, putting away his photos. "You'll have to monitor the drainage for the next two weeks, then come and see me. I'll have my nurse set up an appointment for you."

"You want me to write down how much we get out?" Andrea asked, having done this before.

"You can, or just keep a running total, that's all I'll need," he picked up his equipment and started to leave.

"I'll see you in two weeks," he said moving off down the hallway. "Oh, Lori's out of surgery, she's in recovery. They'll be calling you soon."

"Thanks," we both called after him as he left. He waved to us as he turned the corner and was gone.

Back in recovery we found a sleepy little girl with a tube coming out of her back connected to a drain bag, but otherwise about the same as we had left her. She was cranky, as usual, in recovery and I took her off the bed to let her stand between my knees. She calmed down immediately and began looking around. Within an hour we had her out of recovery, dressed and in the van headed home.

For the next two weeks we measured bloody fluid which drained out of the tube into her bag, emptied the bag several times a day, and tried to keep the bag from dragging on the floor as she ran around the house. Her temperature never fluctuated and her appetite never lagged. Andrea dutifully measured each bag that was drained and wrote down the growing total day by day. Two weeks after surgery I took Lori to see Dr. Hill.

"How much fluid did we get?" he asked and I repeated the figure. He shook his head and went on. "I called a colleague of mine in Kansas City. He's had ten cases with cysts like these. That's about eight more than I've seen. I asked him what he did and he said that he just let them go. There is a drug that I could give Lori that would reduce the size of the cyst, but there are side effects that I would rather not deal with in her case. So, I've decided that my friend has the best idea. He's got more experience at it than I do."

"You're just going to leave it," I asked, unprepared for such a turn of events.

"Yeah," he smiled. "Just let it reduce on its own. She had any fevers? Anything like that?"

"None," I confirmed.

"Good," Hill said, getting up from his stool. "Put her up here on the table on her stomach and hold her down. I'm going to take the tube out."

"Here? Now?" I asked, not relishing what I suspected was coming.

"Why not," he grinned.

I laid Lori on the table on her stomach and pulled her clothing out of the way. Dr. Hill removed the gauze covering the tube's entry point into her body. The tube disappeared into Lori flesh without redness or swelling. Putting one hand against her back and grasping the tube in the other he began pulling on the plastic. The tubing slipped out inches at a time. Lori squirmed and fought but did not cry. My stomach felt queasy and I decided not to watch. In a moment the end of the tube popped free and dangled in front of me for an instant before Dr. Hill deposited it in a wastebasket. Putting a piece of tape over the hole in Lori's back he had me set her up and looked her over.

Lori was happy to be up from the table and when I set her down on the floor she began clapping her hands together as she backed way from us.

"I'll see you in October," Dr. Hill said as he showed us to the door. "We'll do an ultrasound and see how the cyst is doing by that time."

"That's it," I asked, somewhat bewildered.

"That's it," he said, and went off down the hall to other patients.

After I had made an appointment for October with the receptionist and was walking Lori down the hall toward the parking garage, I thought back on all that Dr. Hill had done, all the crises he had helped us get through, all the tragedies he had been through with us. We were reaching the end of all those dark days when no one but he had any hope. I knew that he was too humble a man to ever tell anyone what wonderful things he had done for us. I looked down at Lori walking along beside me and knew that if not for this one man she would probably not be alive today.

"Well," I said to Lori who looked up at me with smiling, blue eyes, " that's O.K., we'll tell people what wonderful things he did, won't we?"

Lori's smile widened as if she understood and agreed. And to this day we have done just that. To the whole world, I say for us all, we love you, Dr. Hill.

Chapter XIX
Lori's Miracle

In the fullness of time I have come to realize that Lori's physical survival is not the true miracle of her story. Yes, she lived in spite of all the problems she had and despite all reasonable medical explanations of modern science to the contrary. As miraculous as the fact of her survival may be, the miracle she actually delivered was the understanding I, and others, gained about the deeper meanings of life itself.

From the earliest days I have referred to Lori as God's child. And surely she is that, just as we are all God's children, but I have discovered that God can see through the dim light of a mentally retarded child's eyes much clearer than I ever suspected and can penetrate directly into your soul. She was not given to Andrea and me to possess, as many people view their children. No, we have come to understand that she is only on loan from the Creator; we are merely temporary custodians, transitory caretakers at best, for one of His special creations.

I have come to understand that Lori represents a living testament to the values that matter most in life. The same values sacred to God and illuminated by the life and teachings of Jesus the Christ. Lori doesn't care one whit for anyone's possessions. She does not want presents or gifts. Wealth, power, nor station in life does not impress her. We have a mound of stuffed animals and other gifts that were given to her during her many hospital stays. They are all packed and stored away, untouched, and unused in the attic. Lori has no interest in such things. What Lori really wants is the one thing that most people are completely unprepared and ill equipped to give: all she wants is time and attention.

What Lori values is the time you spend interacting with her. She enjoys having people talk to her, pay attention to her. Occasionally she might want a hug, but usually she is satisfied with merely your attention to her presence. Unlike most young ladies, a new dress holds no interest for her in the least, but she will spend hours smiling at you and looking you in the eyes. She appreciates only the most basic of human exchanges, one living creature relating to another. I have begun to understand that she is most happy simply listening to the music of your soul.

Her joys are simple. She will play endlessly in a wading pool of water, but she wastes no time on toys or games. She will laugh and smile if you feed her but she has no interest in parties or fancy eating-places. She will joyously ride for hours but cares not one iota for what kind of vehicle you own. She will walk endlessly down store aisles but cares nothing for what is on the shelves.

Lori loves beautiful colors but assigns no significance to their value. Money is meaningless to her, as is fame, property, and influence. None of the things that we work so hard to acquire have any importance to Lori. Conversely, all the things that we take for granted, and usually forget we possess, are priceless treasures to her.

This, then, is part of Lori's true miracle. She brings into my modern world of computers and advanced intellect a disdain for anything beyond the human. She has become the living definition of the essential meaning of life and the reason we are all born into this world to begin with. To answer the question, "Why am I here?" I need only to look into her smiling eyes and there I find the answer, which evades so many. Lori's simplicity of life is profound, her love is boundless and without guile. She is a living testament to Christ's lone commandment, *that ye love one another, as I have loved you* (John 15:12). With her life Lori reminds us that in the end all we really have is one another. Wealth, possessions, accomplishments and titles, all must be left behind when we die; love goes with us, the only treasure of our souls, the only currency between us and God that is of any value.

Lori's greatest miracle was her teaching me the true value of love and the grace of life with others. Through her I have come to understand that love is the only language our hearts understand, and the only path our souls can travel. All else is vanity, and vanity is empty death.

One of my mother's friends's has a mentally retarded son. She once told my mother that all the children like Lori and her son were just angels without wings. I believe that is exactly what they are. Such children as Lori are God's gifts to us in an attempt to force us to restructure our values and priorities. As long as such people like Lori exist we "normal" folk are forced to deal with them. And how we deal with them is our salvation, or our damnation.

It is a little known fact of history, but heartbreakingly true, that the first people killed by Hitler were not Jews, nor even political enemies. The very first people exterminated by the Nazis were the physically and mentally handicapped in Germany. I once viewed film footage of the propaganda campaign designed to sway the German people into accepting euthanasia as a legitimate public policy designed to solve the problem the handicapped imposed on their society by draining it of vital resources.

In one segment there was a little boy who exhibited a trait Lori has. When she is excited she will grab her lower jaw by putting her fingers in her mouth and pulling downwards. The little boy in the film did the same thing. He was excited because there were people paying attention to him and he felt special. His eyes were bright with the same thrill and liquid smile that I have seen in my daughter's eyes so many times. But a lump came to my throat as I watched this familiar gesture from across the span of years because I knew that when the filming was finished they took this happy little boy out and killed him, just as they would do to Lori, if she had been born at that time and in that place.

After watching the film a profound sadness overwhelmed me, an oppressive guilt at the collective sin of humankind. Deep inside me I had a sudden realization that when they took that smiling little boy out and killed him they killed God too. The horror of what they did was crushing to my heart, because I knew that the killers were not some particular, singular breed that have been wiped off the face of the Earth fifty years ago with the end of World War II and were no longer a threat to us. The real horror of what I saw, was that people just like those who killed that little boy are still with us. I recalled seeing recent news film of what were called the starvation rooms in China. In these horrid places mentally and physically handicapped children were left to perish from neglect as they slowly starved to death. About the same time I saw another newscast, which reported the deaths of many children from neglect in cold, dingy mental wards in Bosnia. In each news report I saw Lori, endless Loris', and I saw their happiness made into pain, their laughter turned into cries of abandonment and hunger, all for political and economic expediency. There was other cases, far too many cases that pressed upon me the inescapable truth that the heartless dogs of intolerance nip eternally at our heels, through all time.

Too many people see the Loris' of this world as drains on our economy and spend endless hours devising plans to reduce their depletion of our resources. I once made the observation to a group I addressed that Lori had nothing anyone would want, but the truth is she has the one thing that everyone wishes they had. In her simplicity Lori embodies the music of the universe. In her silence can be heard the voice of God. And in her profound, simple way is the way of our Lord. Christ admonished his disciples, "Suffer the little children to come unto me, for theirs is the kingdom of heaven."

Through Lori I experience God. I do not mean to say that I see God, hear God speak audibly, but I do experience Him as surely as I have experienced joy or sadness, exaltation or pain. These sensations are real, yet I do not see them. They can alter my life, yet make not a sound. The most profound of all things in life are inexplicable truths that can be felt but not examined. They cannot be explained in verbal expressions, but they can and must be experienced to be understood. Trying to explain joy to a person who has not experienced it is like trying to explain the color red to a person who was born blind. That is how I have experienced God.

There was no defining moment when electrical charges riveted through my body, or lighting flashes arched around me. There was no theatrical laser light-pierced environment that swirled in mists down corridors while electronic sounds resonated through the hallways like we see so often in theatrical productions. There were no melodramatics or histrionics that demarcated one moment from another in my realization, but there was the overall experience that permeated my being with the essence of what happened, how it happened, and all that it involved.

I call Vanderbilt Hospital my Sinai because during those tenuous beginnings I found it was where God lived, where God spoke to me. To that towering structure of brick and steel I pilgrimaged daily in a fatiguing journey of discovery. There are many people involved in Lori's story within that structure; Jews and Christians, East Indians and South Americans, Whites and Blacks, men and women, the highly educated and the uneducated. They were all there, the good, and the bad, and the indifferent, and each one played a unique piece in the story. Without even one of them the mosaic would not have been complete.

In my Sinai of discovery I did not see God's face, burning bushes, signs falling from Heaven, nor ethereal fire.

And, unlike Moses, my face did not glow with an inner light from the experience, but I think my soul did. I experienced God in the mount called Vanderbilt. There in the antiseptic halls and sterilized corridors I walked with Him, beside Him, and through Him. He was everywhere, as if the very place had distilled Him from the concentrated emotions that saturated that place from the prayers and tears of all those desperate people who came together within those lamentable walls.

There were times when I was astounded as I watched young doctors in training walk nonchalantly down the hallways of my Sinai, completely oblivious to the wonders that I saw. They seemed to be blinded to the miracles occurring daily in their midst. They took the miraculous as commonplace, the extraordinary as insignificant, as they pursued their personal aspirations. They were blind men and women standing hip deep in a mother lode of precious treasures that they could not, or would not, see.

But I know that these unseeing people are no different from the rest of us who wander blindly through life ignorant of its wonders and blind to its miracles. I have always heard it said that God speaks in a quiet, still voice. If He does, He speaks too softly for most of us to hear amid the clatter of our daily lives. His voice is not to be found in the din of daily life nor in the hymns and songs, praises and shouts, chanting and speeches that so often fill the spaces of our religious worship. The reality of our religion is not found in what we attend but what we attend to.

I was the man who did not believe in miracles who experienced the miraculous. I was the unworthy to whom a treasure was given. I was the intellectual to whom the unexplainable happened. I was the least of God's servants to whom a talent was entrusted. I have now invested that talent in you. Hear my words, hear Lori's testament, and know the truth the Psalmist knew:

"Be still, and know that I am God (Psalm 46:10)."

I have told you the story, as best I can, just as it really happened. The truth of that story is not just for me anymore, the truth of it is for you.

Deo Volente

Chapter XX
Epilogue

Before I leave this story I feel there are two things that need to be addressed. The first is the subject of guilt, and the second to offer some suggestions about what you can do when confronted with a handicapped child.

The reason I want to say a few words about guilt is because it is something I have found people in my situation must learn to deal with just as surely as they must learn to deal with all the other problems of their special children. I have come to realize that there are a variety of guilt's associated with handicapped children, and that the phenomenon of guilt is not so simple as people might think.

Often the parents of handicapped children look to themselves in an attempt to find a reason for the problems their children are experiencing. Often they blame themselves for their child's condition. Such feelings are not based on any rational thoughts, they are based upon a need to know the answer to the question "Why", when in truth there is no other answer. Guilt is an emotion and, as such, it exists whether or not it has a reason to exist, and whether or not it is based upon any rational logic. Guilt lives almost of its own accord and, like all self-sufficient things, it tends to grow if neglected, feeding upon itself.

I have learned that the best way to deal with guilt is to find out what makes it tick, where it comes from, what makes it live. Just like facing fear, guilt can only be overcome if it is confronted head on. Otherwise, guilt continues to grow until it takes over your life. Unrestrained guilt will come to rule you, if you do not rule it.

As the developmental assessment panel told us when they informed us that Lori was mentally retarded, there may never be an explanation of why she is the way she is. As one panelist put it, "Lori is what Lori is." If we were so predisposed we could think up a hundred reasons why she is the way she is. Andrea could convince herself that she is at fault, just as I could equally convince myself that my inattention on the night of her breathing distress caused the damage to her brain and that it was I alone who was at fault. In other words, you can justify your guilt by convincing yourself that it is worthy of existing.

But guilt, in this context, does have one alluring feature; it offers an explanation of why things are as they are. To reject the guilt, and its accompanying explanation, is to assign yourself to the unknown where mystery is the order of the day and the unknown is the only knowable reality. Insecure people prefer the known to the unknown, no matter what consequences may attend the attachment. The courage you must have to refute such guilt is the courage to accept the unknown, and the unknowable, as the only reality and live with it. It is not easy, but it is truth.

Then there are the other guilts you must face, at some time or another, with special children. Perhaps the most terrible for me is the guilt of miracles. Before Lori, I had never thought of miracles as having accompanying guilt attached to them. To me, miracles were the marvelous workings of God that were awe-inspiring events, somehow isolated from the normal context of the world.

But in reality, miracles bring on a wealth of guilt. As your child survives others around you die. The parents of those children who do not survive wanted them to live just as much as you want your child to live, but they did not. You find yourself feeling guilty because of your child's survival. You feel that the parents of those children who died must be looking at you and asking, "Why did your child live? Why could mine not have lived and yours have died?"

To make matters worse, you do not have a rational reason why your child survived. Practically speaking, our daughter should have died. Why did she live? You feel guilty, but twice over, because you had nothing to do with your child living, or the others dying, and in truth you feel happy that your child lived. I have heard this called, survivor's guilt. But this happiness amid the ever-present grief that surrounds you makes your guilt acutely painful.

And then there is the associated guilt of the unanswerable question, "Why did my child live?" There is the uneasy feeling that you "owe" God. But at the same time you are distressed to explain what it is exactly that you do owe him. First and forcmost you can never answer the question, Why me? And then you are faced with the other half of the question, and that is "What now?"

You immediately realize that you, of all people, have not lived such an exemplary life that you deserve such a miracle. Then why did it happen to you? And if you have not lived the life of a saint, should you do so now? Is it even possible? Could you? How on Earth do you pay such an awful debt?

The truth is, after all my experience, I have not the slightest idea how to answer any of these questions. All that came to mind when I pondered these questions was the admonition from Psalms; "Be still, and know that I am God...(Psalm 46:10)" Be still! A nice way of saying, shut up! I realized I had no idea why this happened. Personally, based upon my life experience, I did not deserve any of the miracles that happened, but I realized that whether or not I deserved such a miracle was beside the point. It was what God wanted. "Deo Volente", not what I wanted. And who was I to ask anyway? God did as God wanted, not what I wanted. Then who am I to be guilty? It was not my decision. It was His. Miracles are burdens. Part of my ordeal was to accept the burden. In the beginning I said I would abide by whatever God wanted to happen, and that is what I must do, or admit that I lied to God.

Guilt can be a crushingly heavy burden that comes with a miracle, and not one easily borne, until you come to the realization that the miracle is not of your making. It is not up to you to justify the miracle, or explain it. Your job is to accept and continue, not to reason about why it happened, or justify it having happened. Be still!

Once, someone was talking to me about Lori's condition and said, "Why would God do this to you?" Instantly the words came to mind, "He did not DO anything to us." But if he did not, how do you explain what has happened?

The explanation I created in my mind, and shared with my wife, who understands it and believes it herself, was not an accusatory interpretation of the events surrounding Lori's miracles. I decided that God had a very special child he wished to bring into this world, one that not just any one could care for. He looked all over the world for someone to care for His child, and He settled on us. We are the specially selected caretakers of God's special child. No guilt. Honor perhaps, some might say flattery, but that is better than guilt and condemnation, because in truth Lori is special and we would not take the world for her, so are we not honored by having her?

A sign I once saw taped to the wall of an elementary classroom proclaimed, "I'm somebody because God don't make no junk." If you are the parent of a special child then you are indeed most fortunate among mankind because God himself has seen fit to give you that child. Care for it, love it, and honor Him who gave it to you because no matter what is wrong with your child, no matter how hopeless it may seem at times, no matter how hard the road may become, be of good cheer and feel fortunate because God don't make no junk, and he don't choose no losers!

So, I reject guilt as a killer and hater of glory and triumph. Guilt has never built a bridge into the achievements of tomorrow, it has only paved a slide to destruction, and I consciously have chosen not to take that terrible trip into oblivion. I choose life, I choose love, and I choose happiness, positive acts, and not negative accusations.

* * * * * * *

Everyone wants and expects a perfect baby, especially in this age of modern technical and medical achievements. However, the reality is that in spite of advanced medical technology and excellent prenatal care, some babies are born who are mentally and/or physically handicapped. So, how do parents of handicapped children survive the extra stresses that a special child brings? Our experience and the experiences of others have produced a list of suggestions that we hope you will find helpful.

1. Love your child.
2. Accept your child.
3. Enjoy your child.
4. Don't assign blame.
5. Work together to provide and maintain a secure home for your family.
6. Find out about organizations and services in your community that provides support for handicapped children and their families. If none is available, start one. Contact your state ARC for information.
7. Take time for family activities.
8. Participate as fully as possible in community and extended family activities.

9. Spouses should take time for each other. Set aside a special time every week for just the two of you, even if all you do is take a walk or snuggle in front of the TV
10. If your child has to be hospitalized and one of you is with the child, maintain contact by phone. Include intimate conversations in words and tones that communicate how special you are to each other.
11. Share intimate glances and pats in passing that mean "you are mine and I am yours."
12. Be supportive of one another. Help each other out. Let the world know how much you admire your spouse:
" She's really a wonderful mother."
" He's a fantastic father."
" She makes the best beef stew."
" He is truly a gifted artist."
" She is my support."
" He is my rock."
" If it weren't for (him/her) I could not (you fill in the rest)."

Too many parents of handicapped children become divorce statistics. That doesn't have to happen. Couples who find themselves growing apart instead of together should run, not walk, to the nearest counseling professional who understands the unique problems of parents with handicapped children.

If every avenue of reconciliation has been tried and the marriage comes to an end, then accept that and go on with your separate lives as all divorced couples do. The custody of children should be in their best interest and both parents should be full participants in the child's life.

****

I leave you with some thoughts about handicapped children and what you can do to make the world a better place for them. The days when handicapped children were closed off into institutions are over. More and more families are like us, electing to keep their handicapped child at home and offer them full participation in not only family life, but the world at large. You should not be surprised then that you will encounter these children in all the places "normal" people go.

Many people have no experience with handicapped or retarded children and when they meet one face to face in their daily affairs their reactions often range from a surprised sympathy or embarrassment to an outright hostility. Actually none of these reactions are appropriate or necessary. With the aid of some other people with special children we have created a list of suggestions which we feel will afford such people a better understanding of not only the children but themselves as well, and thereby we hope that they may feel a bit more comfortable during such encounters.

Suggestions

1. First, and foremost, understand that everyone is a right-to-life child, even the handicapped. Everyone, no matter their condition or circumstance, has a right to be here and to fully participate in the events of a full and complete life.

2. Realize that not everyone is born with a healthy body. Most everyone has some small thing wrong with them, even you. In that regard the handicapped are not so much different than you. Only by degrees do any of us differ.

3. Expect to see handicapped children out and about, and you won't be surprised. How do you prepare yourself for such a condition? The same way we prepared to be parents of a retarded child, it happened and we accepted it. Simple.

4. Accept that some children are handicapped and that many parents no longer feel that such children should be hidden away.

5. Respect the family's right to bring the child with them into public places. Life is hard enough for them without you adding to their discomfort, and besides it is their business, not yours. Parents with handicapped children only want their kids to have as full a life as they are able to have. Isn't that all you want for your child? So, what's the difference? They have the same right you have and they are exercising it.

6. Bear in mind that many of these handicapped children have undergone surgeries, therapies, or procedures and that they must wear casts, braces, or devices and the appearance of such things is by no means an indicator of abuse. We see what we are predisposed to see. Do not be predisposed to see evil where there is none. If you do, that is what you will see.

7. Respect the privacy of a handicapped child and their family. People are NOT sideshows for your amusement. Treat them as you would any other family; if you know them, speak to them. If you don't, act as you would with any stranger you meet.

8. Treat the handicapped child as you would any other child. It is perfectly permissible to speak to a handicapped child, just as you would any other child. If circumstances are such that you would not speak to a "normal" child, then do not

speak to a handicapped child. Treat them as if they are just any other child and you can't go wrong. Treat them as if they are different and you can't do right.

9. Believe that everyone is "special" to God. If you know this in your heart, then you know that we are all God's children and are to be treated no differently than anyone else.

10. Don't assign blame. We are a great nation of blame seekers. We hunt eternally for who is to blame for things. Handicapped children are not events for which we must find a cause. They are human beings who are as they are and in many cases no one knows the reason why. Judge not, lest you also be judged by the standards that you yourself have set.

11. DO NOT *pity* handicapped children. First, they do not deserve it and second, they do not need it. Many of these children do not even know they are different. So why tell them with you reactions. And if they already know they are different, why make it more pronounced by pitying them? Pity has no place in a handicapped child's life.

* * * * * * *

If you know a family of a handicapped child fairly well, there are several things you can do to make their life better.

- Offer to sit with the child, if you can. Parents of handicapped children get precious little time to be alone or go out. Their lives are bound up in the needs of the child most of the time. Anything you could do to relieve that situation would, usually, be greatly appreciated.

- Be supportive, lend an ear, or a shoulder, or a hand - if you can. Parents with special children are just like other people, sometimes it all becomes too much and we just need someone to talk to. Sometimes we may actually need somebody to yell at because we think God gets tired of hearing it.

- Parents with handicapped children seldom, if ever, get the opportunity to take a vacation like other people. If you can, arrange, or help arrange, a way to let the parents take a few days away.

- Pay attention to the child. Notice when he/she has made improvements or learns a new skill. The parents are so close to the child that many times they do not see the forest for the trees. Also, it is encouraging to hear others say that things are improving.

- Pay attention to siblings of the handicapped child. Many times "normal" children feel left out when all the attention, time, and effort is focused on the handicapped brother or sister. Siblings of handicapped children are less apt to view them as "special" and see them only as brothers or sisters.

- Ask if there is anything you can do to help. You might be surprised at the answers you get.

- Be yourself. Don't "put on airs" as the old people used to say. If you know a family very well with a handicapped child, they know you too. If you start acting differently they'll know it and know why you are doing it. Just be yourself, that's all anyone wants.

* * * * * * *

In closing I'll share a story with you that I believe sheds a light on the value handicapped children holds for all of us. Recently I was talking to a man who helped run the state wide Special Olympics for handicapped children in Tennessee. He told me that he had been at a meeting a year or two ago at which handicapped children from all over the world were in attendance. He watched Israeli children playing and laughing with Arab children, and Northern Ireland Roman Catholic children hugging Protestant children. He said race or nationality made no difference what so ever to those children in their affection for one another.

"We need to listen to these handicapped kids." He said with a wink and a smile. "They really are God's children, and I think they know something we don't."

I agree. I know they do, and all we have to do is listen.